UNCLE GRANDPA

CREATED BY
PETER BROWNGARDT

ROSS RICHIE CEO & Founder • MARK SMYLIE Founder of Archaia • MATT GAGNON Editor-in-Chief • FILIP SABLIK President of Publishing & Marketing • STEPHEN CHRISTY President of Development
LANCE KREITER VP of Licensing & Merchandising • PHIL BARBARO VP of Finance • BRYCE CARLSON Managing Editor • MEL CAYLO Marketing Manager • SCOTT NEWMAN Production Design Manager
IRENE BRADISH Operations Manager • CHRISTINE DINH Brand Communications Manager • DAFNA PLEBAN Editor • SHANNON WATTERS Editor • ERIC HARBURN Editor • IAN BRILL Editor • WHITNEY LEOPARD Associate Editor
JASMINE AMIRI Associate Editor • CHRIS ROSA Associate Editor • ALEX GALER Assistant Editor • CAMERON CHITTOCK Assistant Editor • MARY GUMPORT Assistant Editor • KELSEY DIETERICH Production Designer
JILLIAN CRAB Production Designer • KARA LEOPARD Production Designer • MICHELLE ANKLEY Production Design Assistant • DEVIN FUNCHES E-Commerce & Inventory Coordinator • AARON FERRARA Operations Coordinator
JOSÉ MEZA Sales Assistant • ELIZABETH LOUGHRIDGE Accounting Assistant • STEPHANIE HOCUTT Marketing Assistant • HILLARY LEVI Executive Assistant • KATE ALBIN Administrative Assistant • JAMES ARRIOLA Mailroom Assistant

UNCLE GRANDPA, November 2015. Published by KaBOOM!, a division of Boom Entertainment, Inc. UNCLE GRANDPA, CARTOON NETWORK, the logos, and all related
characters and elements are trademarks of © of Cartoon Network. (S15) Originally published in single magazine form as UNCLE GRANDPA No. 1-4; STEVEN UNIVERSE
No. 1-2. © Cartoon Network. (S15) All rights reserved. KaBOOM!™ and the KaBOOM! logo are trademarks of Boom Entertainment, Inc., registered in various countries and
categories. All characters, events, and institutions depicted herein are fictional. Any similarity between any of the names, characters, persons, events, and/or institutions
in this publication to actual names, characters, and persons, whether living or dead, events, and/or institutions is unintended and purely coincidental. KaBOOM! does not
read or accept unsolicited submissions of ideas, stories, or artwork.

A catalog record of this book is available from OCLC and from the KaBOOM! Studios website, www.kaboom-studios.com, on the Librarians Page.

BOOM! Studios, 5670 Wilshire Boulevard, Suite 450, Los Angeles, CA 90036-5679. Printed in China. First Printing.

ISBN: 978-1-60886-765-3, eISBN: 978-1-61398-436-9

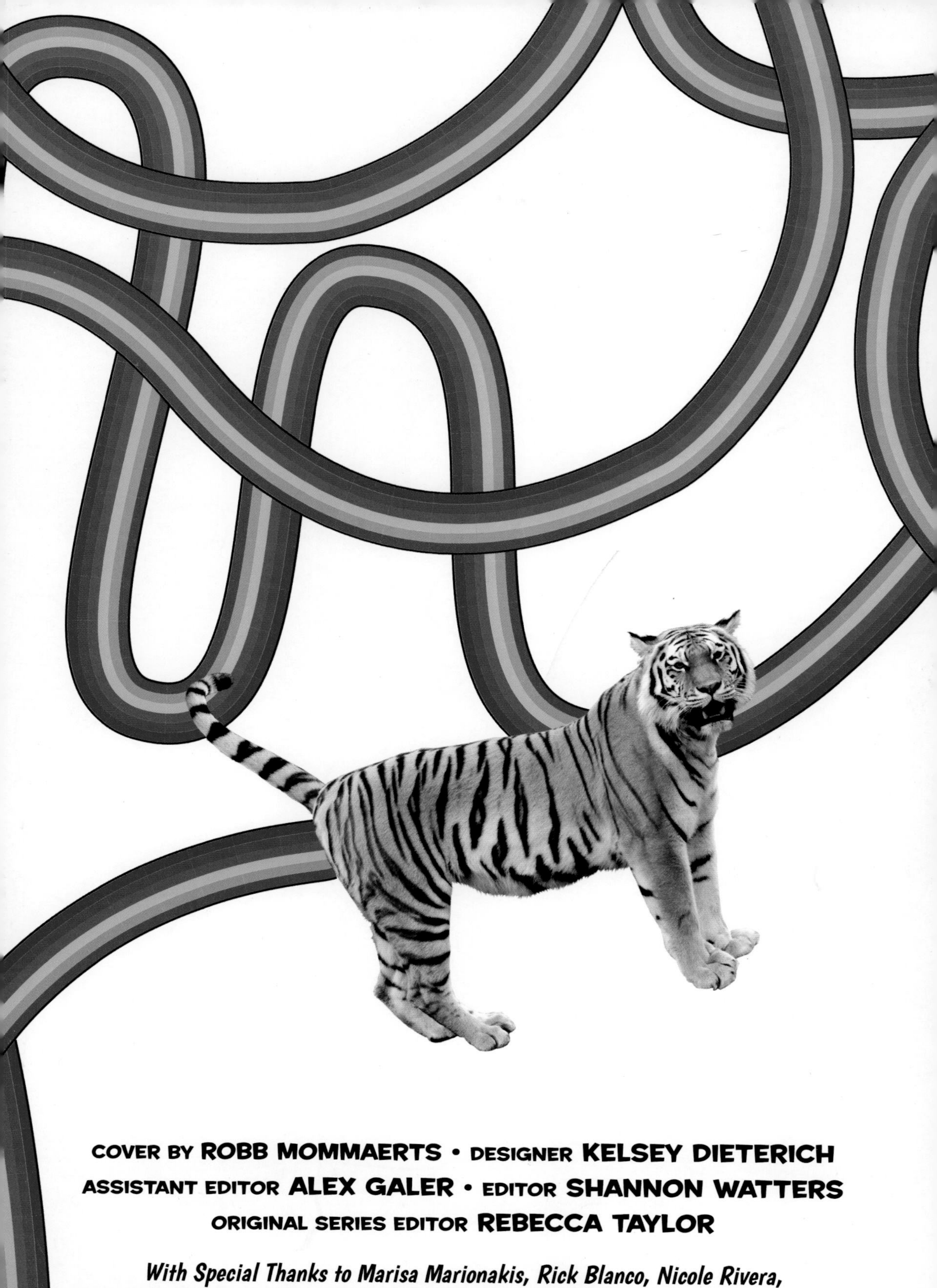

COVER BY ROBB MOMMAERTS • DESIGNER KELSEY DIETERICH
ASSISTANT EDITOR ALEX GALER • EDITOR SHANNON WATTERS
ORIGINAL SERIES EDITOR REBECCA TAYLOR

With Special Thanks to Marisa Marionakis, Rick Blanco, Nicole Rivera, Conrad Montgomery, Meghan Bradley, Curtis Lelash, Kelly Crews and the wonderful folks at Cartoon Network.

ISSUE #1 COVER
BOB FLYNN

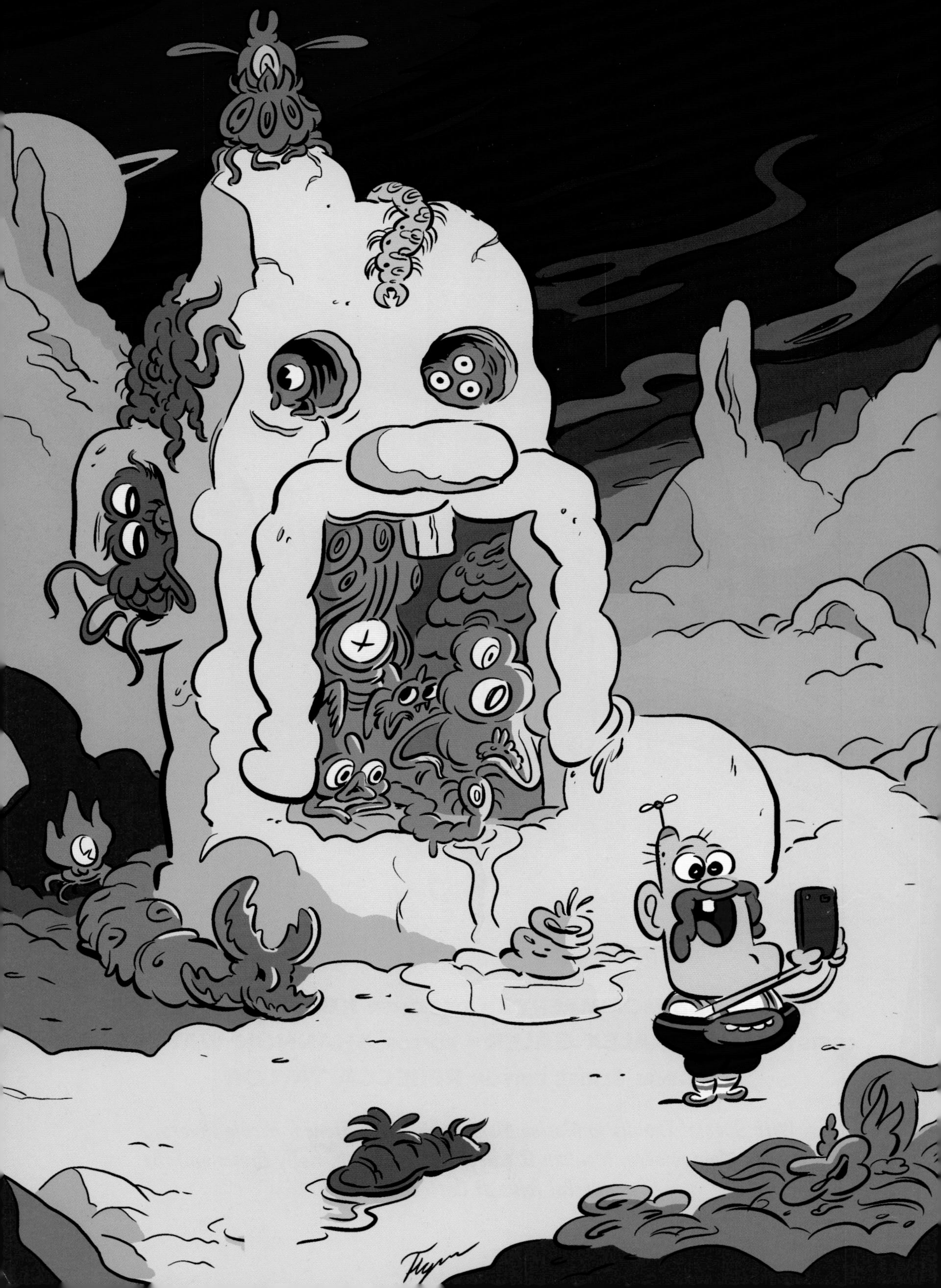
Flynn

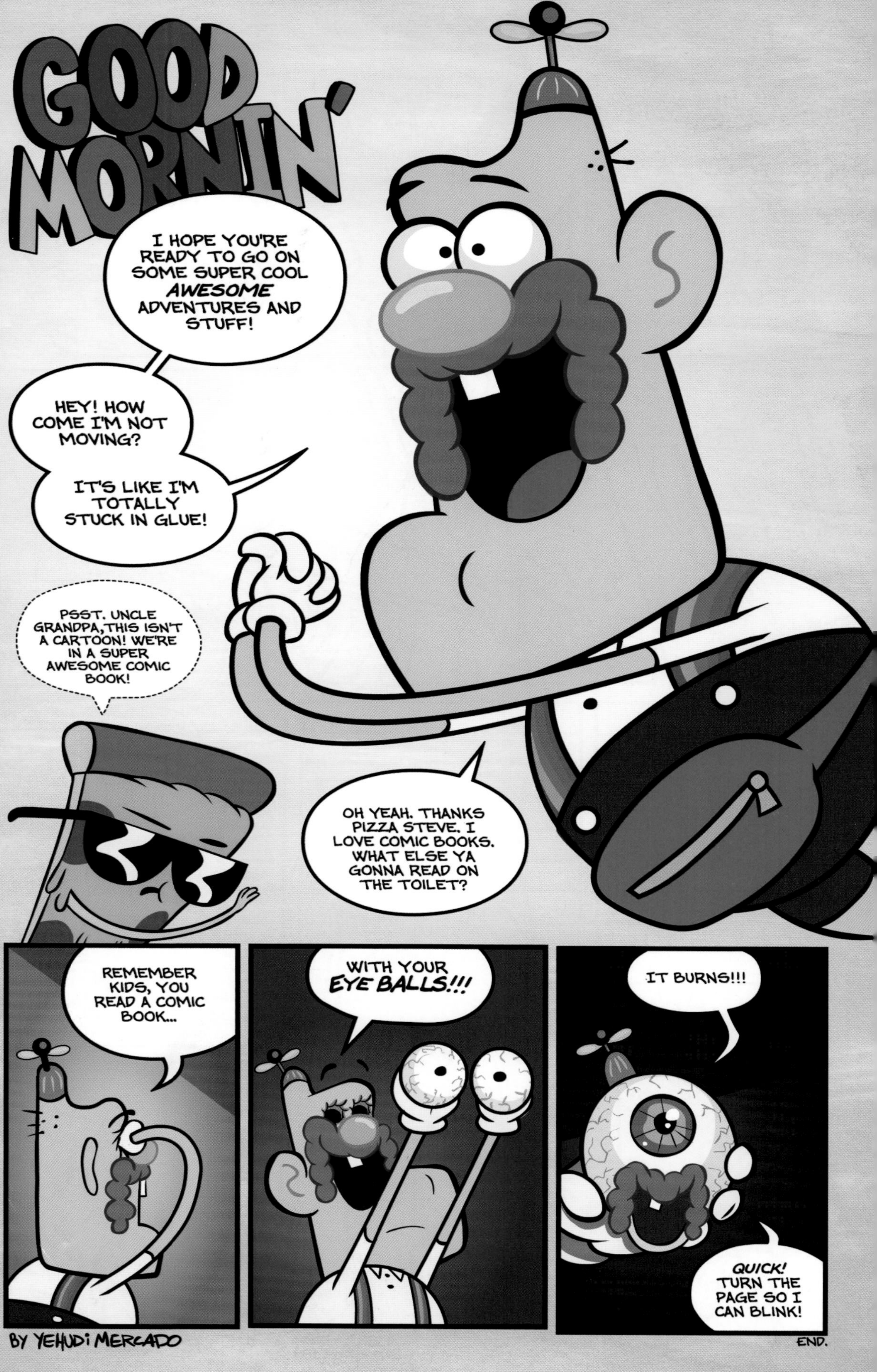
GOOD MORNIN'
I HOPE YOU'RE READY TO GO ON SOME SUPER COOL AWESOME ADVENTURES AND STUFF!
HEY! HOW COME I'M NOT MOVING?
IT'S LIKE I'M TOTALLY STUCK IN GLUE!
PSST. UNCLE GRANDPA, THIS ISN'T A CARTOON! WE'RE IN A SUPER AWESOME COMIC BOOK!
OH YEAH. THANKS PIZZA STEVE. I LOVE COMIC BOOKS. WHAT ELSE YA GONNA READ ON THE TOILET?
REMEMBER KIDS, YOU READ A COMIC BOOK...
WITH YOUR EYE BALLS!!!
IT BURNS!!!
QUICK! TURN THE PAGE SO I CAN BLINK!
BY YEHUDI MERCADO
END.

"PANTRY PANIC"

STORY & ART BY SCOTT ROBERTS - COLORS BY WHITNEY COGAR - LETTERS BY WARREN MONTGOMERY

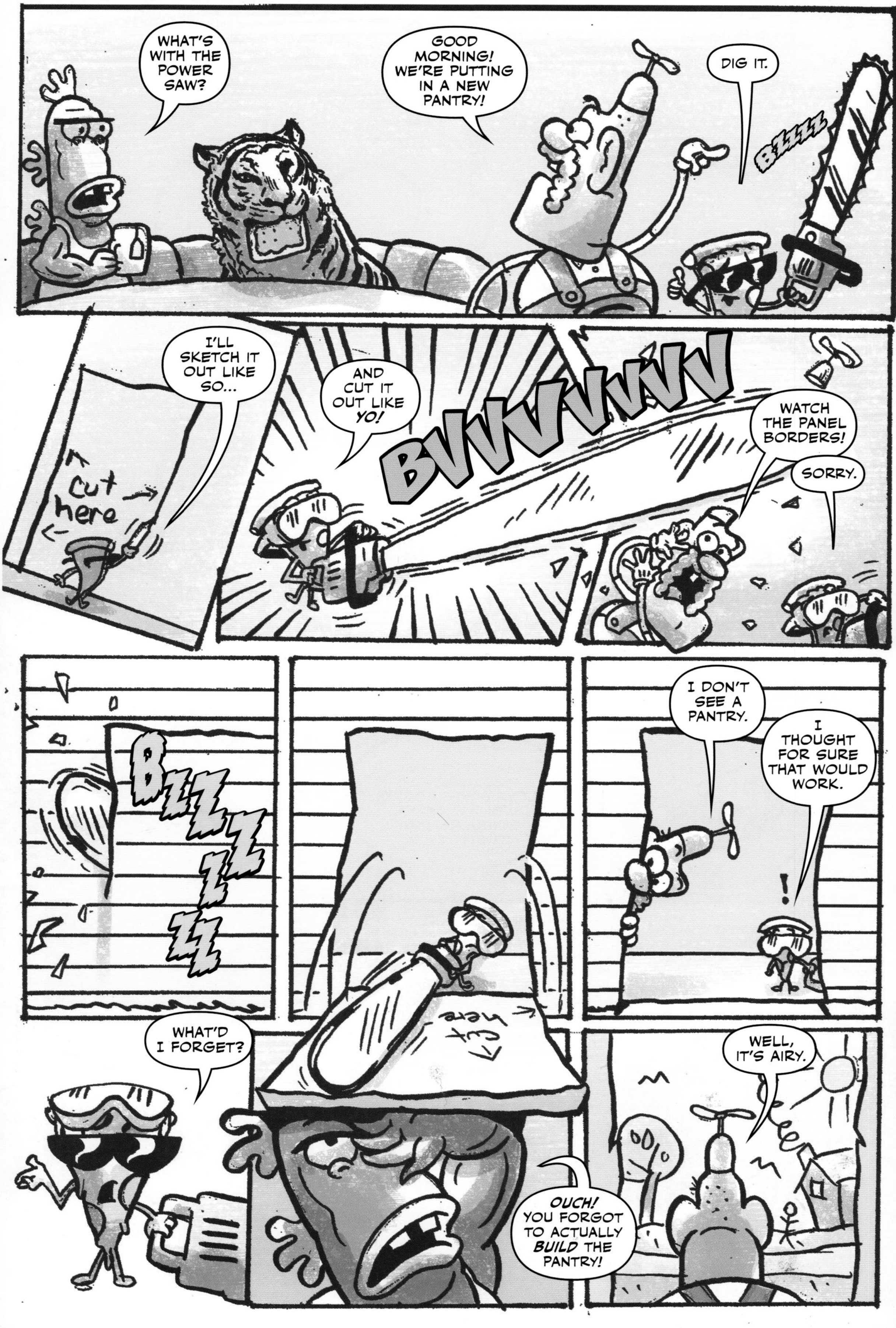

WHAT'S WITH THE POWER SAW?
GOOD MORNING! WE'RE PUTTING IN A NEW PANTRY!
DIG IT.
BZZZZ
I'LL SKETCH IT OUT LIKE SO...
cut here
AND CUT IT OUT LIKE YO!
BVVVVVVV
WATCH THE PANEL BORDERS!
SORRY.
BZZZZZZZ
I DON'T SEE A PANTRY.
I THOUGHT FOR SURE THAT WOULD WORK.
!
WHAT'D I FORGET?
cut here
OUCH! YOU FORGOT TO ACTUALLY BUILD THE PANTRY!
WELL, IT'S AIRY.

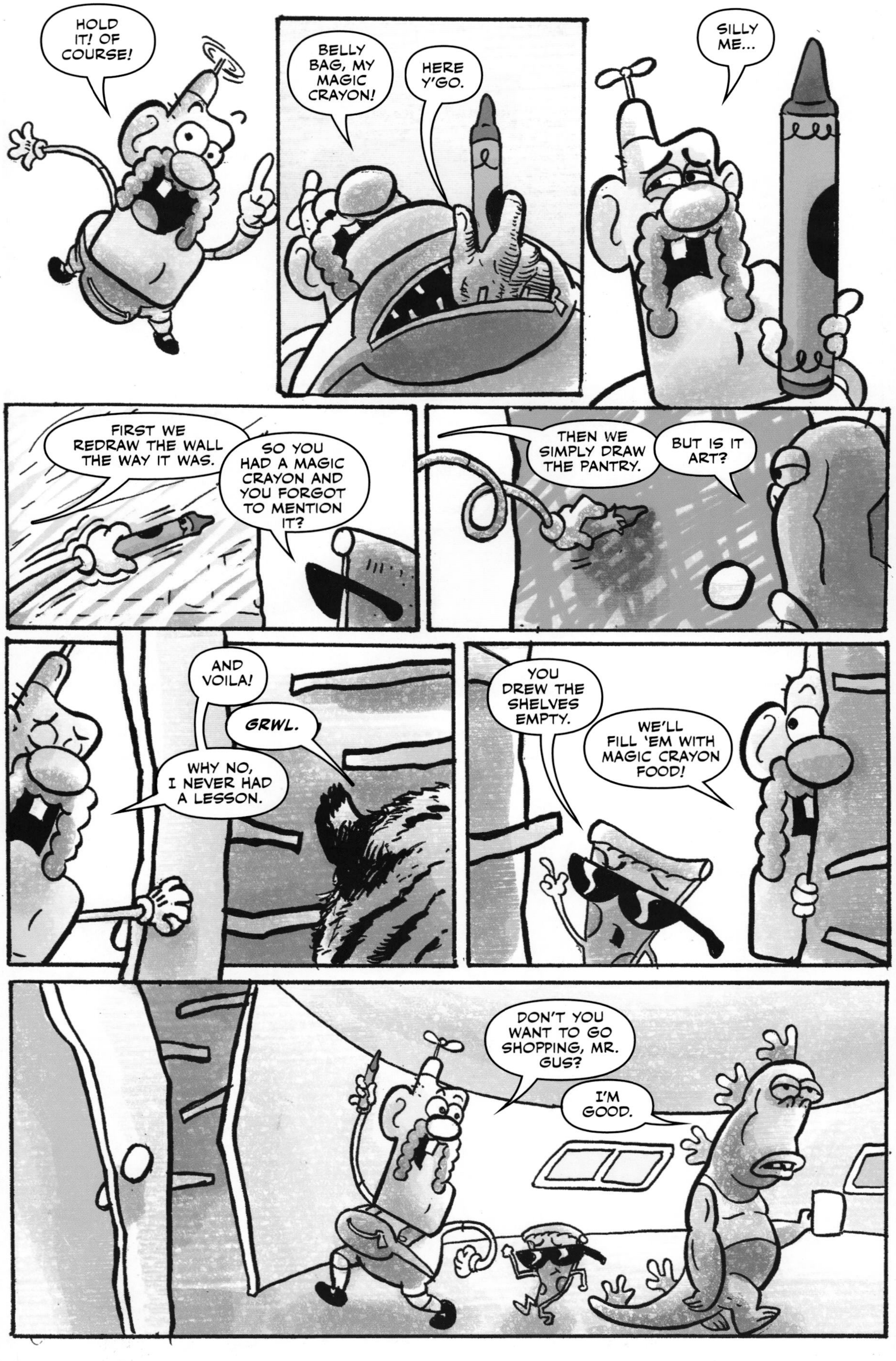
HOLD IT! OF COURSE!
BELLY BAG, MY MAGIC CRAYON!
HERE Y'GO.
SILLY ME...
FIRST WE REDRAW THE WALL THE WAY IT WAS.
SO YOU HAD A MAGIC CRAYON AND YOU FORGOT TO MENTION IT?
THEN WE SIMPLY DRAW THE PANTRY.
BUT IS IT ART?
AND VOILA!
GRWL.
WHY NO, I NEVER HAD A LESSON.
YOU DREW THE SHELVES EMPTY.
WE'LL FILL 'EM WITH MAGIC CRAYON FOOD!
DON'T YOU WANT TO GO SHOPPING, MR. GUS?
I'M GOOD.

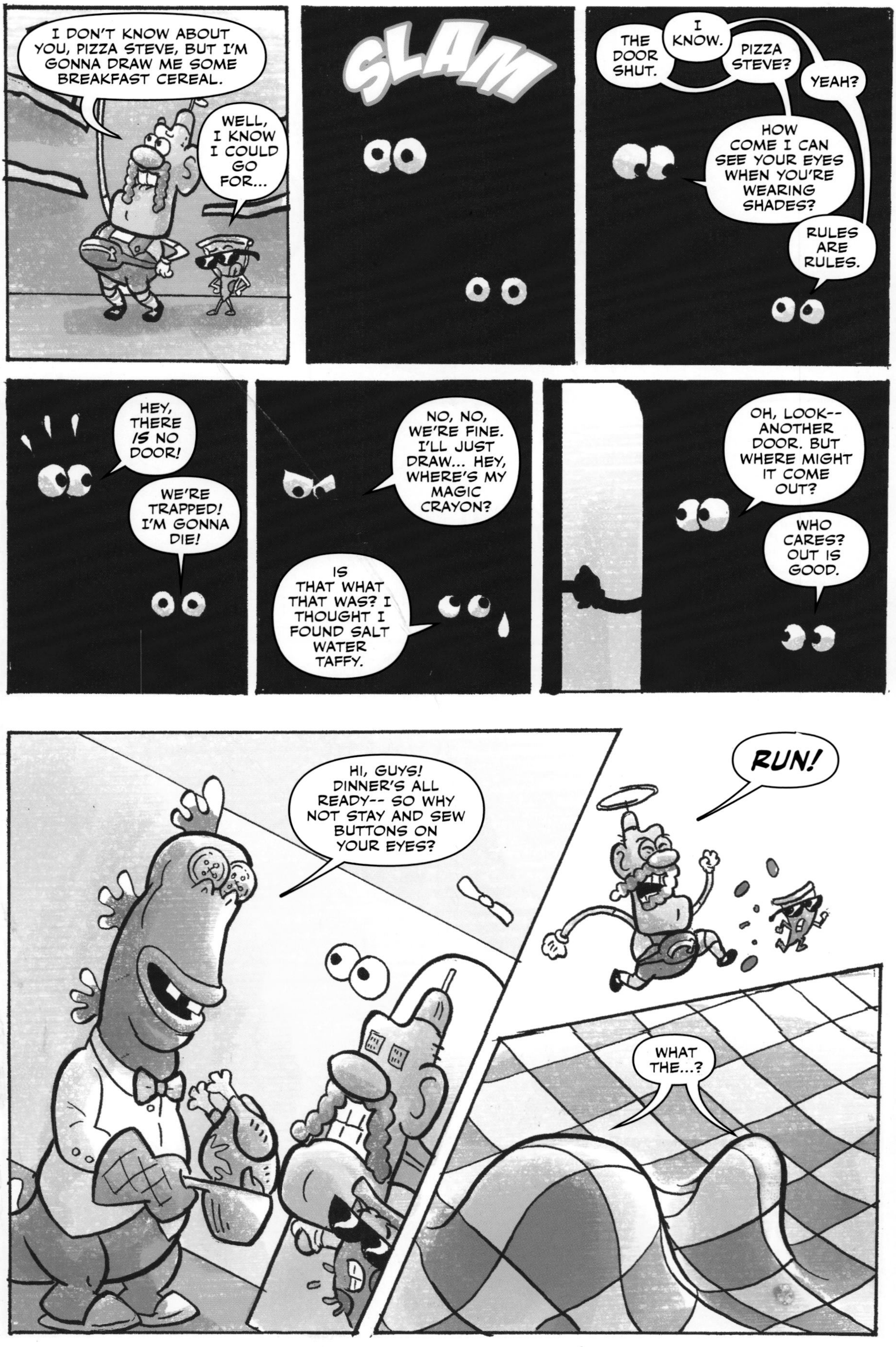
I DON'T KNOW ABOUT YOU, PIZZA STEVE, BUT I'M GONNA DRAW ME SOME BREAKFAST CEREAL.
WELL, I KNOW I COULD GO FOR...
SLAM
THE DOOR SHUT.
I KNOW.
PIZZA STEVE?
YEAH?
HOW COME I CAN SEE YOUR EYES WHEN YOU'RE WEARING SHADES?
RULES ARE RULES.
HEY, THERE *IS* NO DOOR!
WE'RE TRAPPED! I'M GONNA DIE!
NO, NO, WE'RE FINE. I'LL JUST DRAW... HEY, WHERE'S MY MAGIC CRAYON?
IS THAT WHAT THAT WAS? I THOUGHT I FOUND SALT WATER TAFFY.
OH, LOOK-- ANOTHER DOOR. BUT WHERE MIGHT IT COME OUT?
WHO CARES? OUT IS GOOD.
HI, GUYS! DINNER'S ALL READY-- SO WHY NOT STAY AND SEW BUTTONS ON YOUR EYES?
RUN!
WHAT THE...?

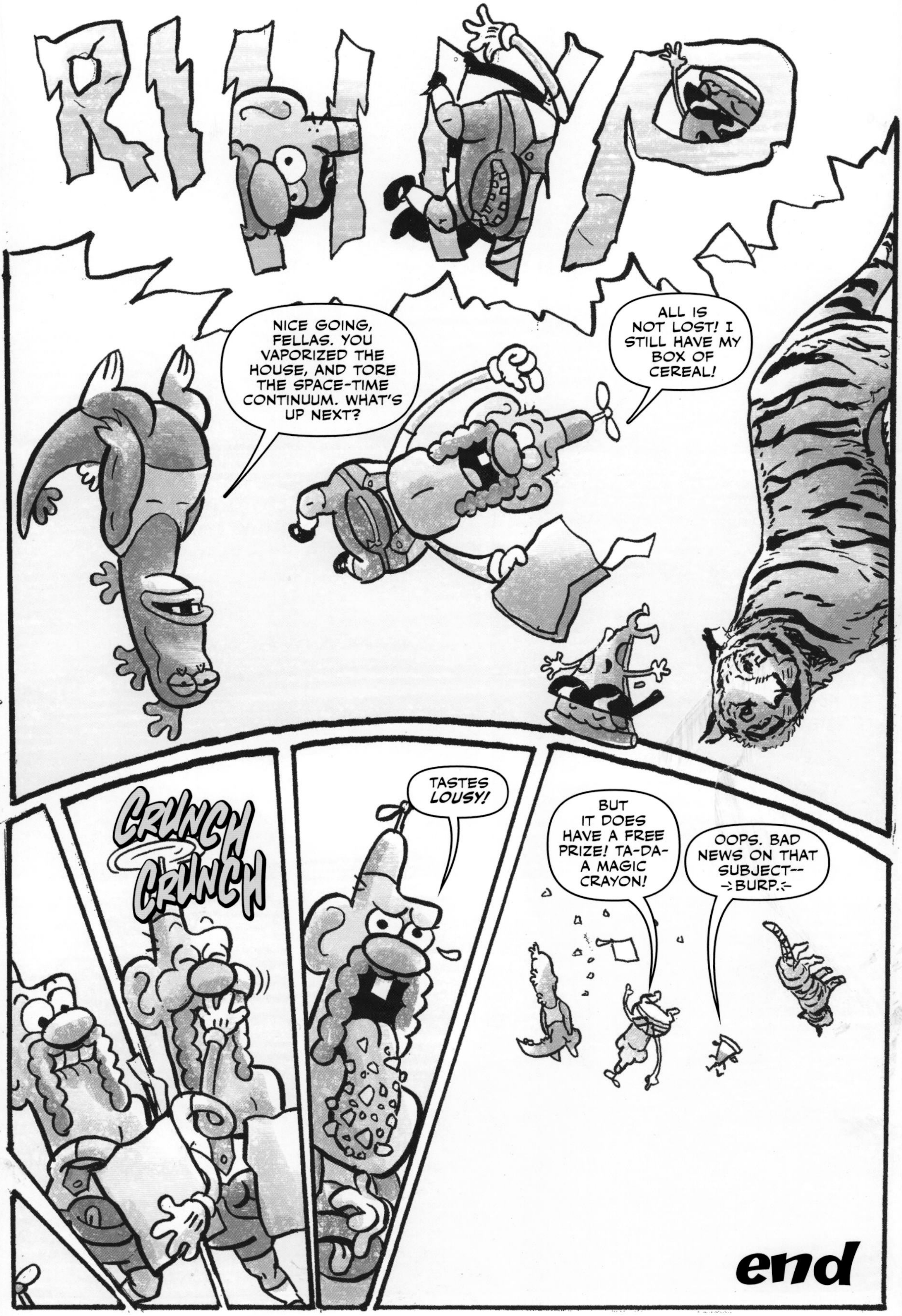
RIIIP
NICE GOING, FELLAS. YOU VAPORIZED THE HOUSE, AND TORE THE SPACE-TIME CONTINUUM. WHAT'S UP NEXT?
ALL IS NOT LOST! I STILL HAVE MY BOX OF CEREAL!
CRUNCH CRUNCH
TASTES LOUSY!
BUT IT DOES HAVE A FREE PRIZE! TA-DA- A MAGIC CRAYON!
OOPS. BAD NEWS ON THAT SUBJECT-- BURP.
end

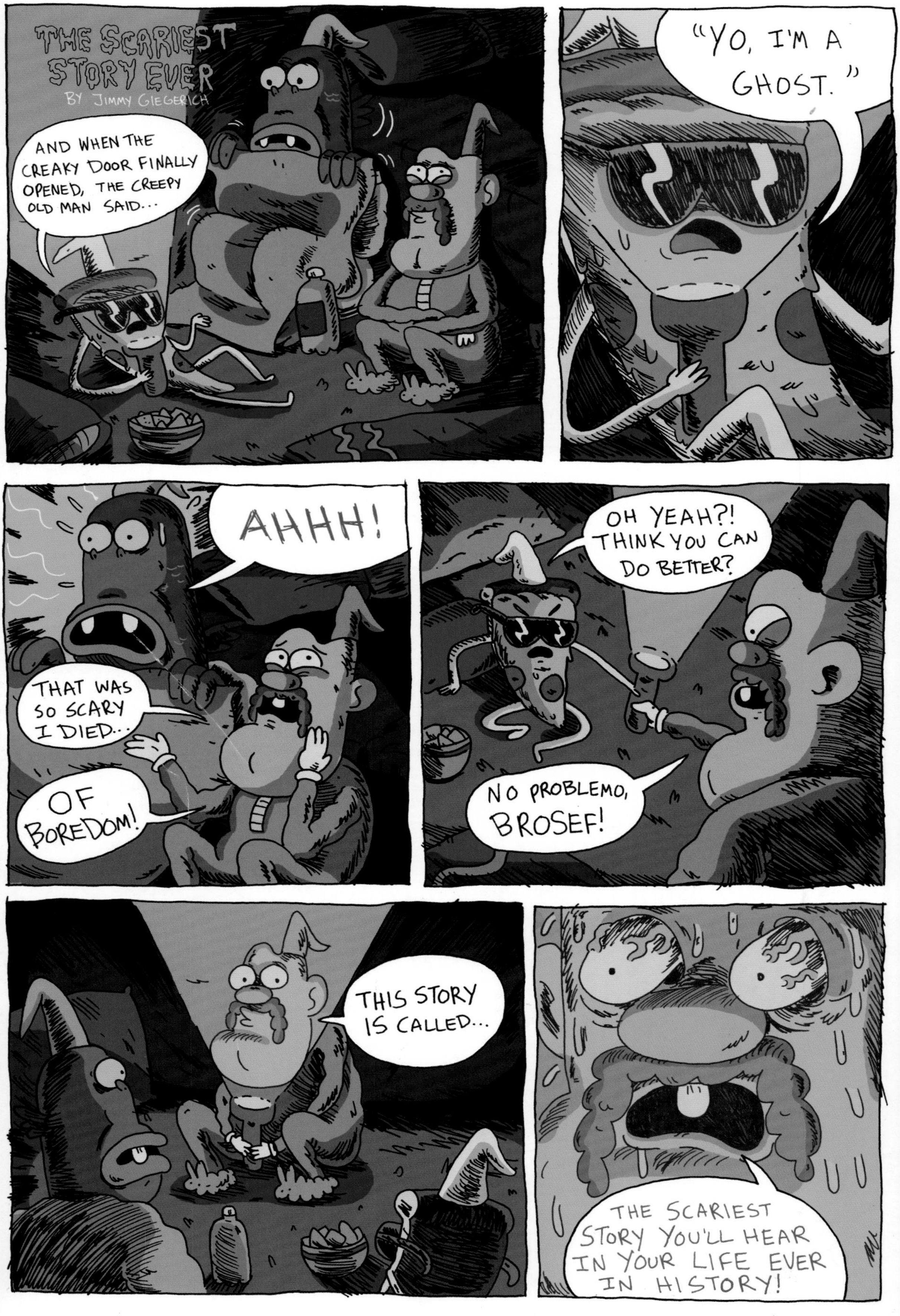
THE SCARIEST STORY EVER
BY JIMMY GIEGERICH
AND WHEN THE CREAKY DOOR FINALLY OPENED, THE CREEPY OLD MAN SAID...
"YO, I'M A GHOST."
AHHH!
THAT WAS SO SCARY I DIED...
OF BOREDOM!
OH YEAH?! THINK YOU CAN DO BETTER?
NO PROBLEMO, BROSEF!
THIS STORY IS CALLED...
THE SCARIEST STORY YOU'LL HEAR IN YOUR LIFE EVER IN HISTORY!

ONCE UPON A TIME, IN THE CREEPIEST FOREST EVER

THERE WAS A MONSTER UNLIKE ANY MONSTER YOU'VE SEEN!

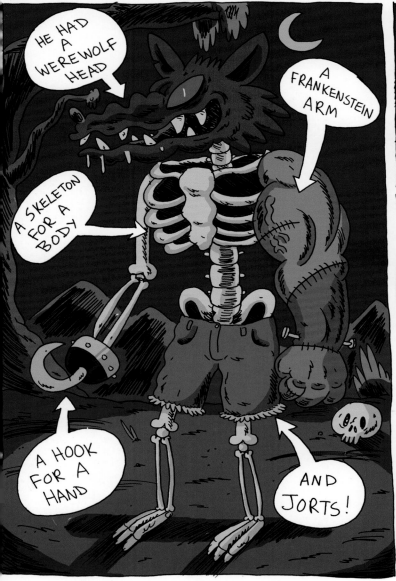

HE HAD A WEREWOLF HEAD

A FRANKENSTEIN ARM

A SKELETON FOR A BODY

A HOOK FOR A HAND

AND JORTS!

ON NIGHTS LIKE TONIGHT, HE'D WAIT FOR PEOPLE LEAVING BURGER HUT...

AND ATTACK THEM!

AND EAT THEIR BURGERS & FRIES ALIVE!

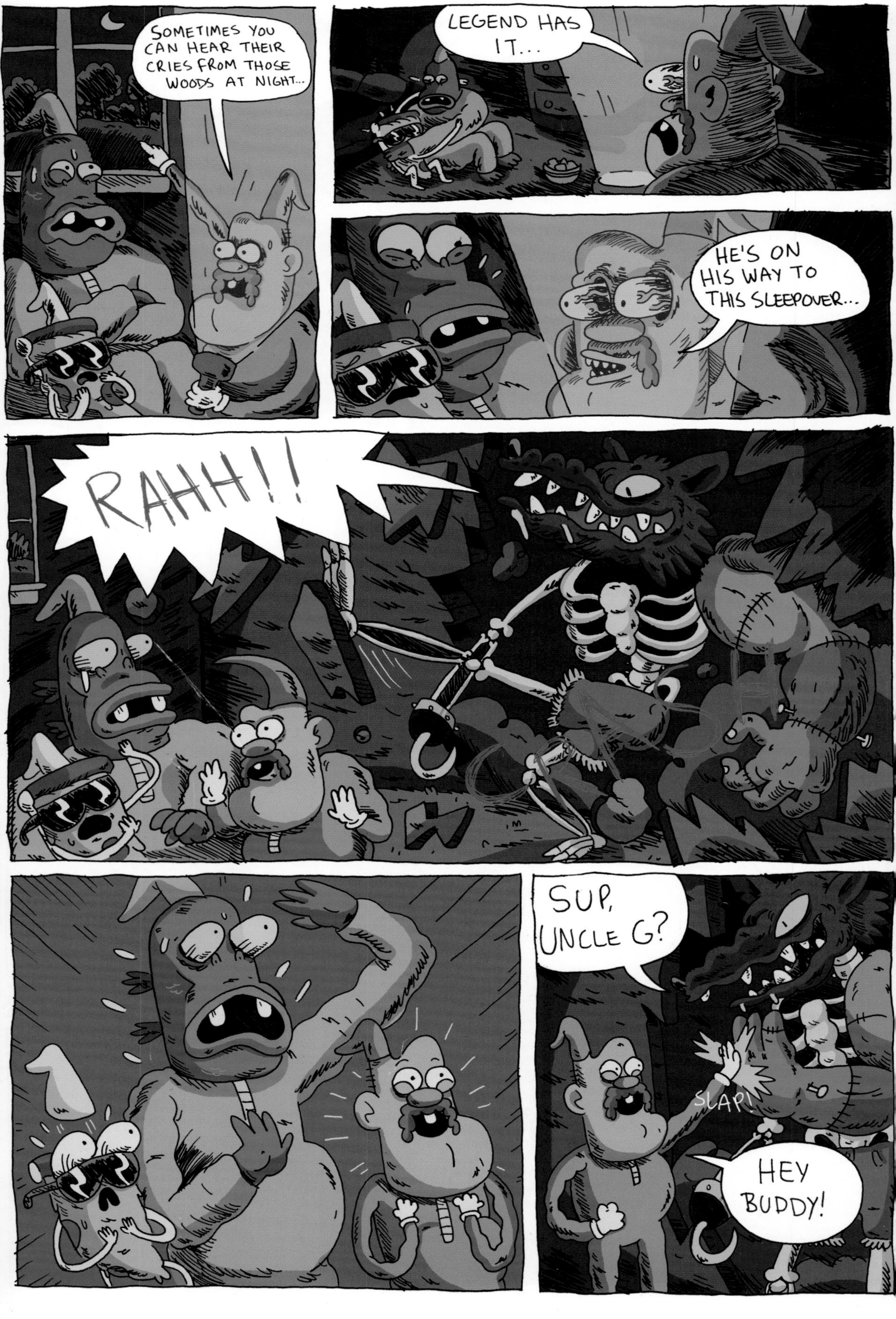
SOMETIMES YOU CAN HEAR THEIR CRIES FROM THOSE WOODS AT NIGHT...
LEGEND HAS IT...
HE'S ON HIS WAY TO THIS SLEEPOVER...
RAHH!!
SUP, UNCLE G?
SLAP!
HEY BUDDY!

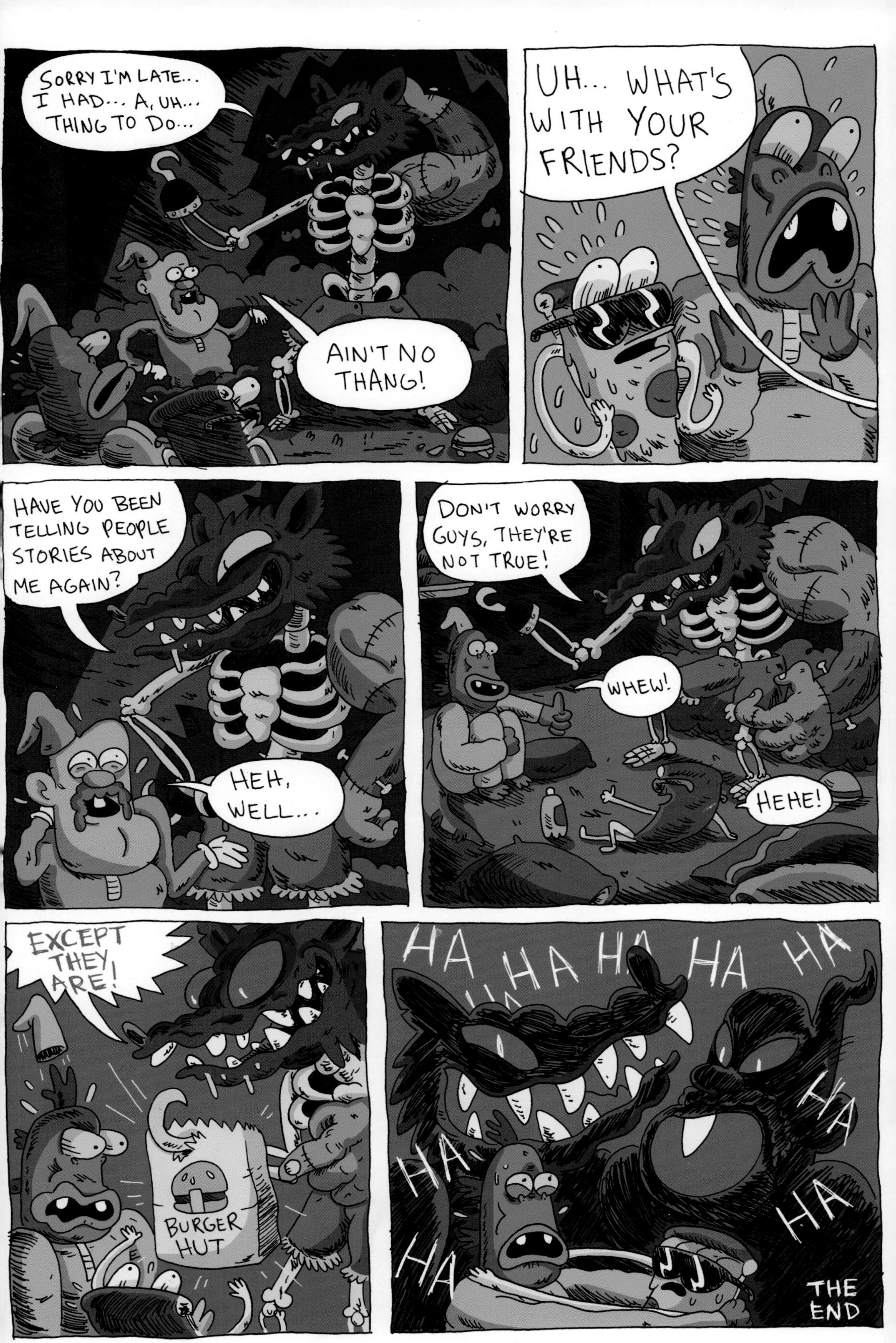
SORRY I'M LATE... I HAD... A, UH... THING TO DO...
AIN'T NO THANG!
UH... WHAT'S WITH YOUR FRIENDS?
HAVE YOU BEEN TELLING PEOPLE STORIES ABOUT ME AGAIN?
HEH, WELL...
DON'T WORRY GUYS, THEY'RE NOT TRUE!
WHEW!
HEHE!
EXCEPT THEY ARE!
BURGER HUT
HA HA HA HA HA HA
HA HA HA HA
THE END

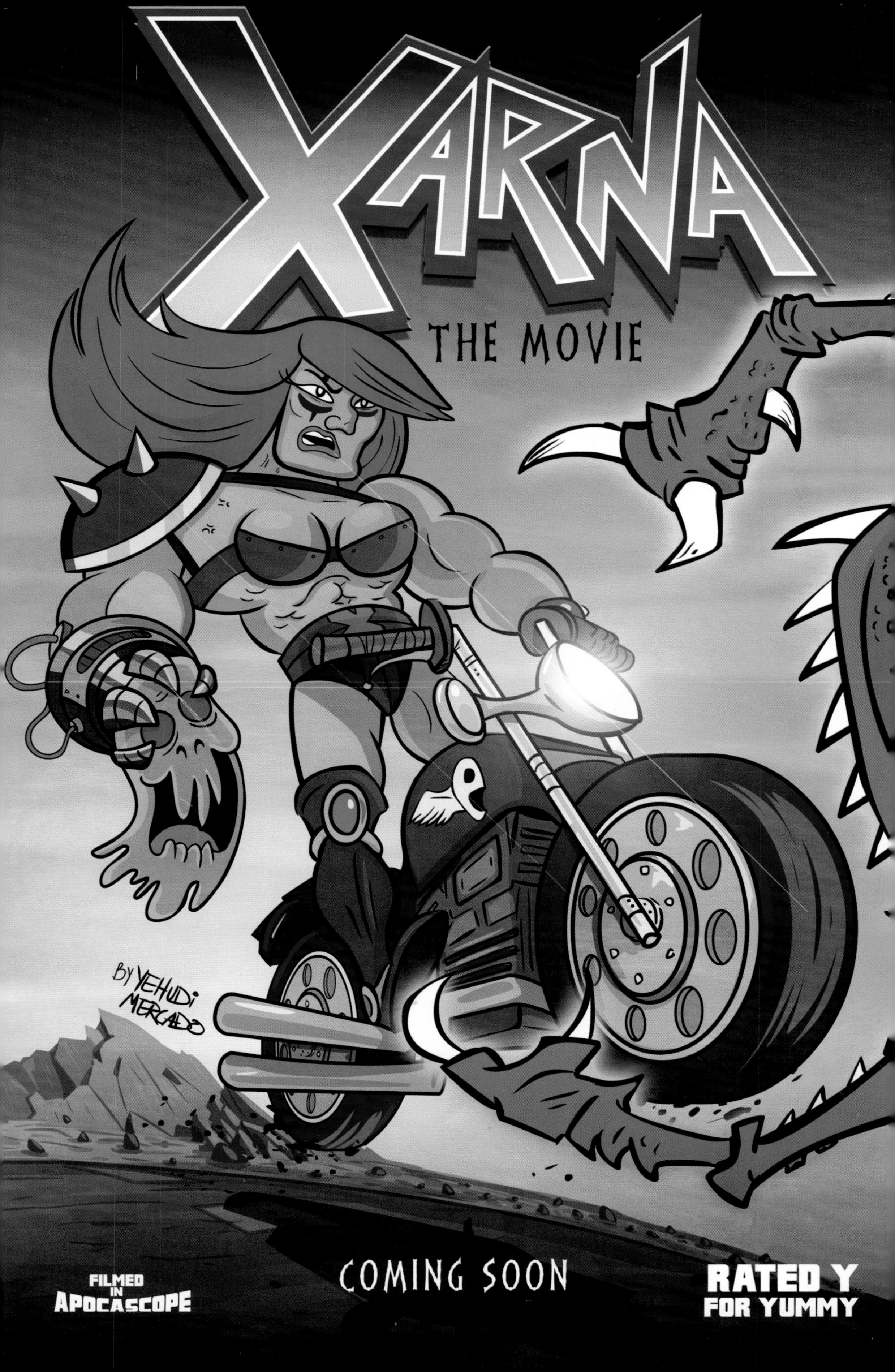
XARNA
THE MOVIE
BY YEHUDI MERCADO
FILMED IN APOCASCOPE
COMING SOON
RATED Y FOR YUMMY

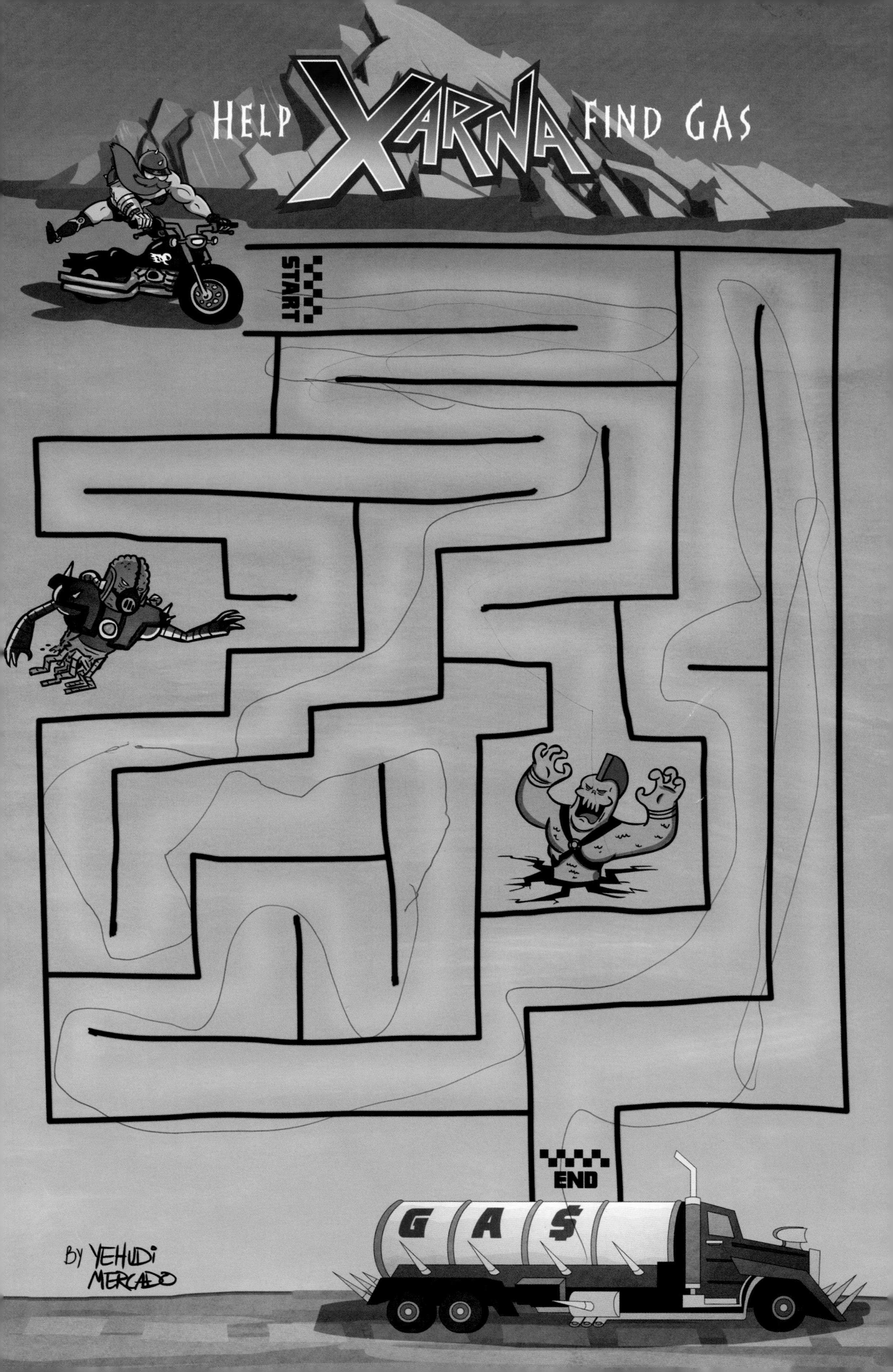
HELP XARNA FIND GAS
START
END
GAS
BY YEHUDI MERCADO

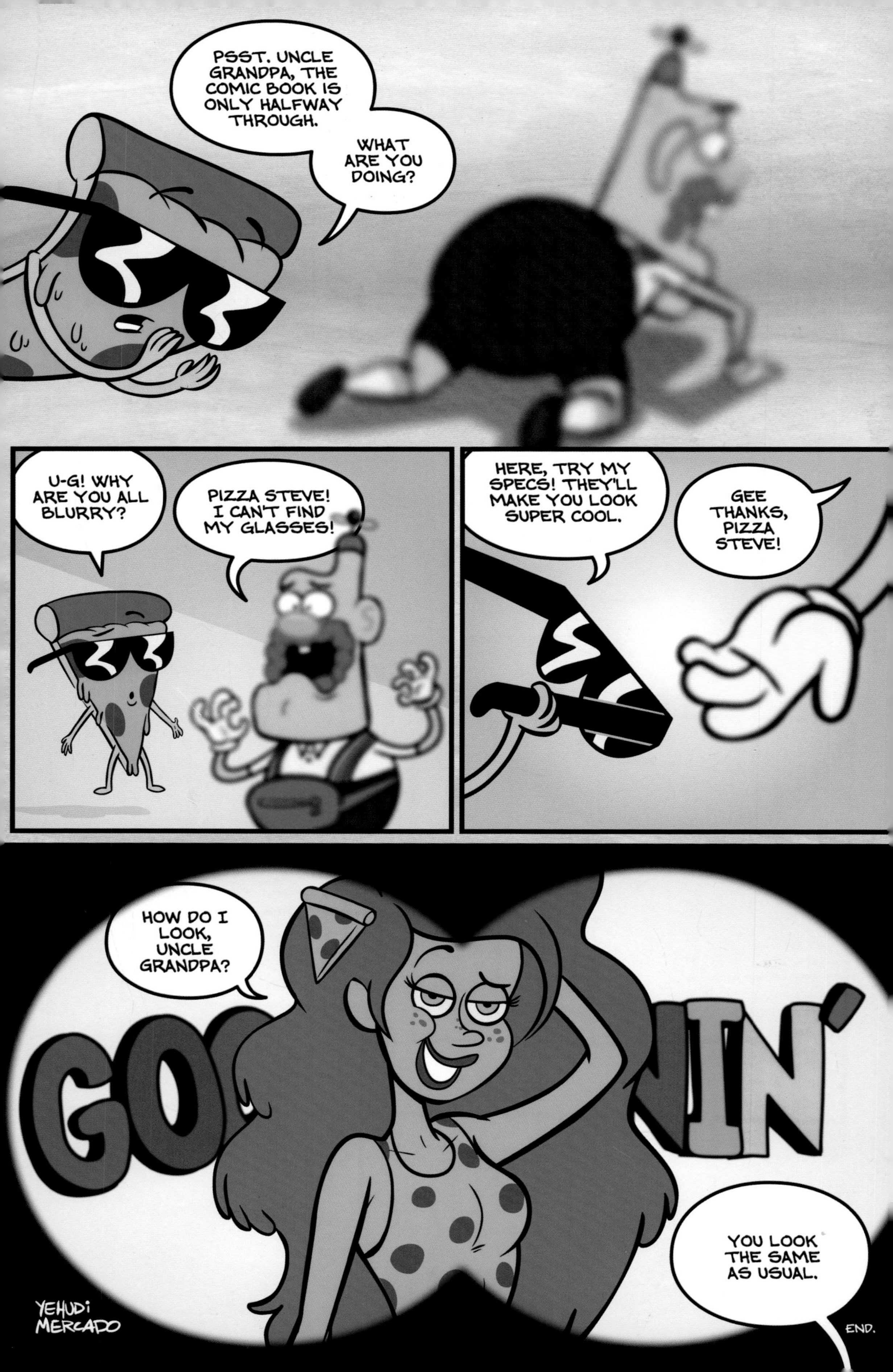
PSST. UNCLE GRANDPA, THE COMIC BOOK IS ONLY HALFWAY THROUGH.
WHAT ARE YOU DOING?
U-G! WHY ARE YOU ALL BLURRY?
PIZZA STEVE! I CAN'T FIND MY GLASSES!
HERE, TRY MY SPECS! THEY'LL MAKE YOU LOOK SUPER COOL.
GEE THANKS, PIZZA STEVE!
HOW DO I LOOK, UNCLE GRANDPA?
GOO
NIN'
YOU LOOK THE SAME AS USUAL.
YEHUDi MERCADO
END.

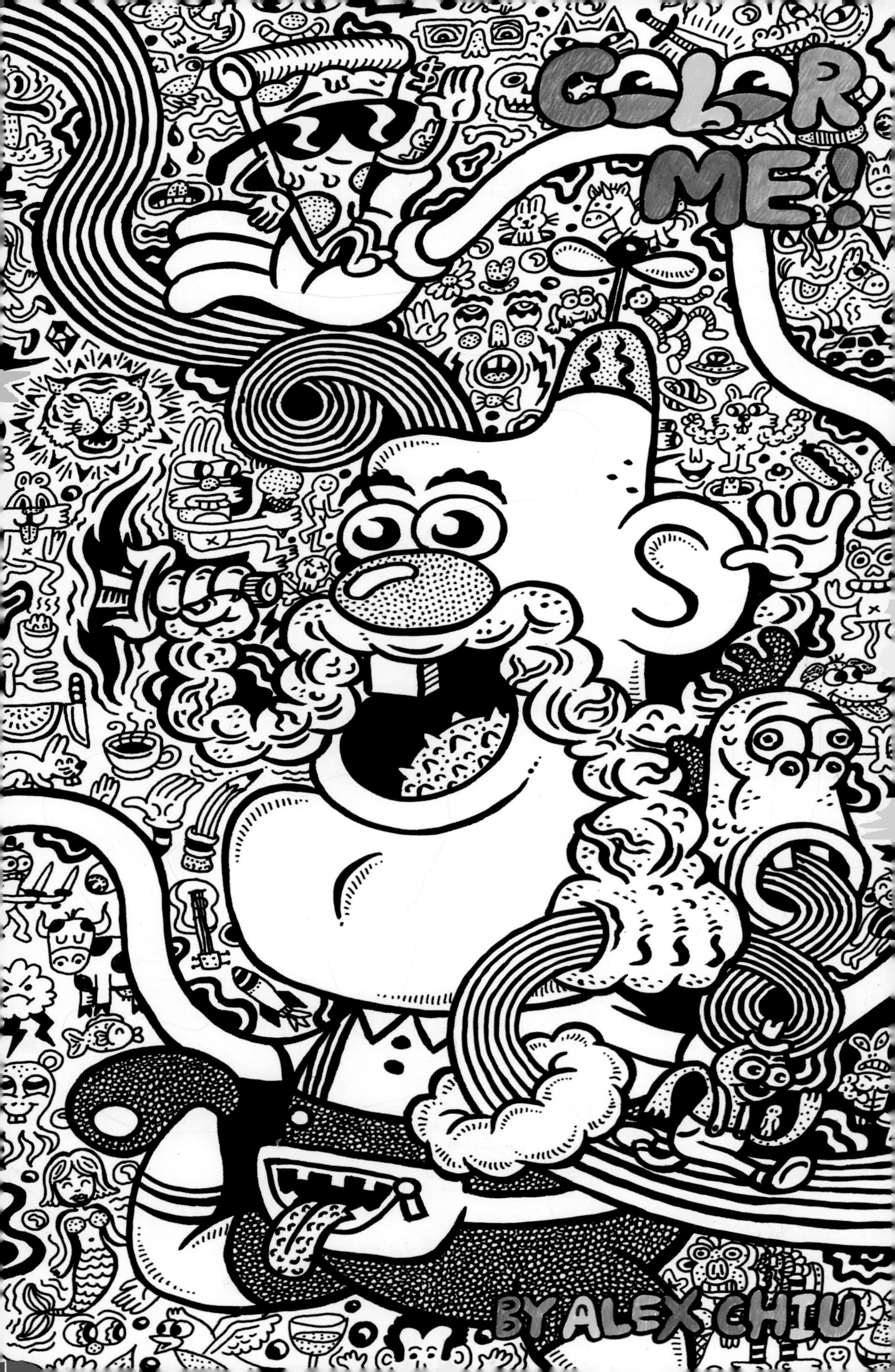
COLOR ME!
BY ALEX CHIU

FEAR OF WATER

EVGENY YAKOVLEV

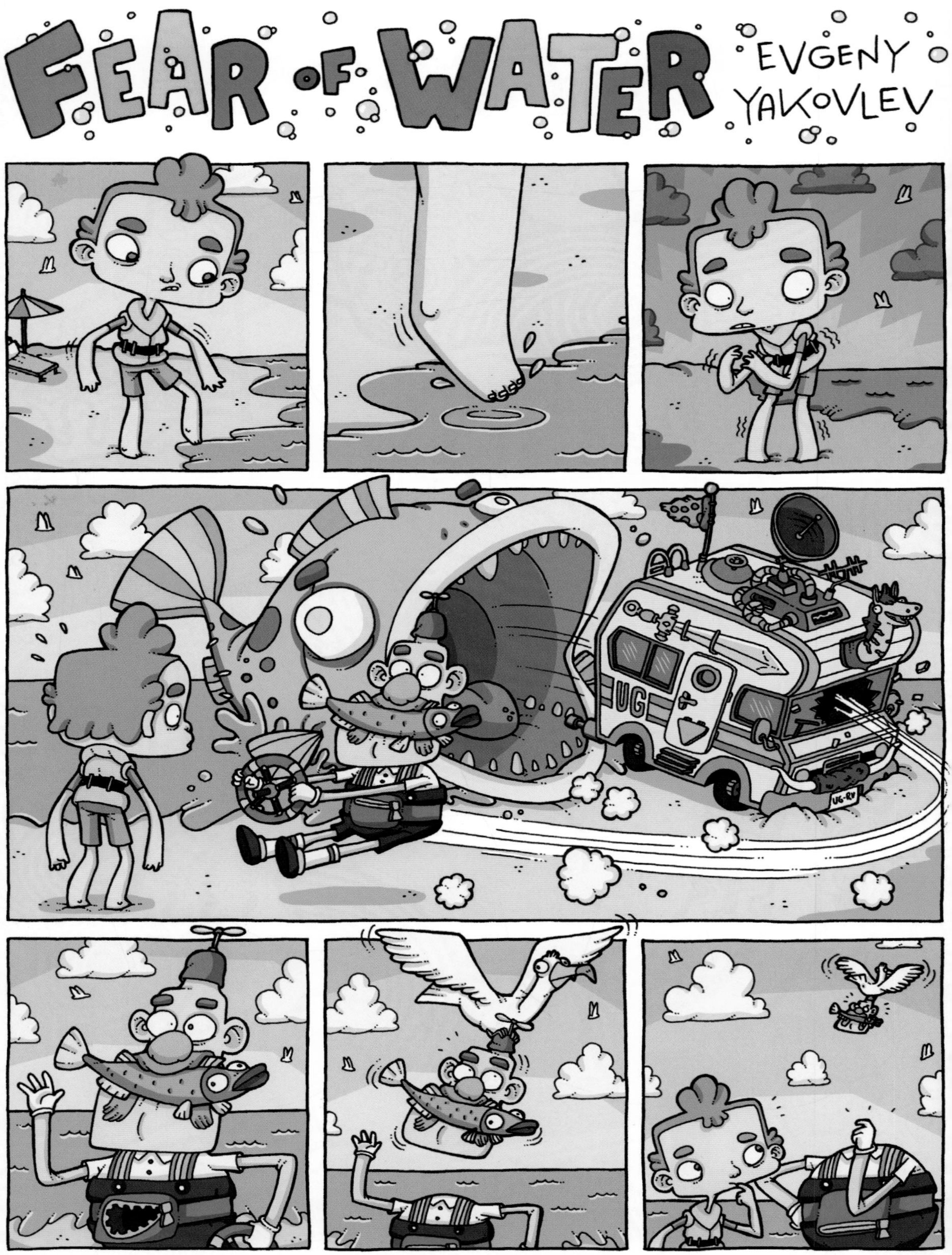
UG

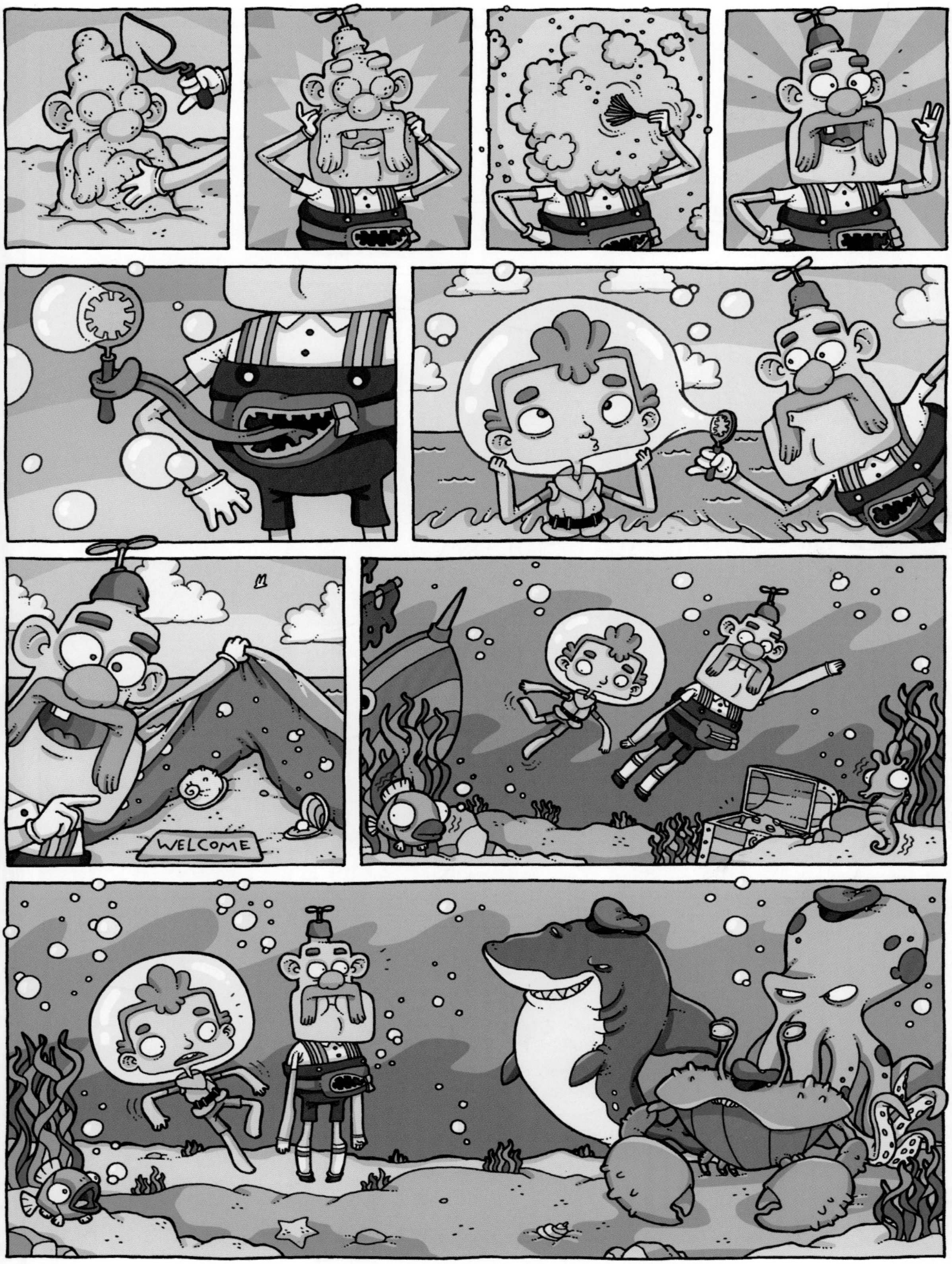
WELCOME

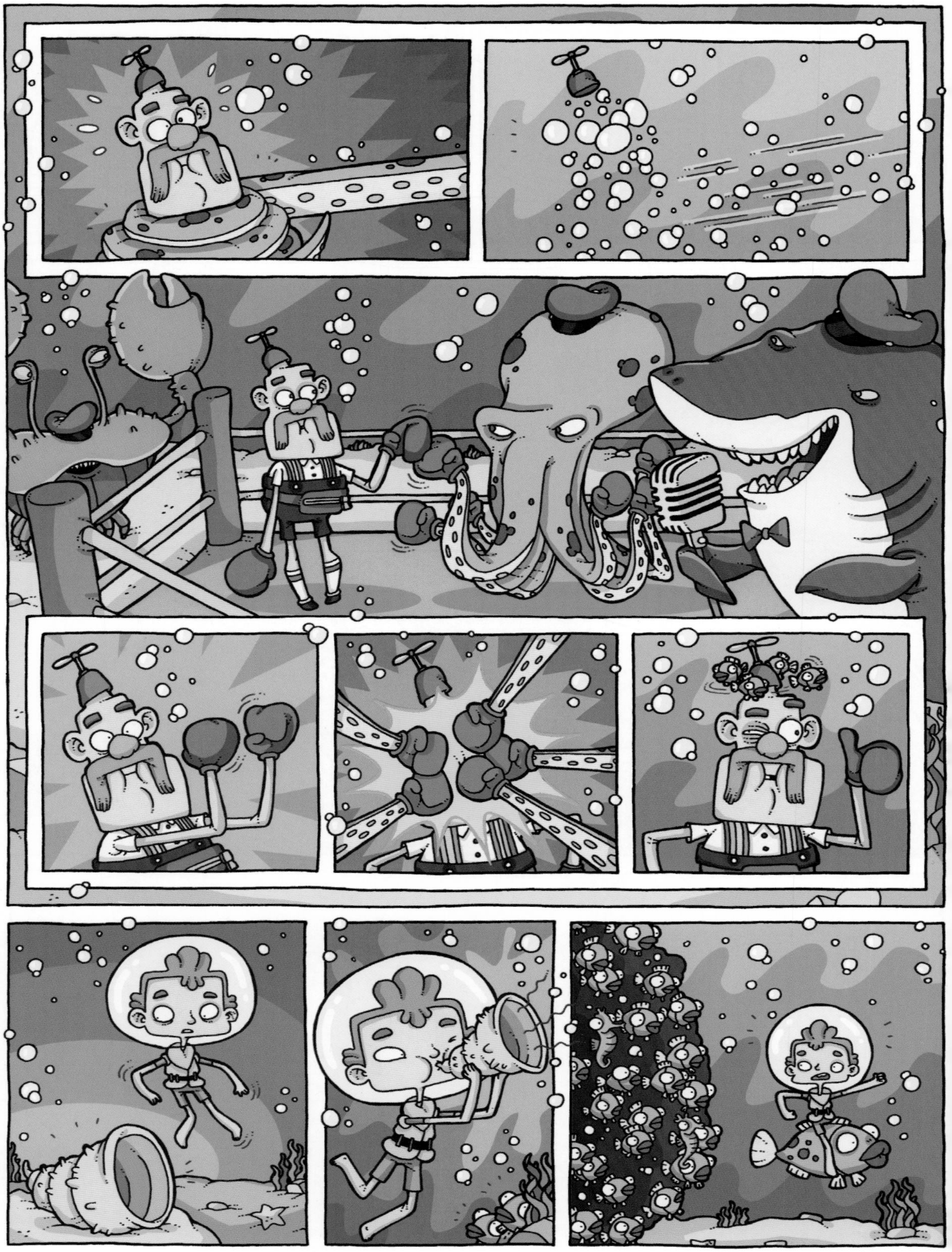

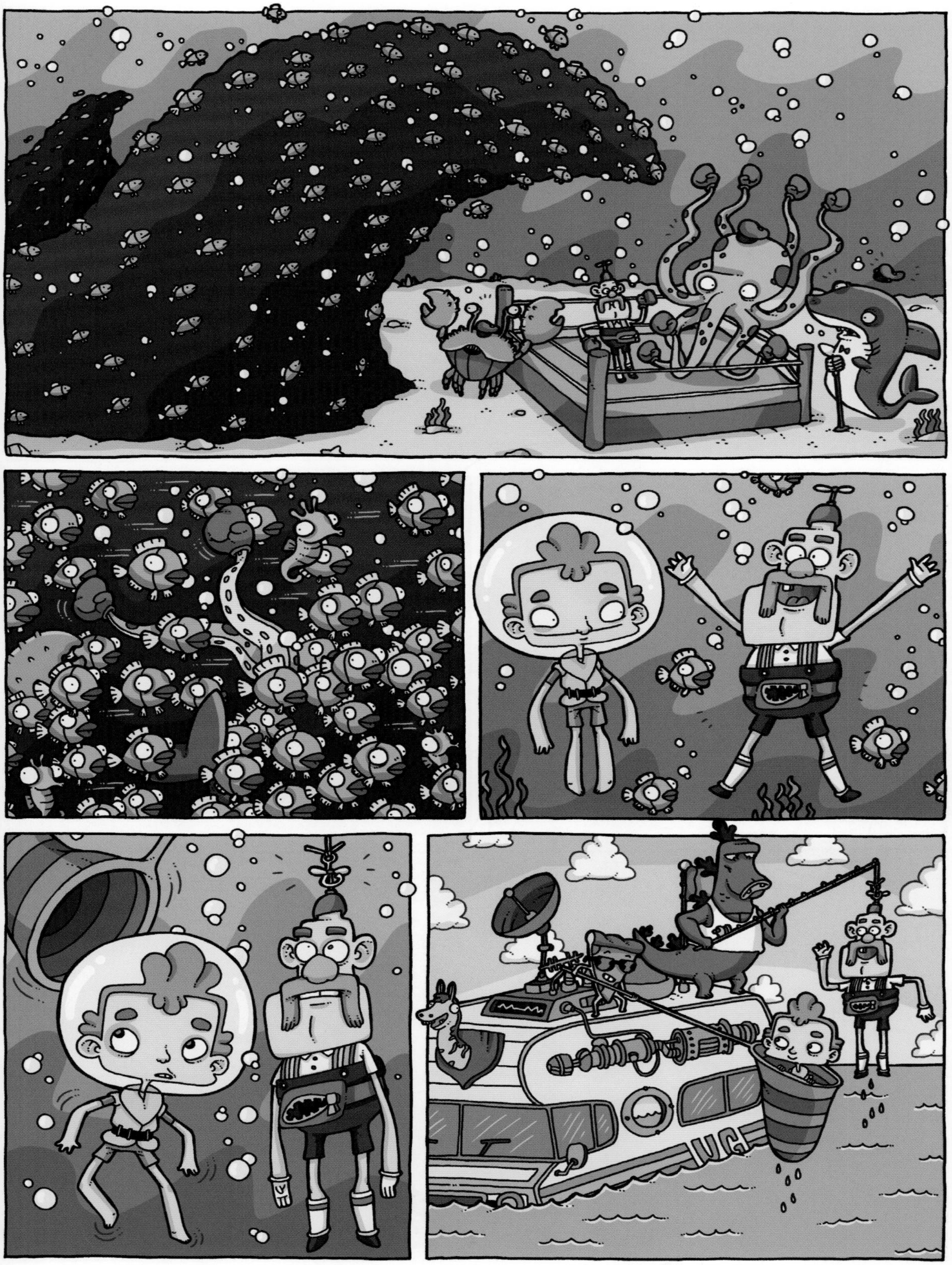
UG

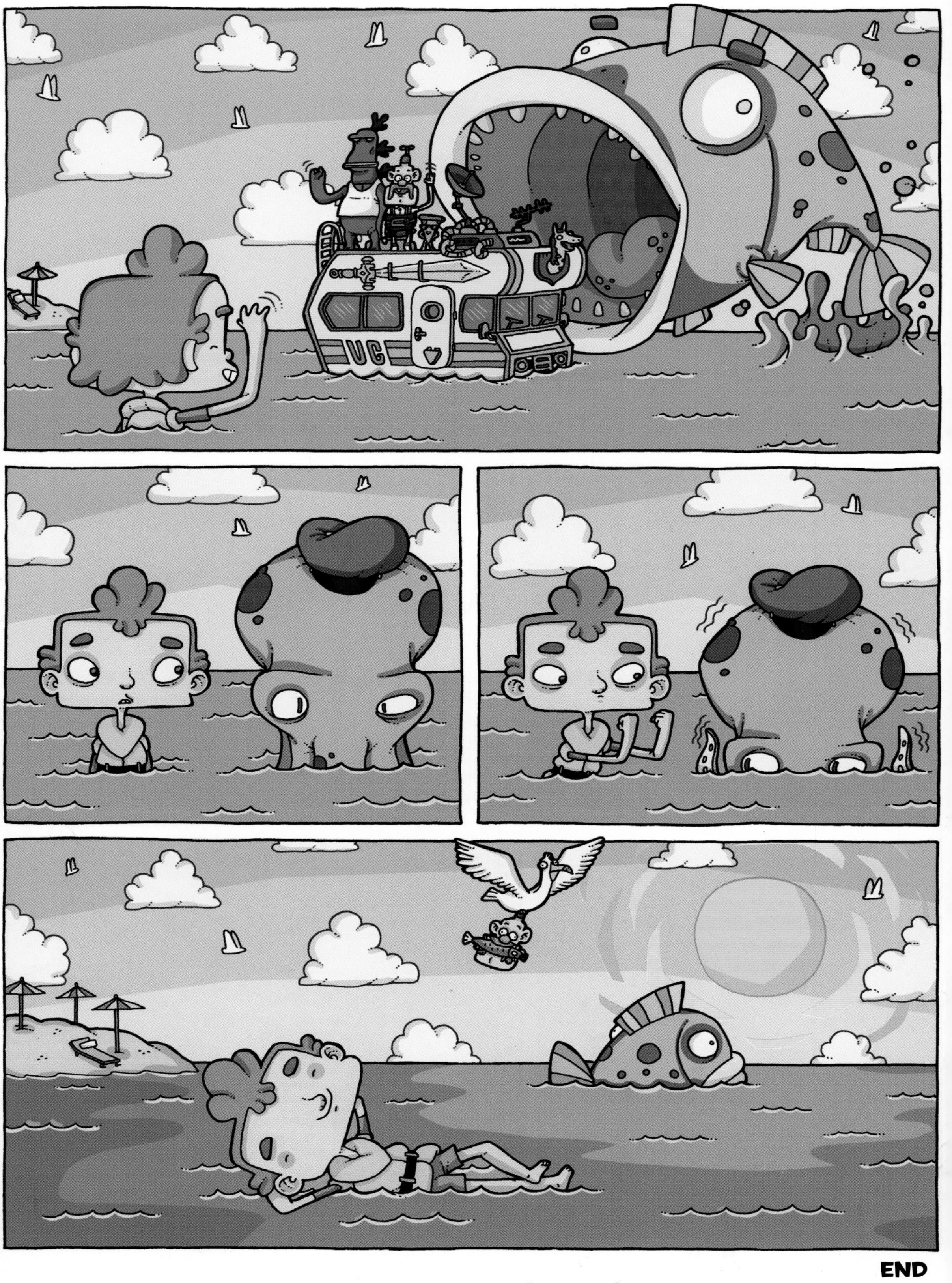
VG

END

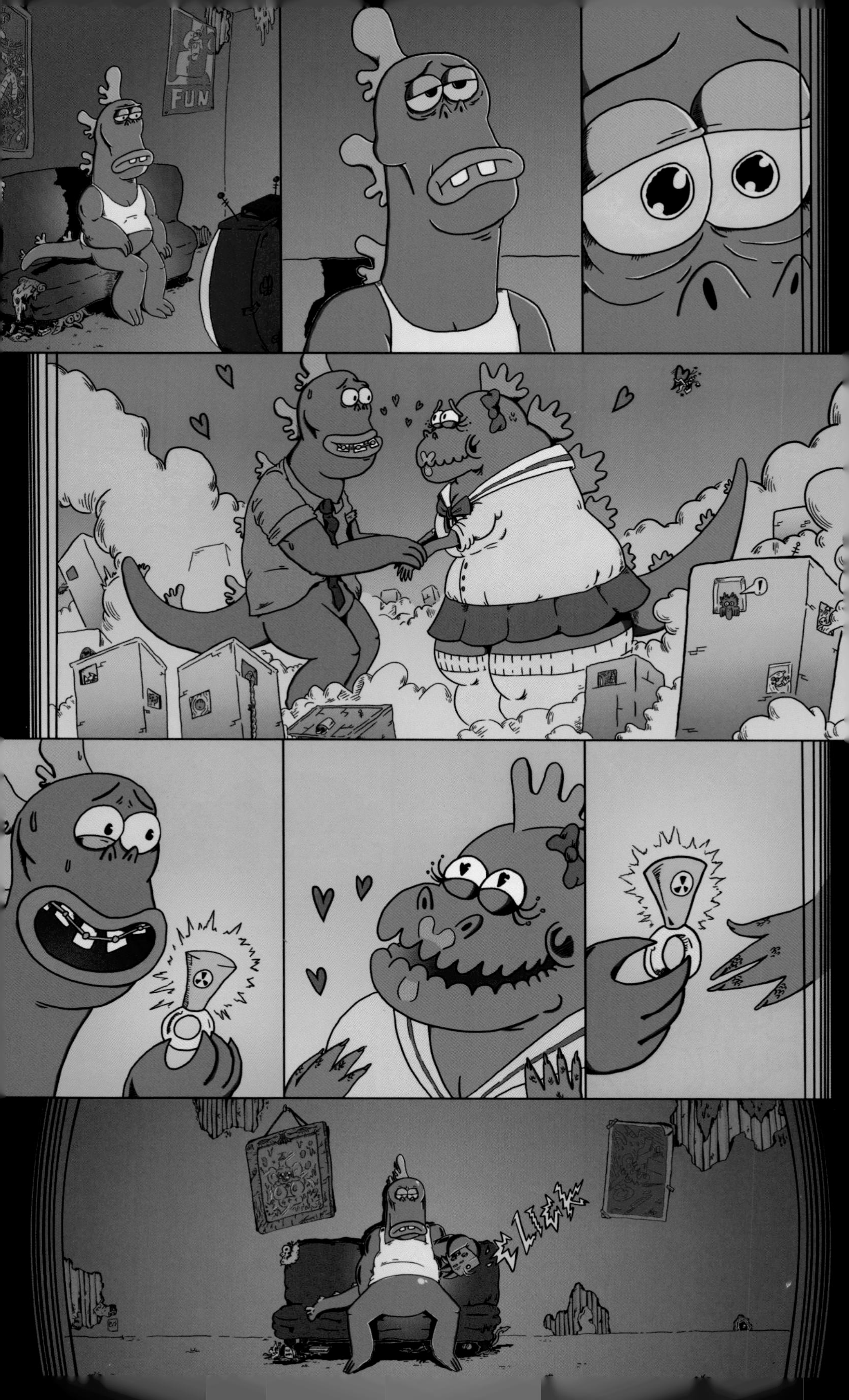
FUN
!
ZLICK

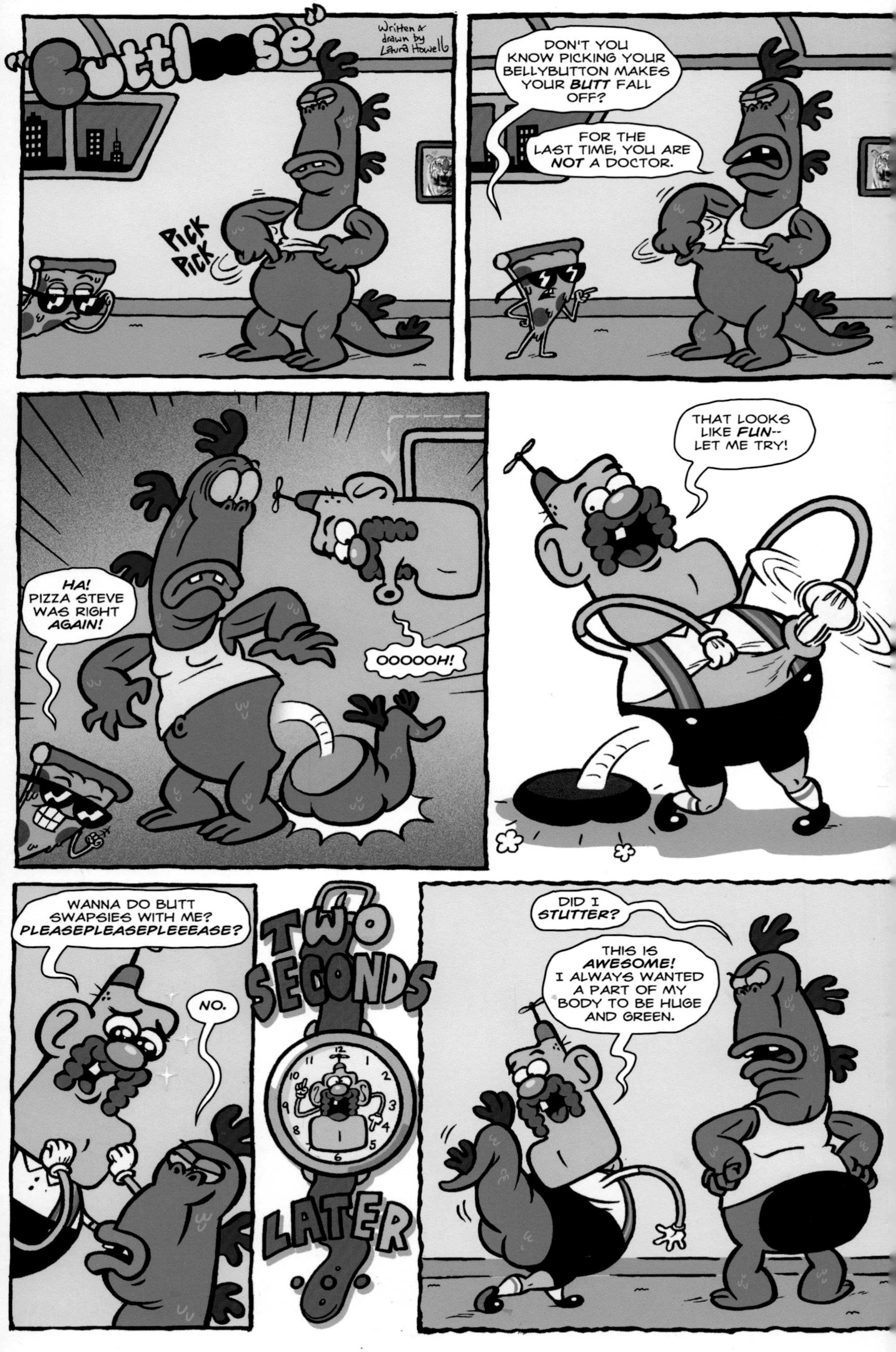
"Buttloose"
Written & drawn by Laura Howell
PICK PICK
DON'T YOU KNOW PICKING YOUR BELLYBUTTON MAKES YOUR BUTT FALL OFF?
FOR THE LAST TIME, YOU ARE NOT A DOCTOR.
HA! PIZZA STEVE WAS RIGHT AGAIN!
OOOOOH!
THAT LOOKS LIKE FUN-- LET ME TRY!
WANNA DO BUTT SWAPSIES WITH ME? PLEASEPLEASEPLEEEASE?
NO.
TWO SECONDS LATER
DID I STUTTER?
THIS IS AWESOME! I ALWAYS WANTED A PART OF MY BODY TO BE HUGE AND GREEN.

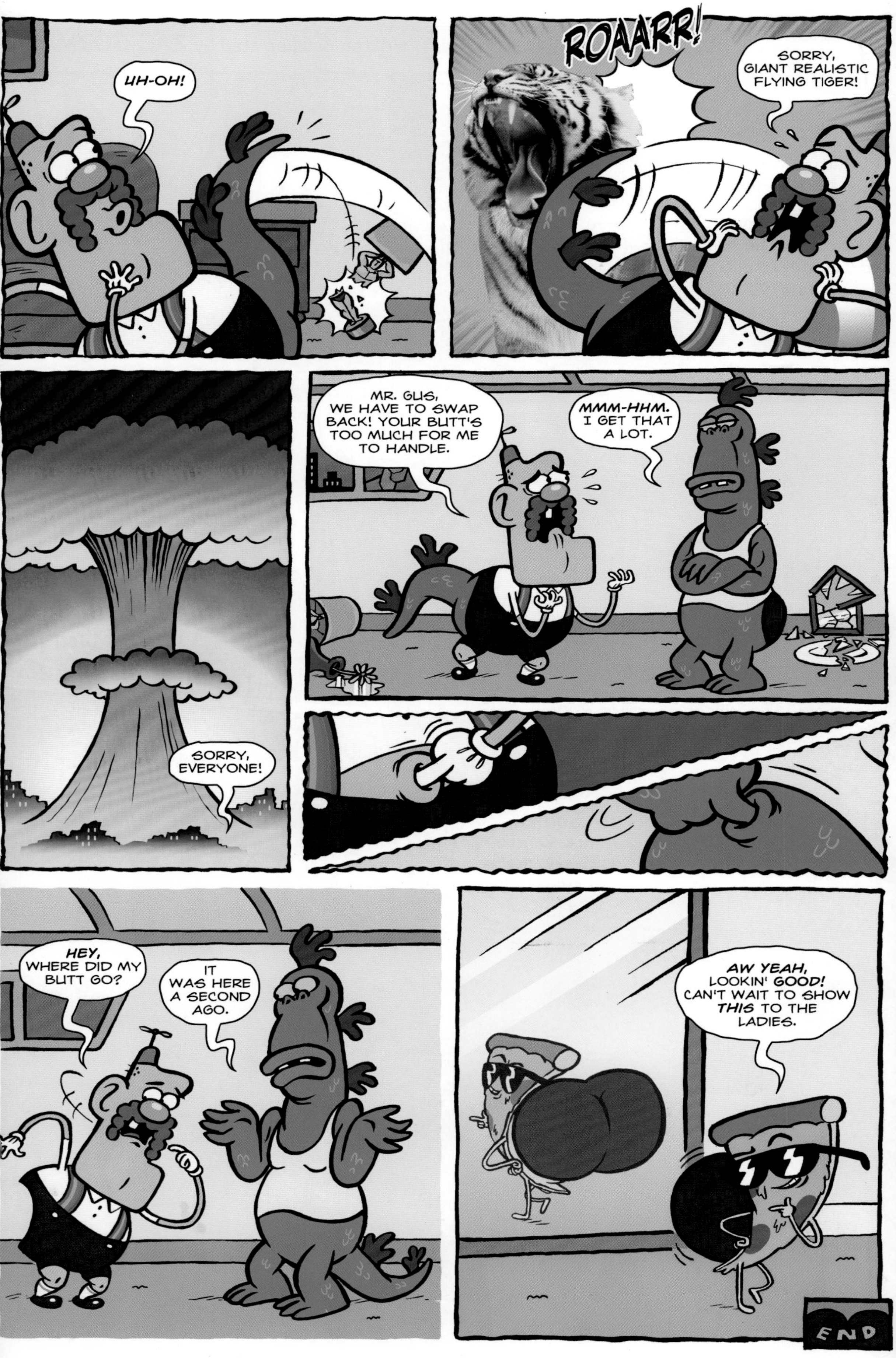
UH-OH!
ROAARR!
SORRY, GIANT REALISTIC FLYING TIGER!
SORRY, EVERYONE!
MR. GUS, WE HAVE TO SWAP BACK! YOUR BUTT'S TOO MUCH FOR ME TO HANDLE.
MMM-HHM. I GET THAT A LOT.
HEY, WHERE DID MY BUTT GO?
IT WAS HERE A SECOND AGO.
AW YEAH, LOOKIN' GOOD! CAN'T WAIT TO SHOW THIS TO THE LADIES.
END

UNCLE GRANDPA™ "VALUABLE LESSON" written & illustrated by ZAC GORMAN

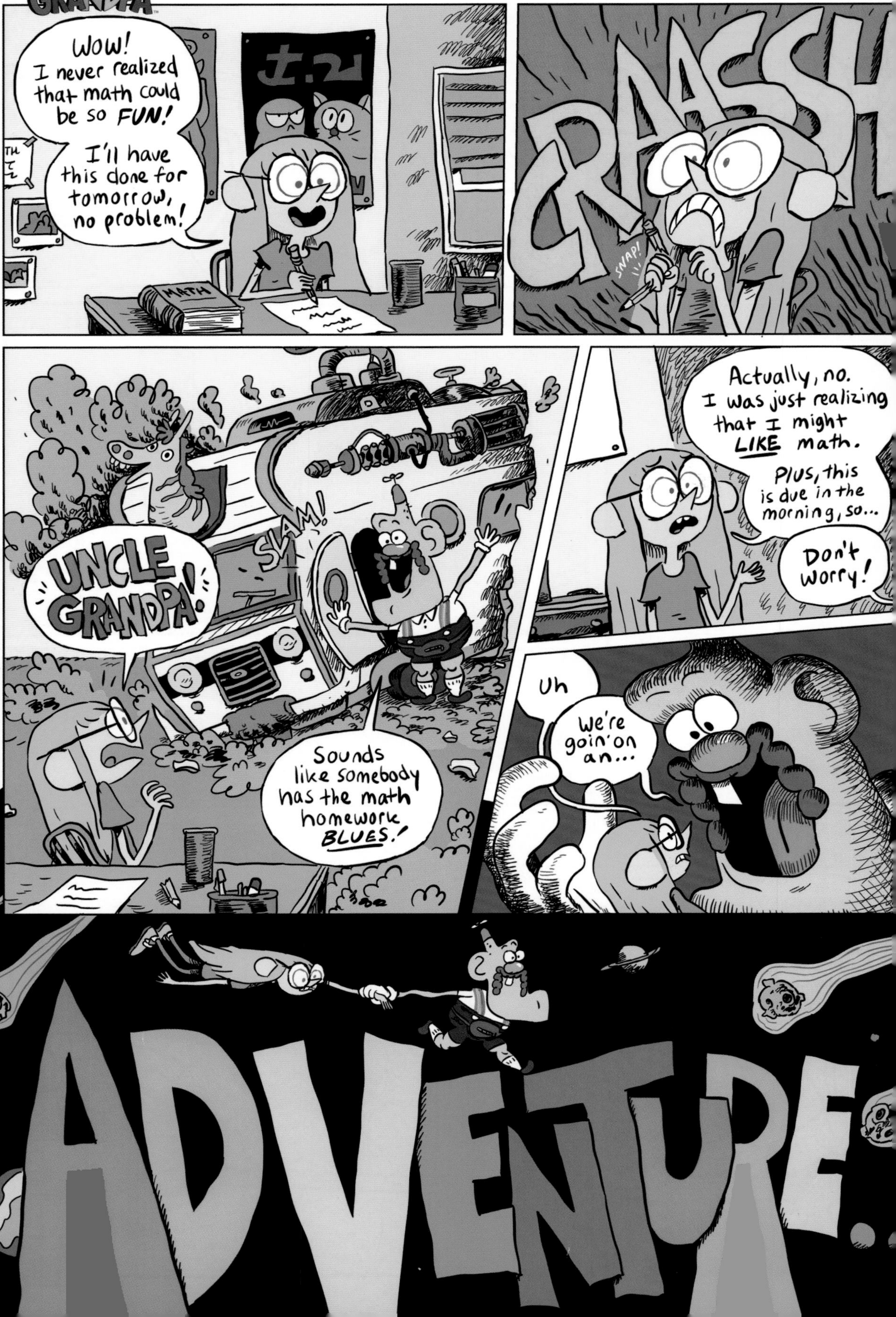
WOW! I never realized that math could be so FUN!
I'll have this done for tomorrow, no problem!
MATH
CRAASSH
SNAP!
SLAM!
UNCLE GRANDPA!
Sounds like somebody has the math homework BLUES!
Actually, no. I was just realizing that I might LIKE math.
PLUS, this is due in the morning, so...
Don't worry!
Uh
We're goin' on an...
ADVENTURE!

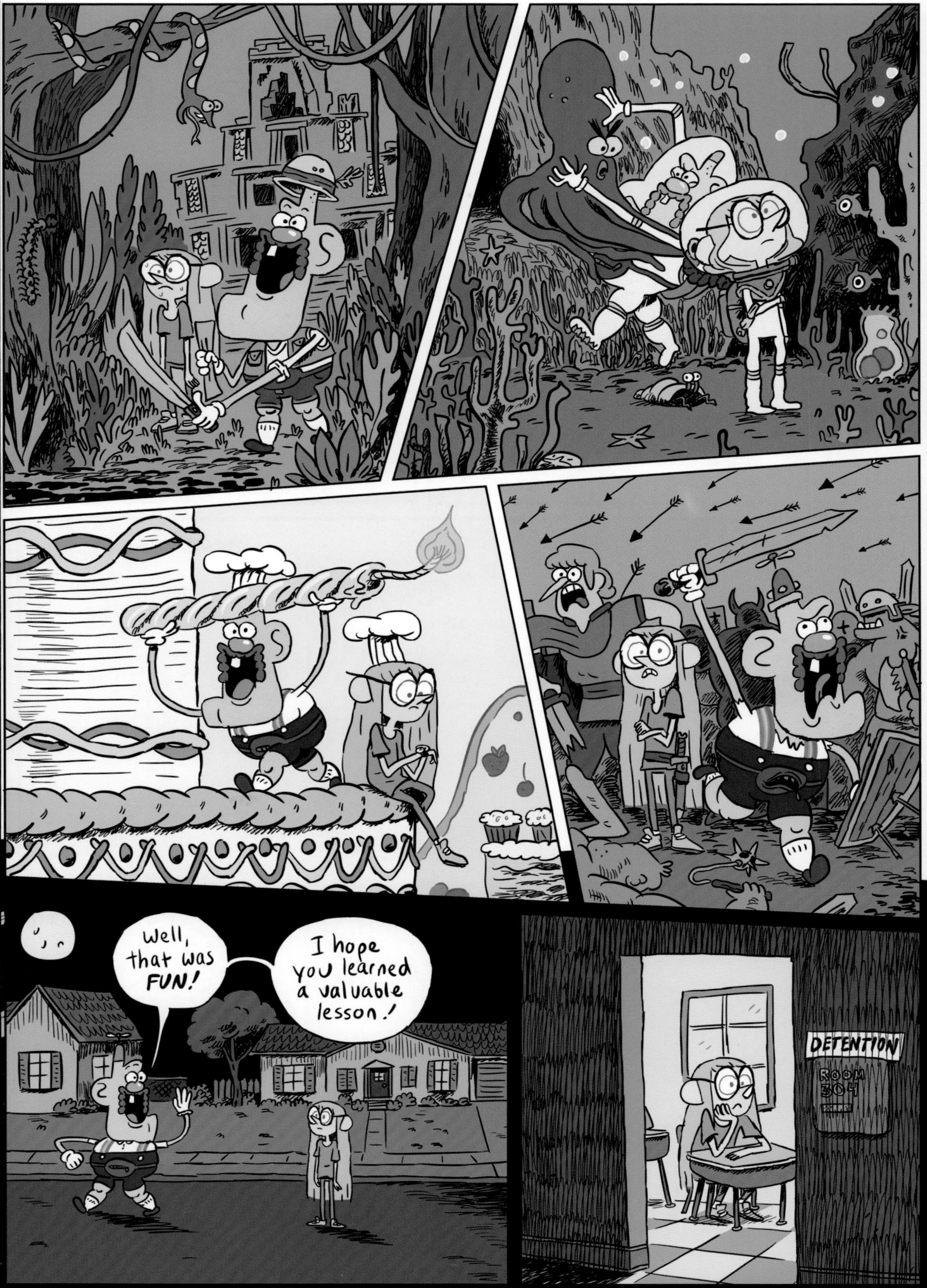
Well, that was FUN!
I hope you learned a valuable lesson!
DETENTION
ROOM 304

- ZAC GORMAN

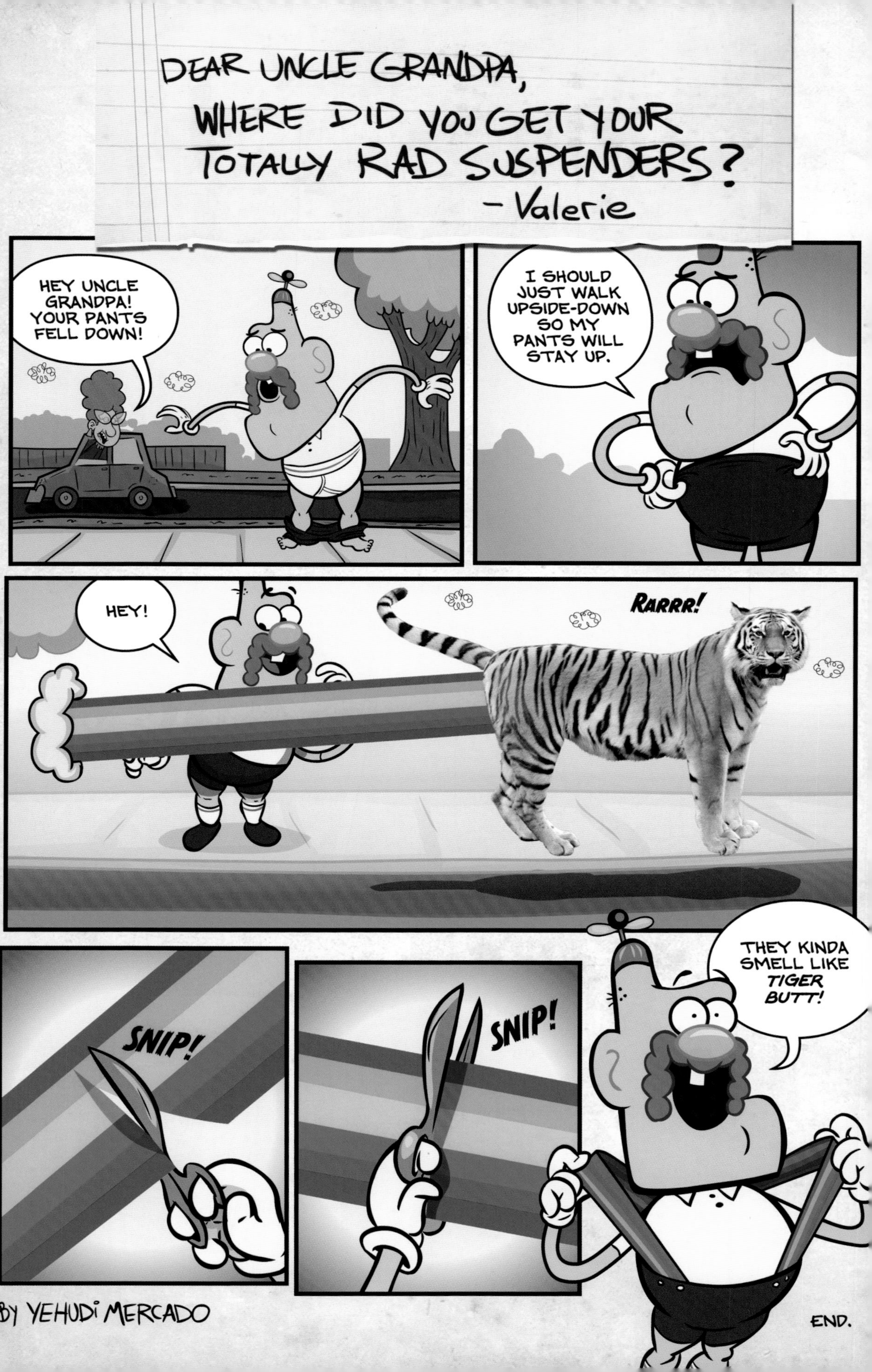
DEAR UNCLE GRANDPA,
WHERE DID YOU GET YOUR TOTALLY RAD SUSPENDERS?
- Valerie
HEY UNCLE GRANDPA! YOUR PANTS FELL DOWN!
I SHOULD JUST WALK UPSIDE-DOWN SO MY PANTS WILL STAY UP.
HEY!
RARRR!
SNIP!
SNIP!
THEY KINDA SMELL LIKE TIGER BUTT!
BY YEHUDI MERCADO
END.

ISSUE #1 VARIANT COVER
TROY LITTLE

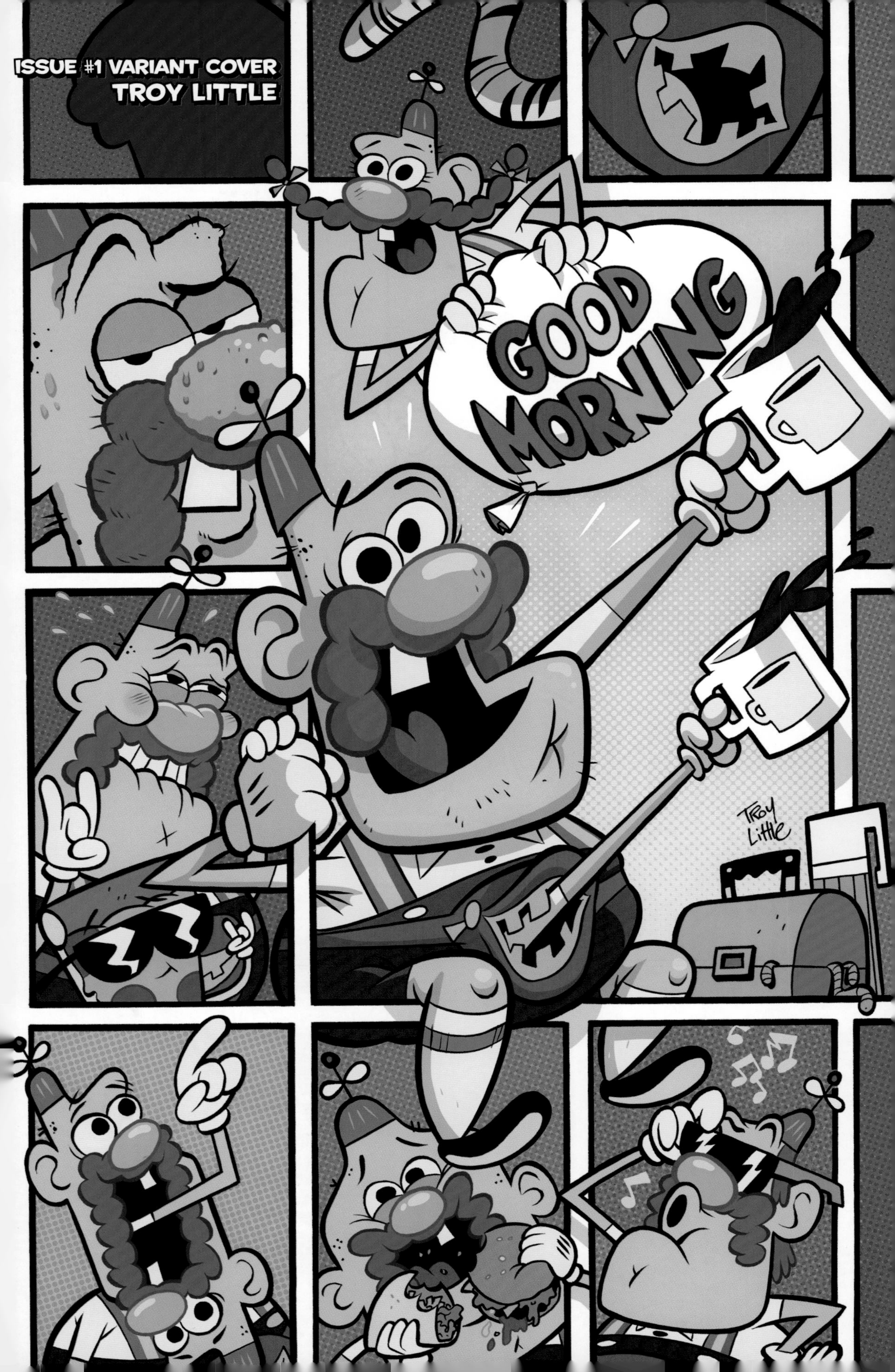
GOOD MORNING
TROY LITTLE

ISSUE #2 COVER
ROBB MOMMAERTS

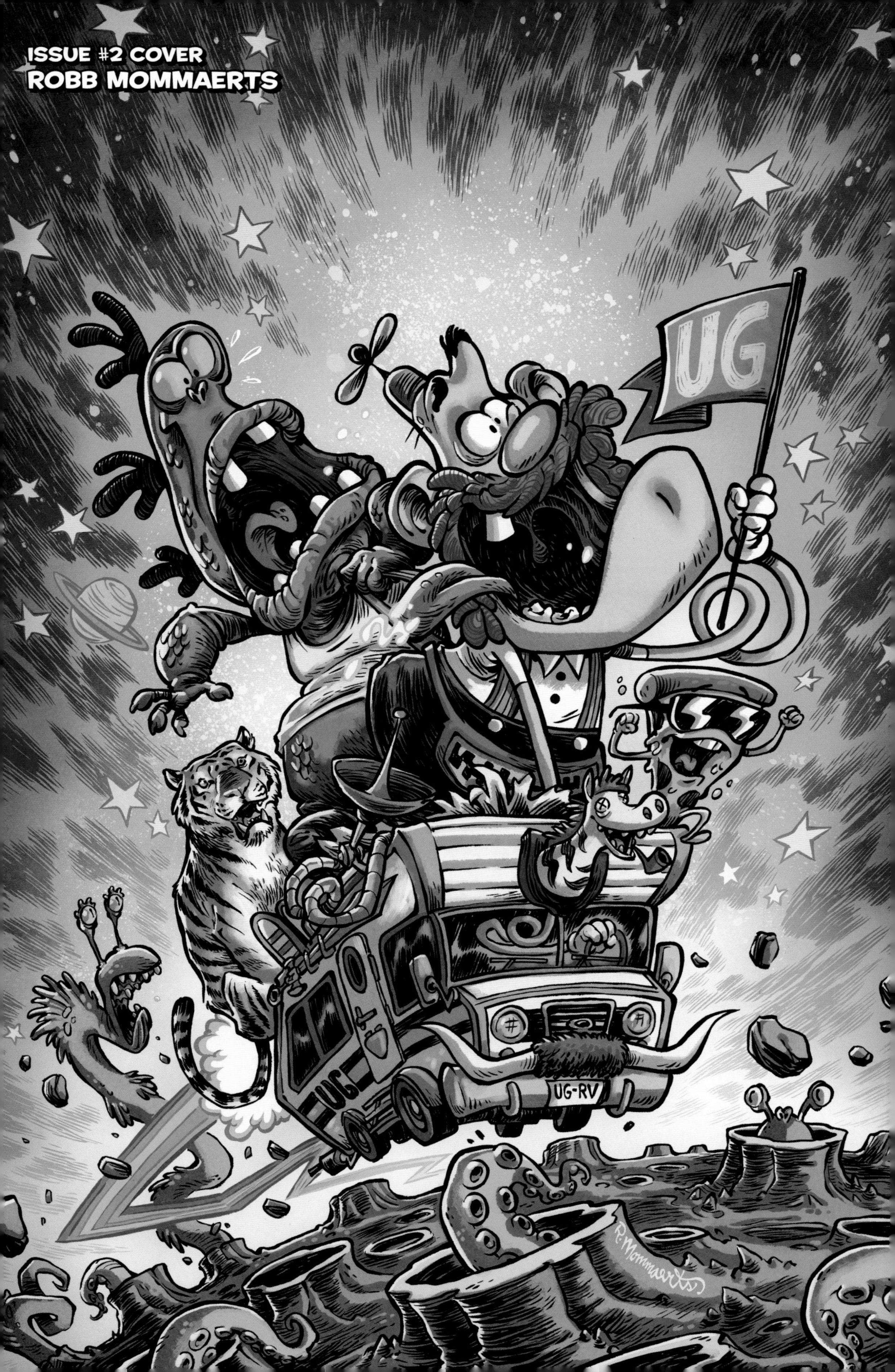
UG
UG
UG-RV
R. Mommaerts

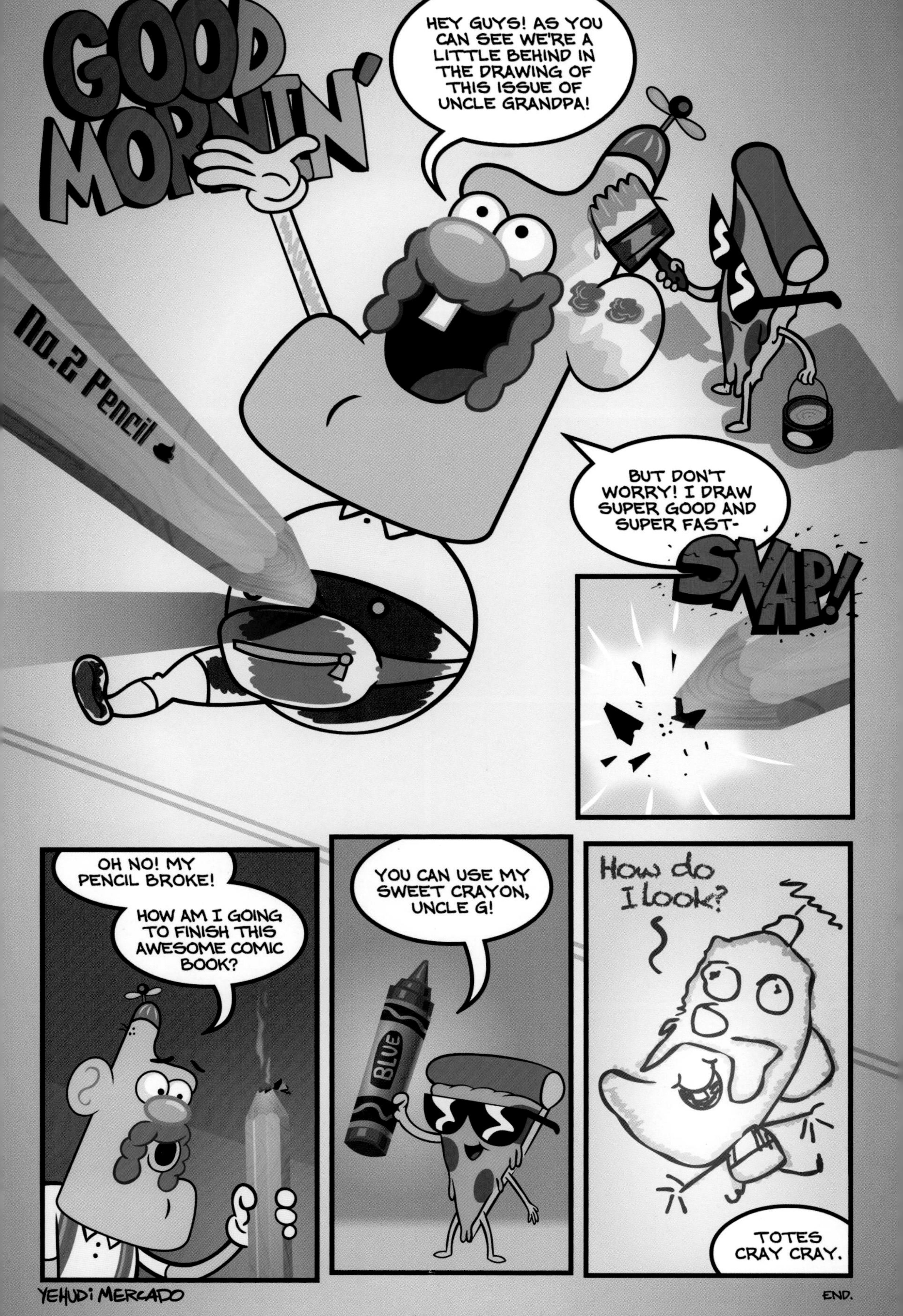
GOOD MORNIN'
HEY GUYS! AS YOU CAN SEE WE'RE A LITTLE BEHIND IN THE DRAWING OF THIS ISSUE OF UNCLE GRANDPA!
No.2 Pencil
BUT DON'T WORRY! I DRAW SUPER GOOD AND SUPER FAST-
SNAP!
OH NO! MY PENCIL BROKE!
HOW AM I GOING TO FINISH THIS AWESOME COMIC BOOK?
YOU CAN USE MY SWEET CRAYON, UNCLE G!
BLUE
How do I look?
TOTES CRAY CRAY.
YEHUDI MERCADO
END.

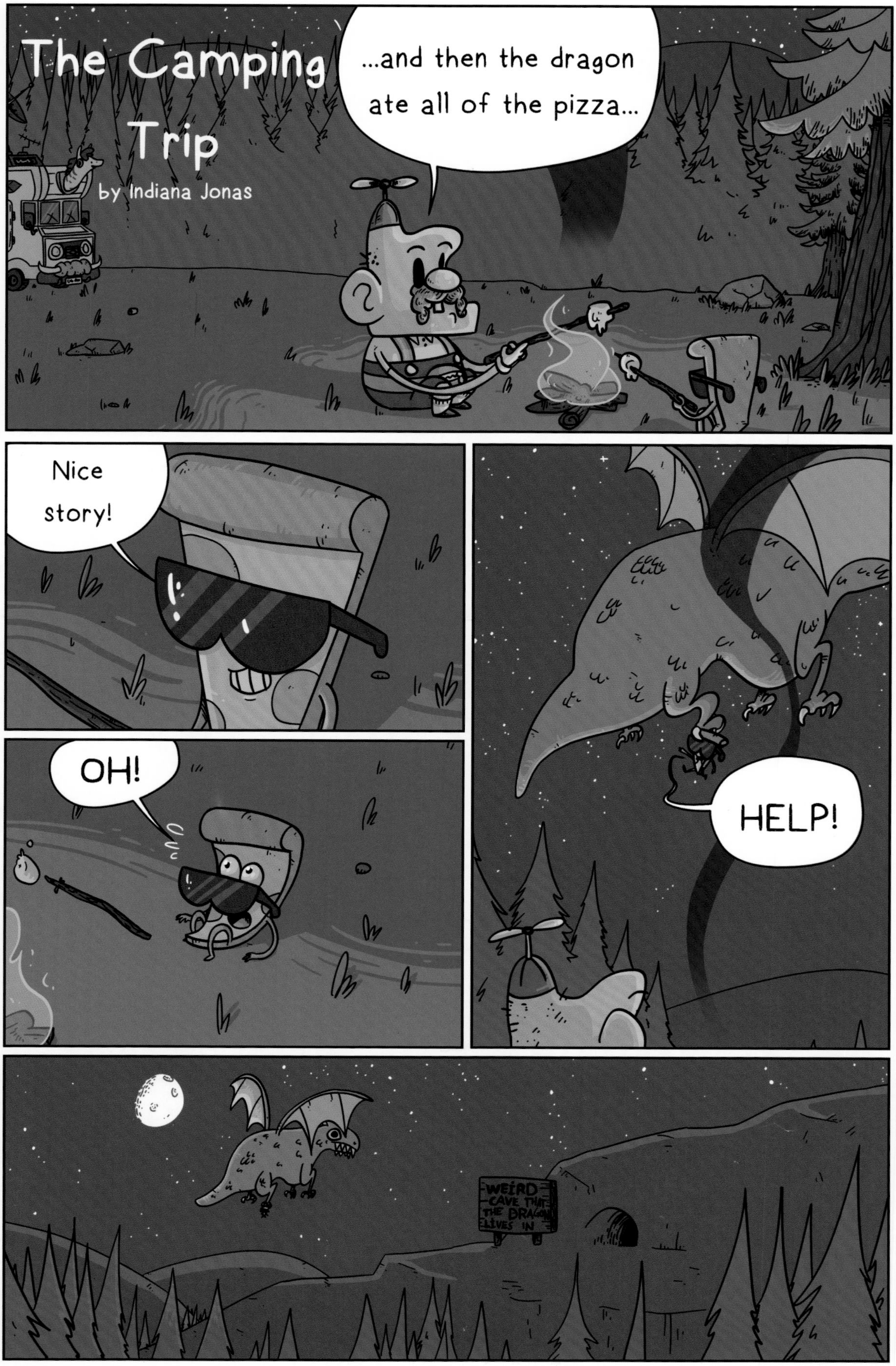
The Camping Trip
by Indiana Jonas
...and then the dragon ate all of the pizza...
Nice story!
OH!
HELP!
WEIRD CAVE THAT THE DRAGON LIVES IN

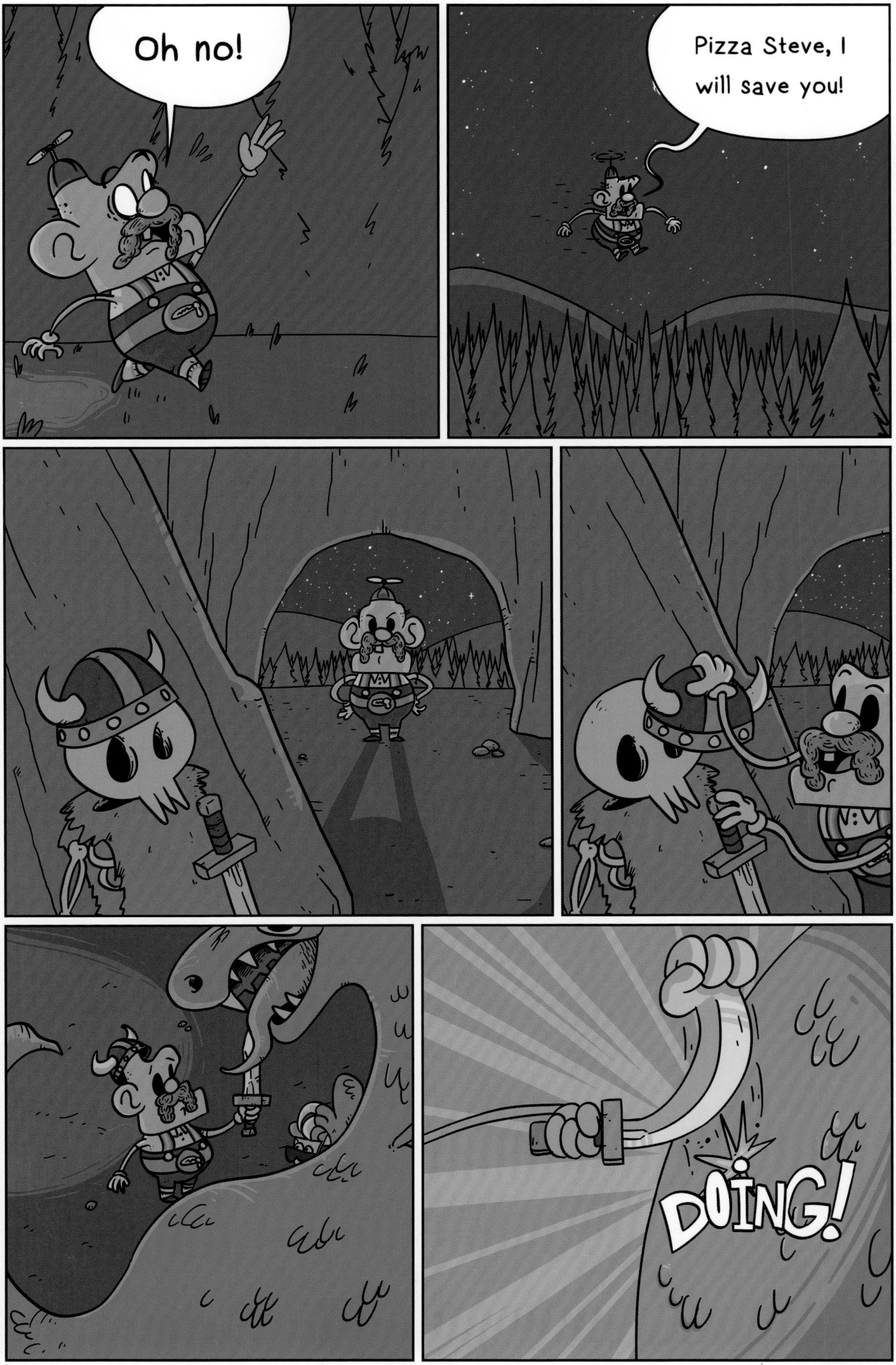
Oh no!
Pizza Steve, I will save you!
DOING!

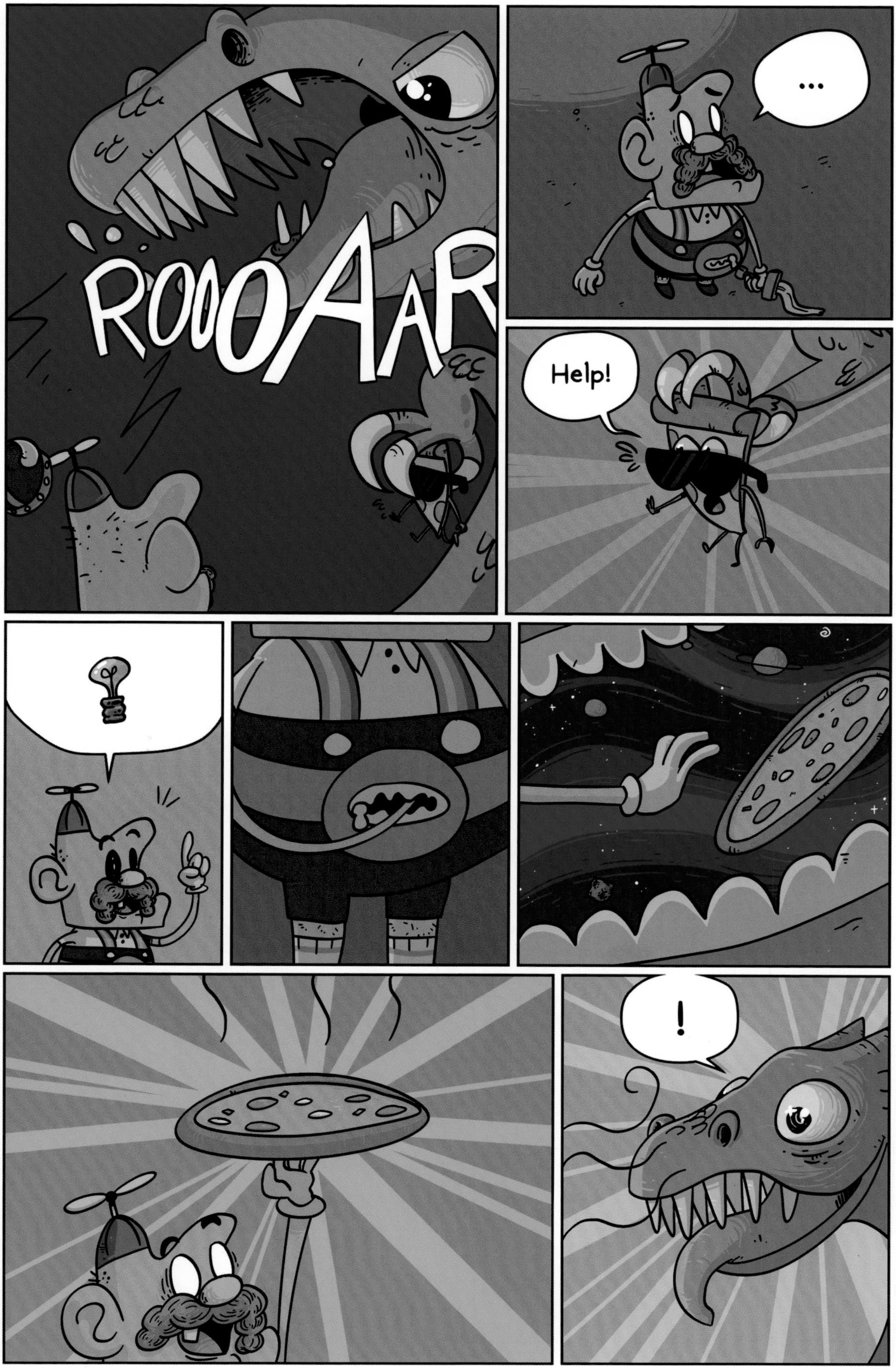
ROOOAAR
...
Help!
!

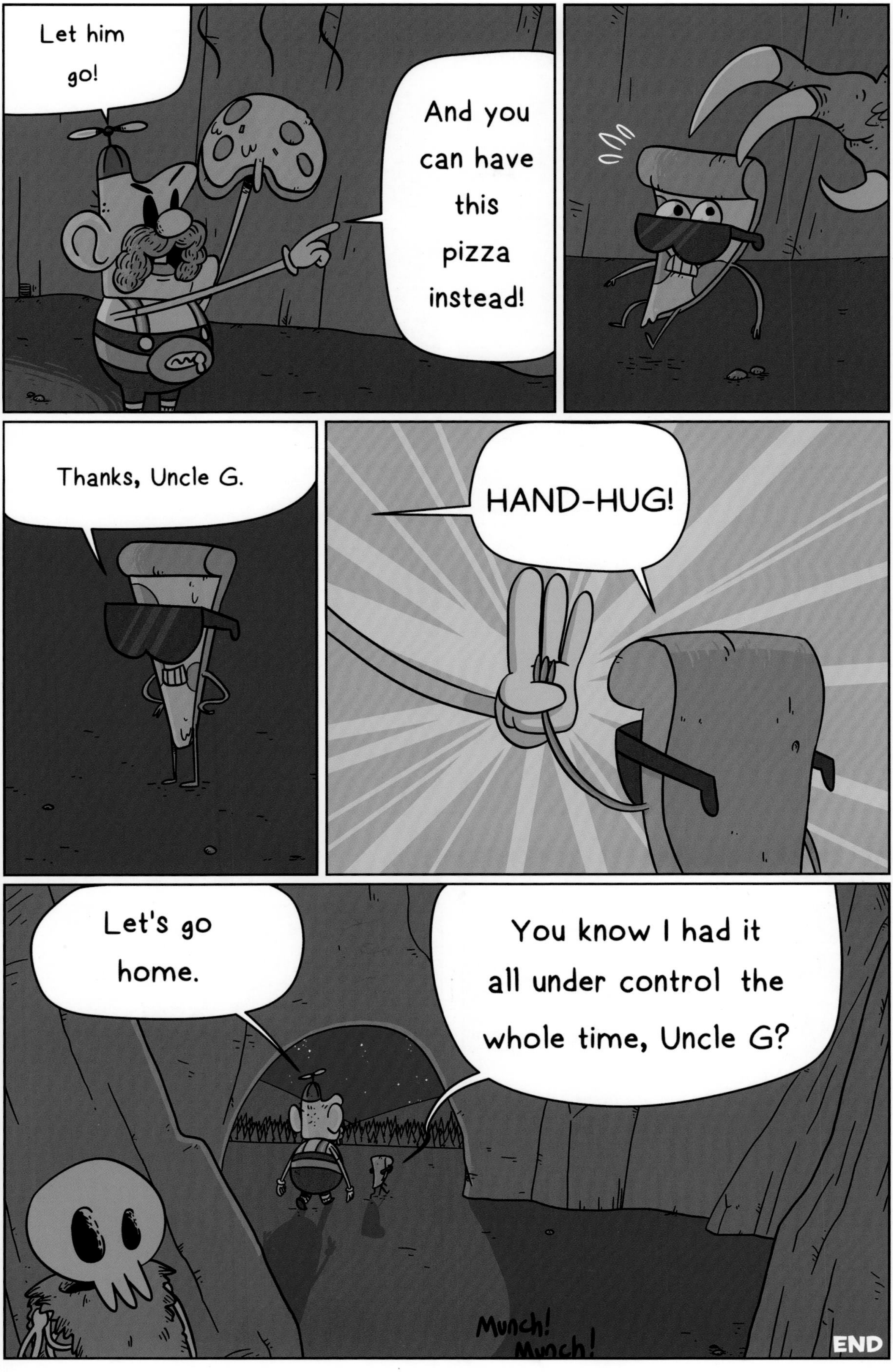
Let him go!
And you can have this pizza instead!
Thanks, Uncle G.
HAND-HUG!
Let's go home.
You know I had it all under control the whole time, Uncle G?
Munch! Munch!
END

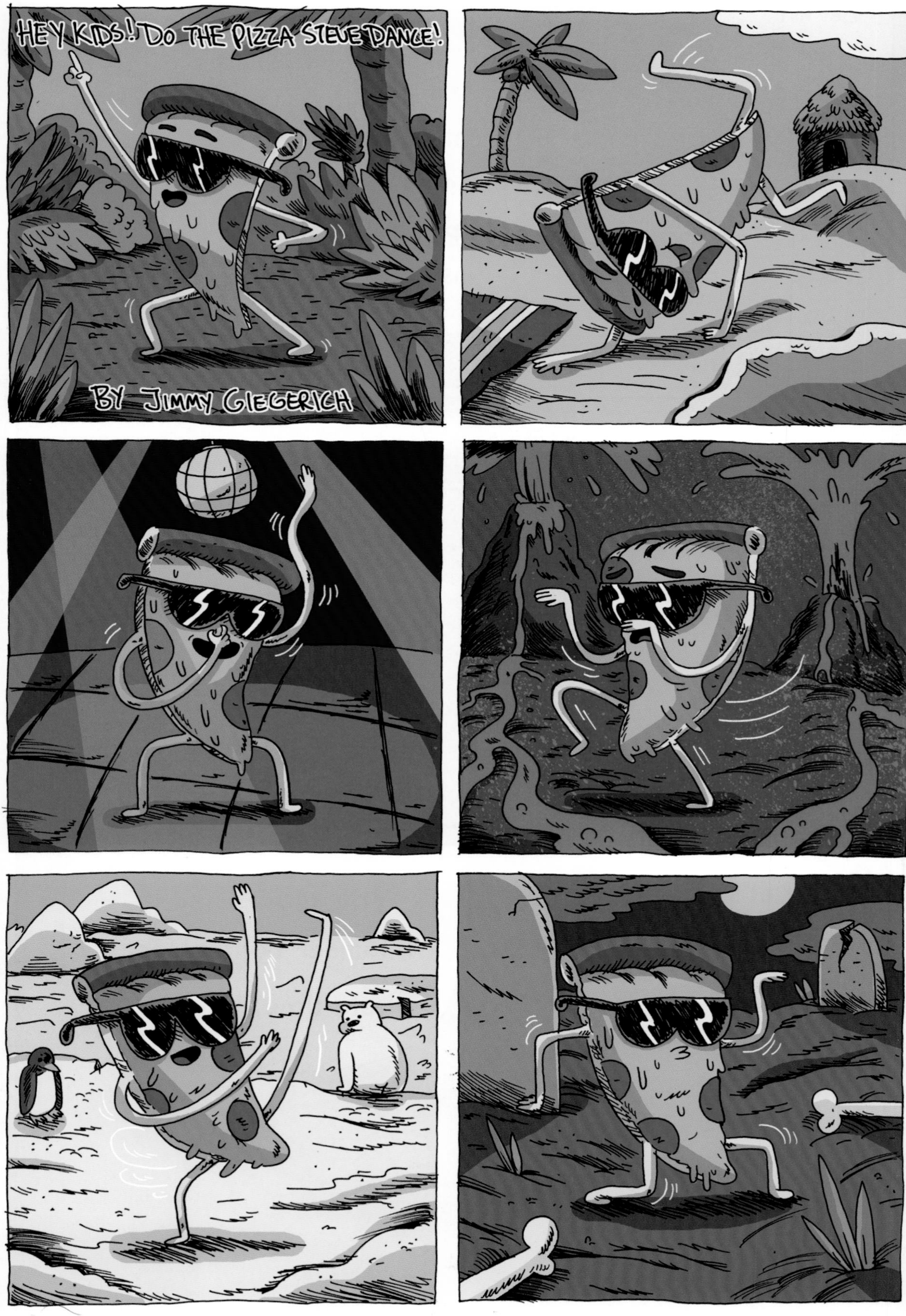
HEY KIDS! DO THE PIZZA STEVE DANCE!
BY JIMMY GIEGERICH

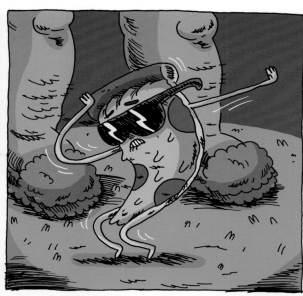

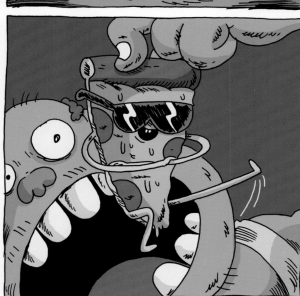

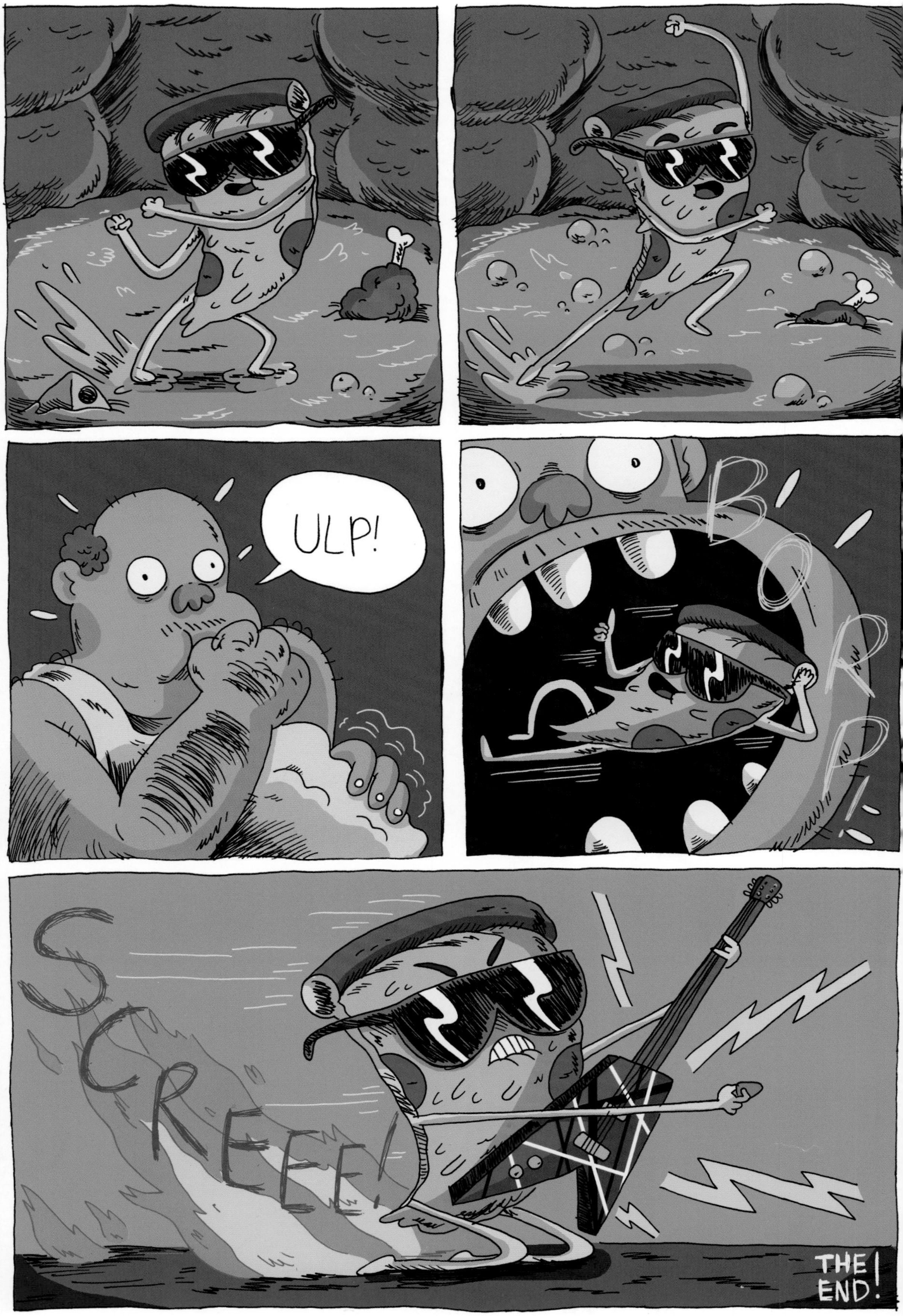
ULP!
BORRP!
SCREEE!
THE END!

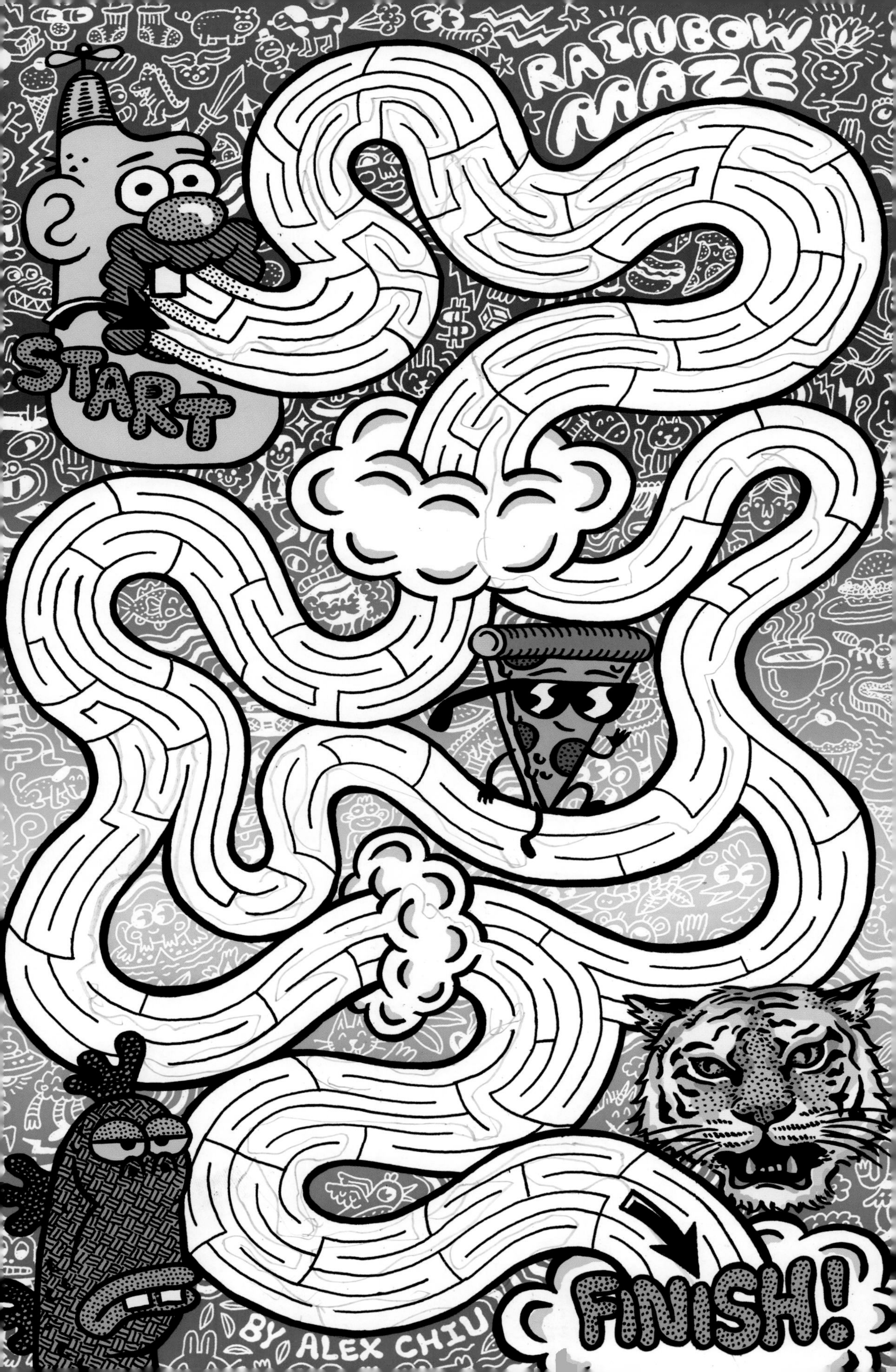
RAINBOW MAZE
START
FINISH!
BY ALEX CHIU

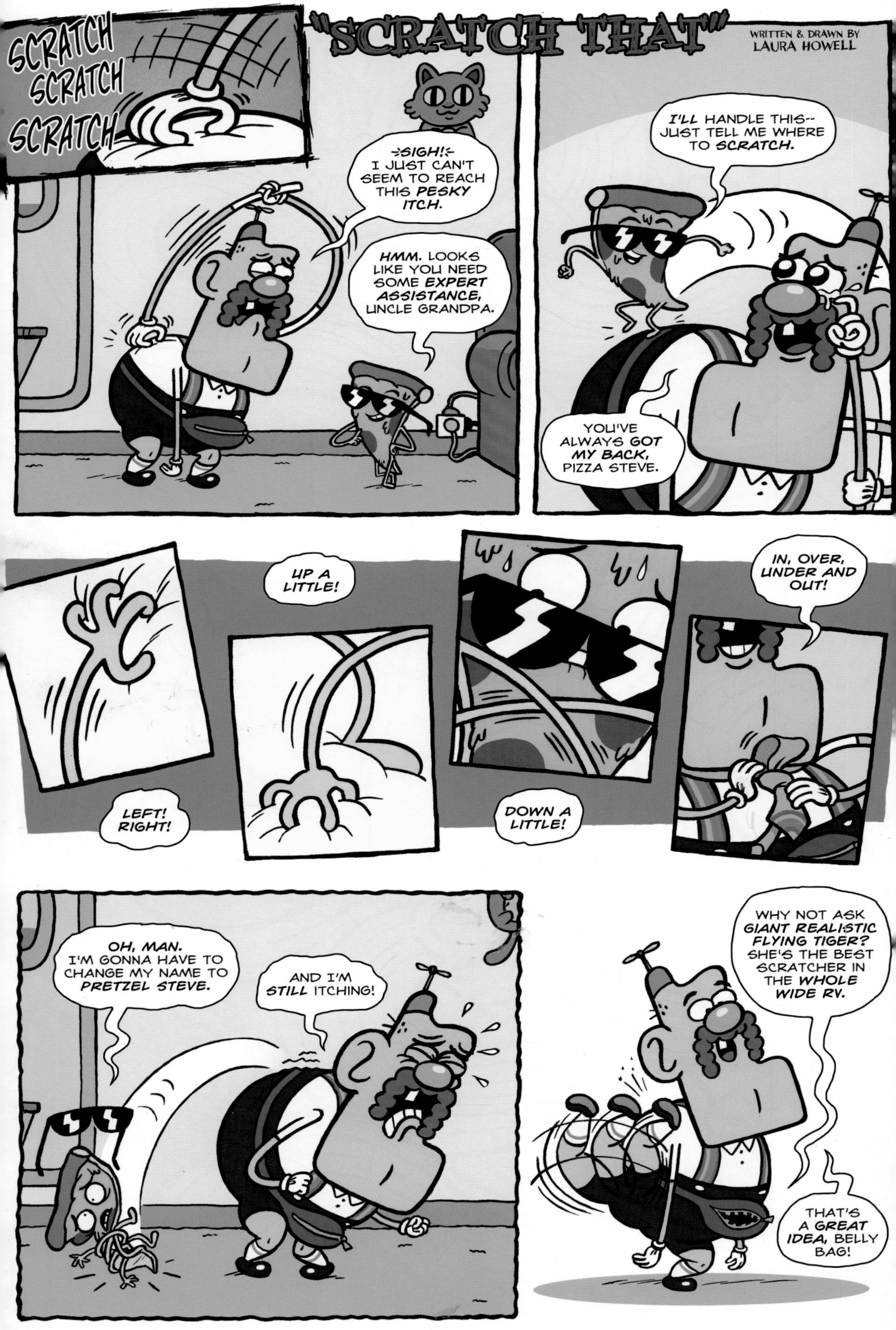
"SCRATCH THAT"
WRITTEN & DRAWN BY LAURA HOWELL
SCRATCH SCRATCH SCRATCH
SIGH! I JUST CAN'T SEEM TO REACH THIS PESKY ITCH.
HMM. LOOKS LIKE YOU NEED SOME EXPERT ASSISTANCE, UNCLE GRANDPA.
I'LL HANDLE THIS-- JUST TELL ME WHERE TO SCRATCH.
YOU'VE ALWAYS GOT MY BACK, PIZZA STEVE.
LEFT! RIGHT!
UP A LITTLE!
DOWN A LITTLE!
IN, OVER, UNDER AND OUT!
OH, MAN. I'M GONNA HAVE TO CHANGE MY NAME TO PRETZEL STEVE.
AND I'M STILL ITCHING!
WHY NOT ASK GIANT REALISTIC FLYING TIGER? SHE'S THE BEST SCRATCHER IN THE WHOLE WIDE RV.
THAT'S A GREAT IDEA, BELLY BAG!

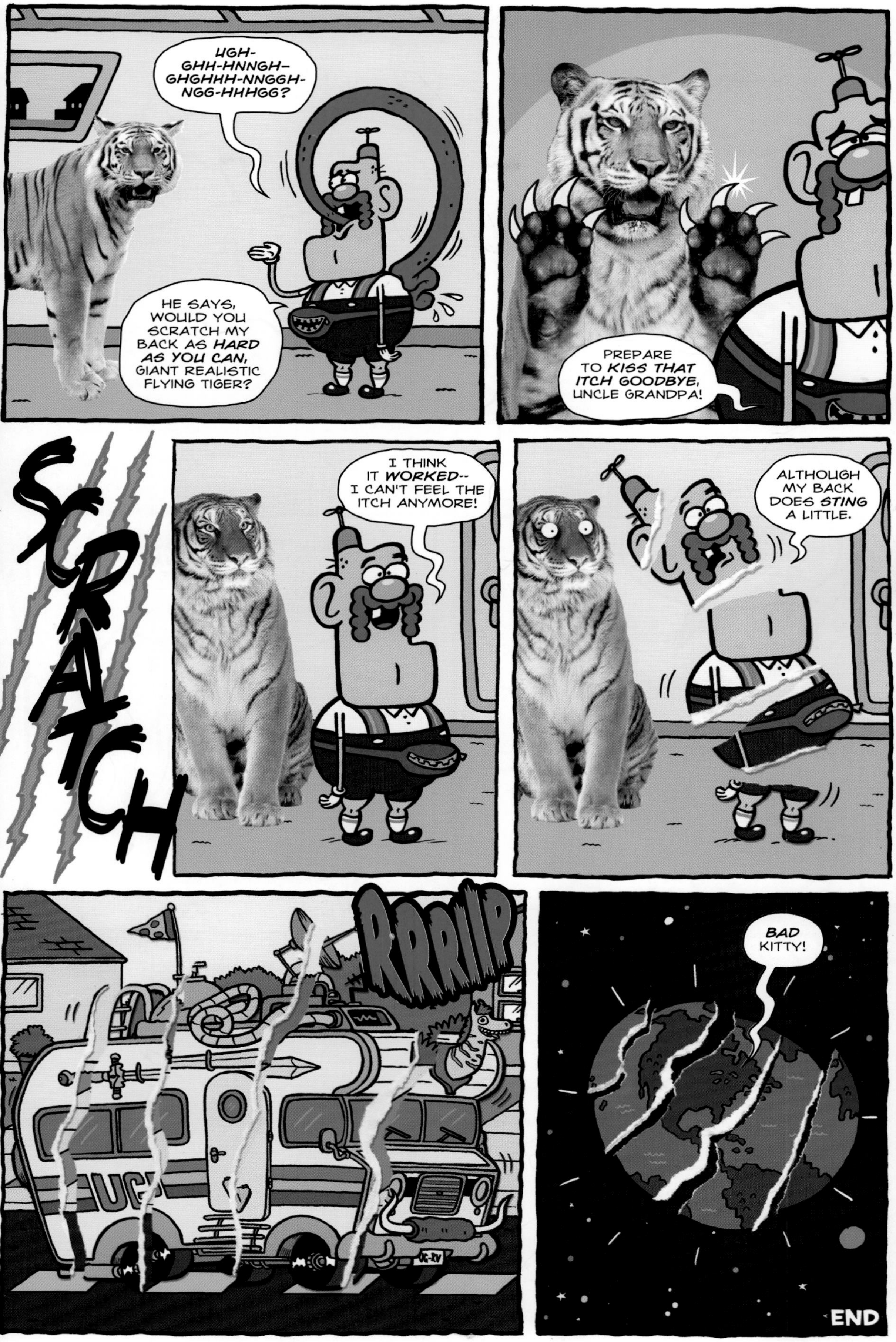
UGH-GHH-HNNGH-GHGHHH-NNGGH-NGG-HHHGG?
HE SAYS, WOULD YOU SCRATCH MY BACK AS HARD AS YOU CAN, GIANT REALISTIC FLYING TIGER?
PREPARE TO KISS THAT ITCH GOODBYE, UNCLE GRANDPA!
SCRATCH
I THINK IT WORKED-- I CAN'T FEEL THE ITCH ANYMORE!
ALTHOUGH MY BACK DOES STING A LITTLE.
RRRIIP
UG
UG-RV
BAD KITTY!
END

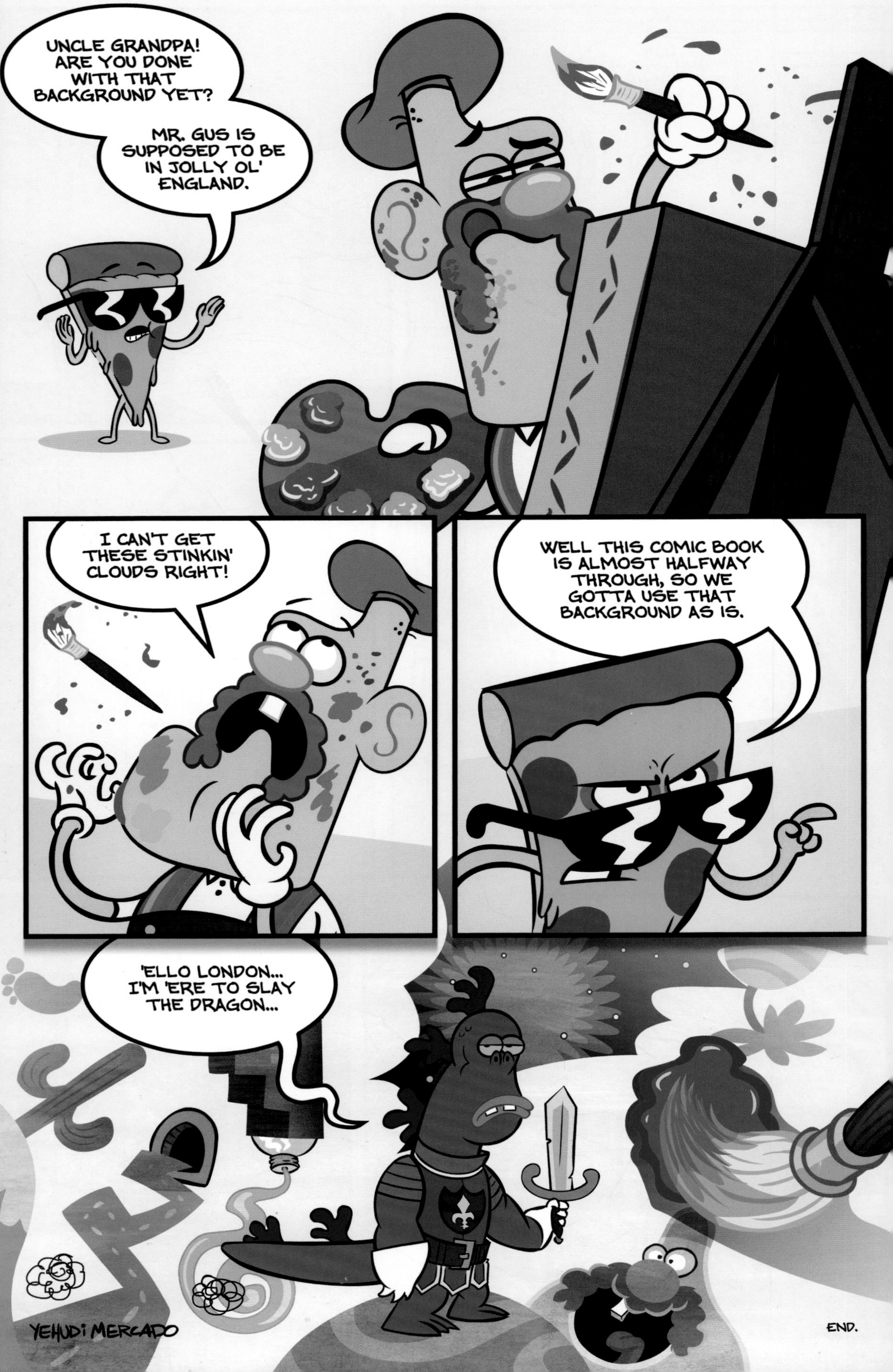
UNCLE GRANDPA! ARE YOU DONE WITH THAT BACKGROUND YET?
MR. GUS IS SUPPOSED TO BE IN JOLLY OL' ENGLAND.
I CAN'T GET THESE STINKIN' CLOUDS RIGHT!
WELL THIS COMIC BOOK IS ALMOST HALFWAY THROUGH, SO WE GOTTA USE THAT BACKGROUND AS IS.
'ELLO LONDON... I'M 'ERE TO SLAY THE DRAGON...
YEHUDI MERCADO
END.

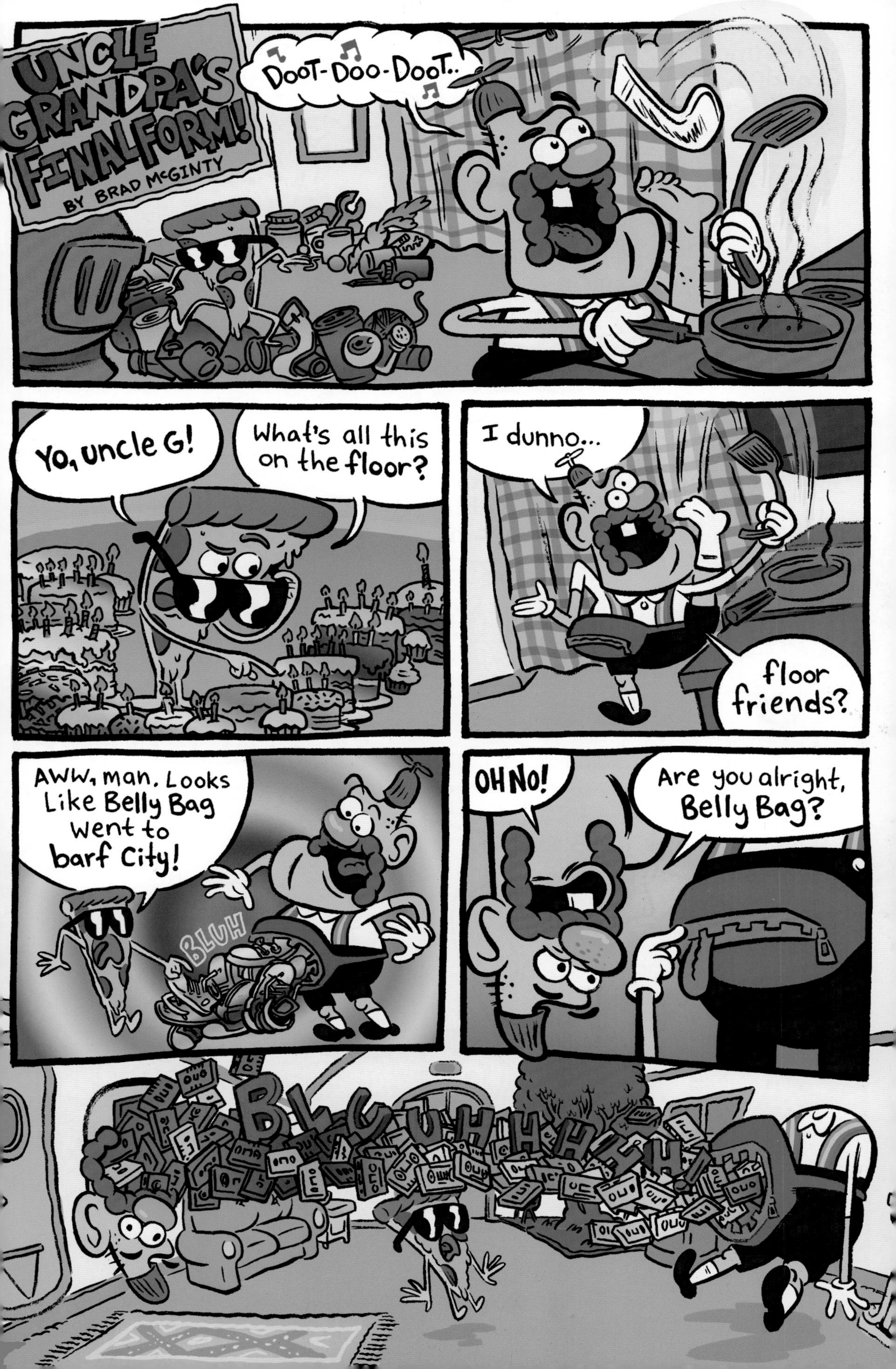
UNCLE GRANDPA'S FINAL FORM!
BY BRAD McGINTY
DOOT-DOO-DOOT..
YO, uncle G!
What's all this on the floor?
I dunno...
floor friends?
AWW, man. Looks Like Belly Bag Went to barf City!
BLUH
OH NO!
Are you alright, Belly Bag?
BLUUHHHHH!

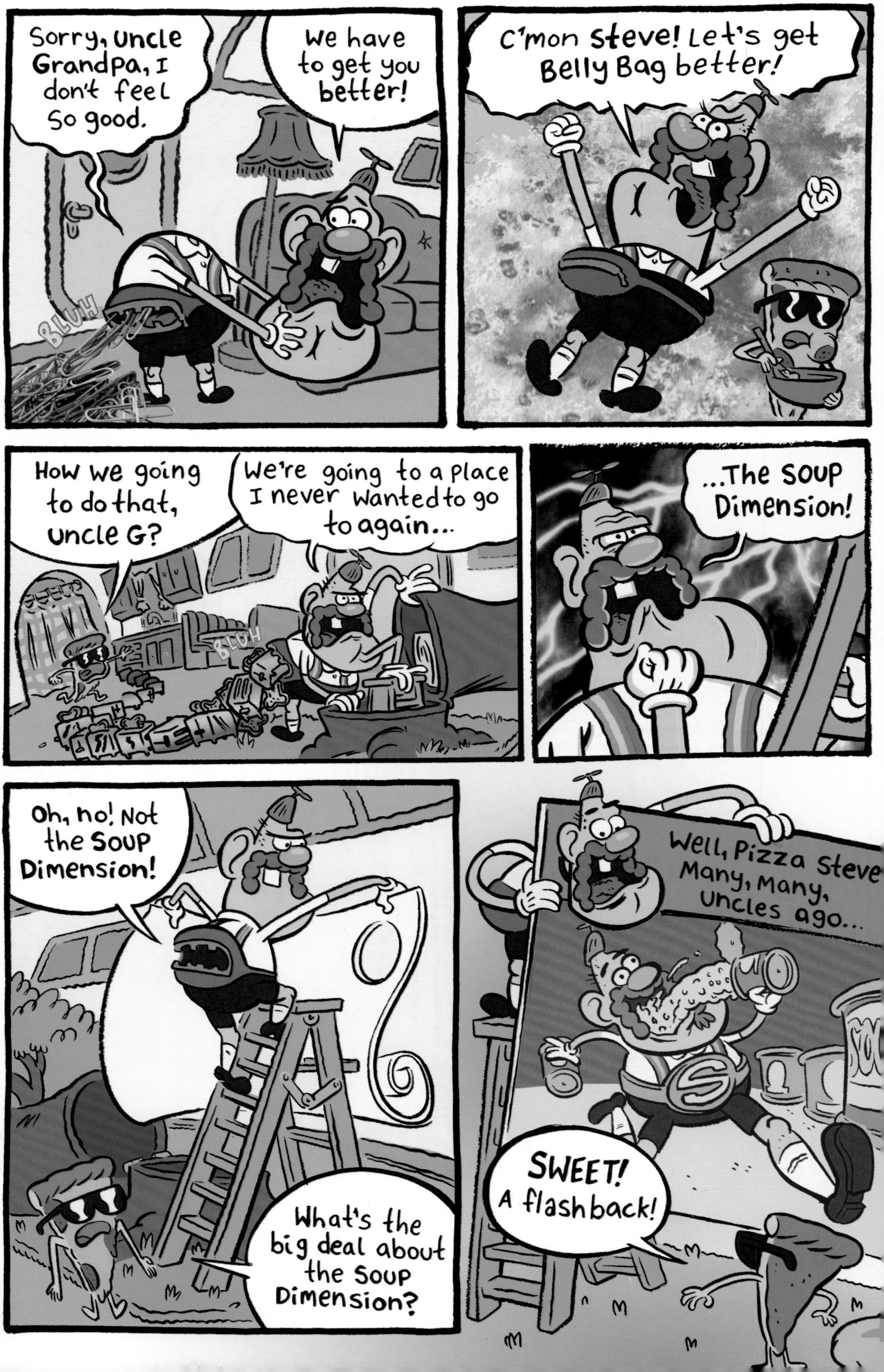

Sorry, Uncle Grandpa, I don't feel so good.
We have to get you better!
BLUH
C'mon Steve! Let's get Belly Bag better!
How we going to do that, Uncle G?
We're going to a place I never wanted to go to again...
BLUH
...The Soup Dimension!
Oh, no! Not the Soup Dimension!
What's the big deal about the Soup Dimension?
Well, Pizza Steve Many, many, Uncles ago...
SWEET! A flashback!

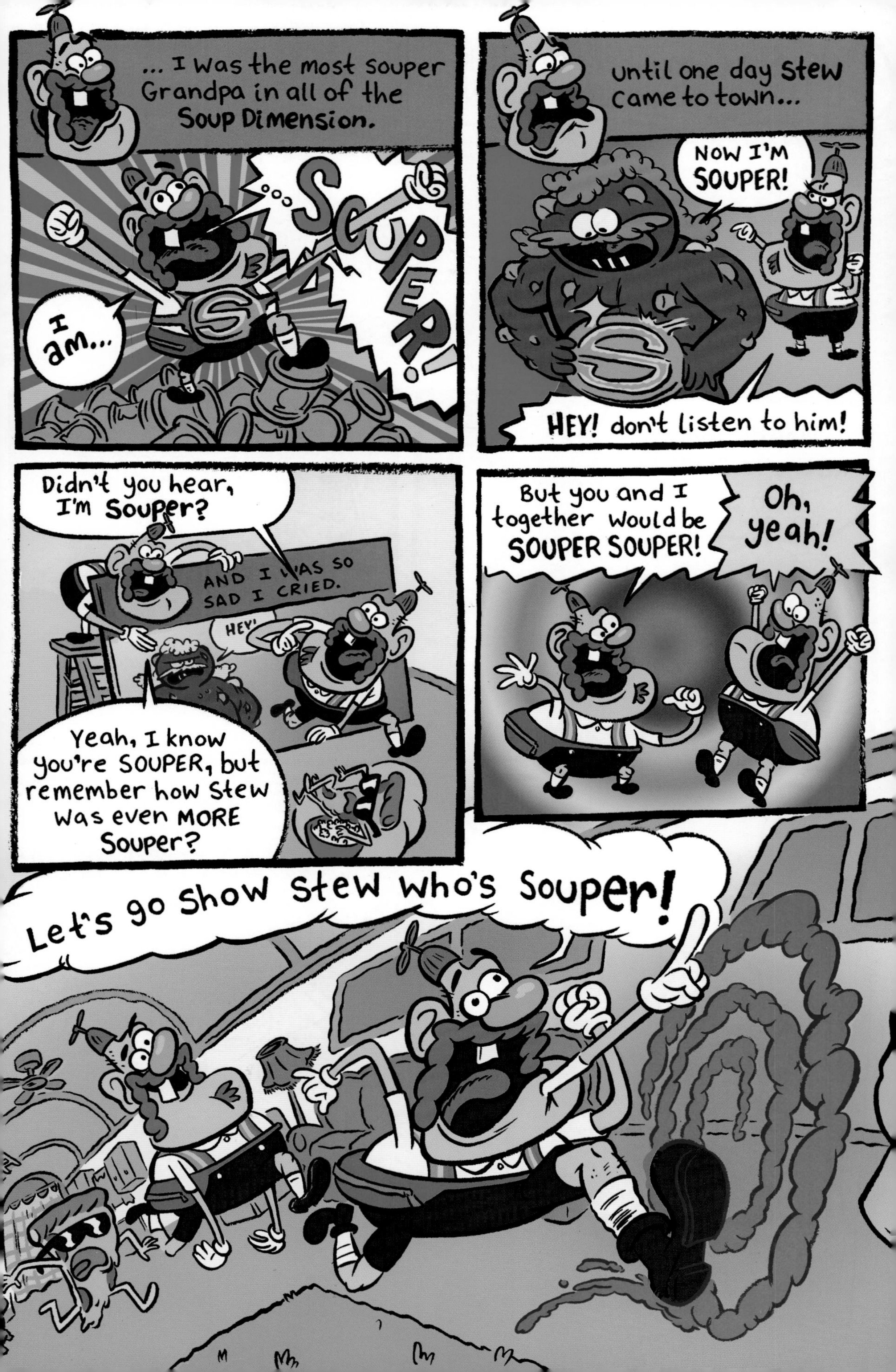

... I was the most souper Grandpa in all of the Soup Dimension.
I am...
...SOUPER!
until one day Stew came to town...
NOW I'M SOUPER!
HEY! don't listen to him!
Didn't you hear, I'm Souper?
AND I WAS SO SAD I CRIED.
HEY!
Yeah, I know you're SOUPER, but remember how Stew was even MORE Souper?
But you and I together would be SOUPER SOUPER!
Oh, yeah!
Let's go show Stew who's Souper!

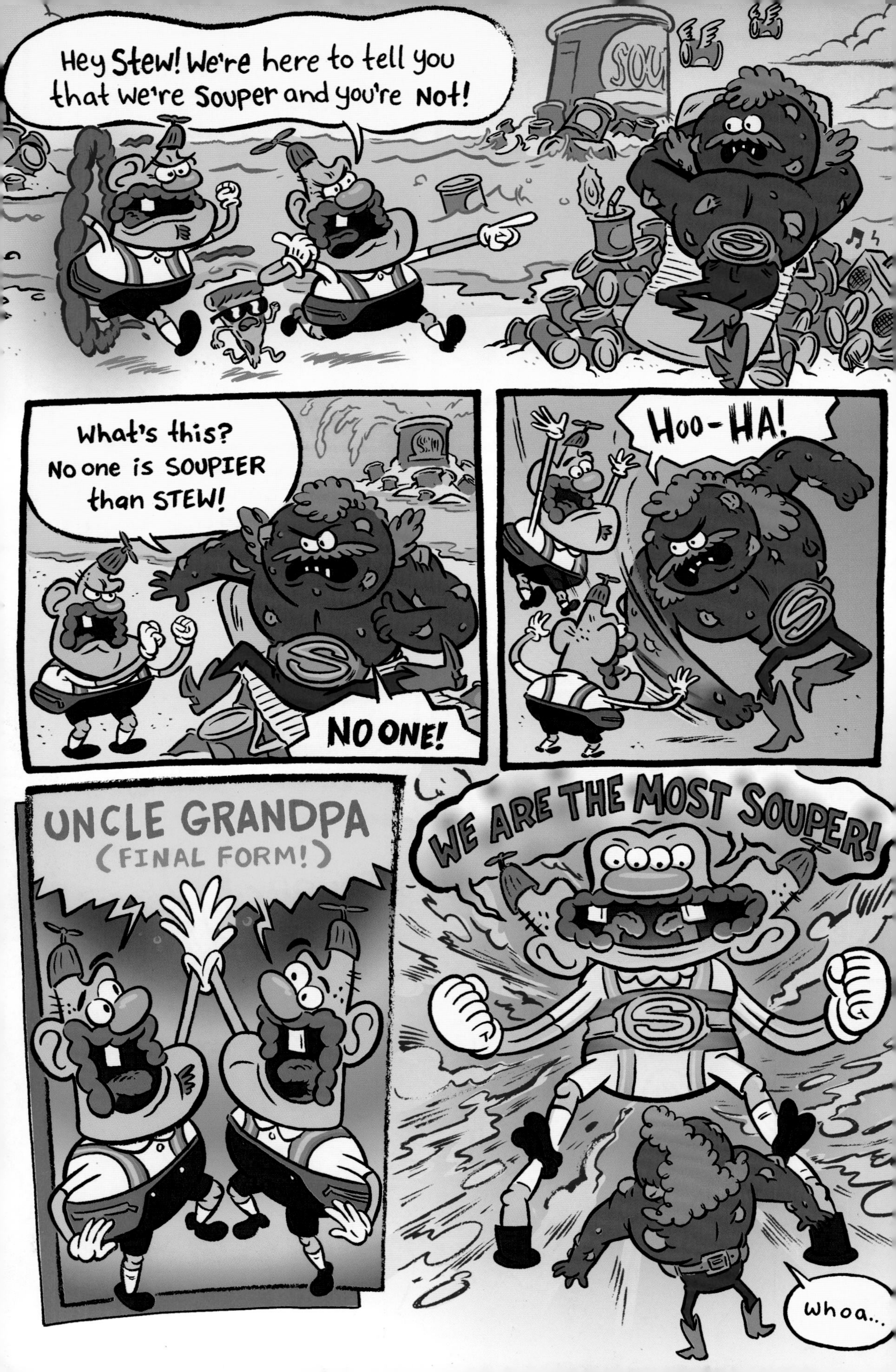
Hey Stew! We're here to tell you that we're Souper and you're Not!
What's this? No one is SOUPIER than STEW!
NO ONE!
HOO-HA!
UNCLE GRANDPA (FINAL FORM!)
WE ARE THE MOST SOUPER!
Whoa...

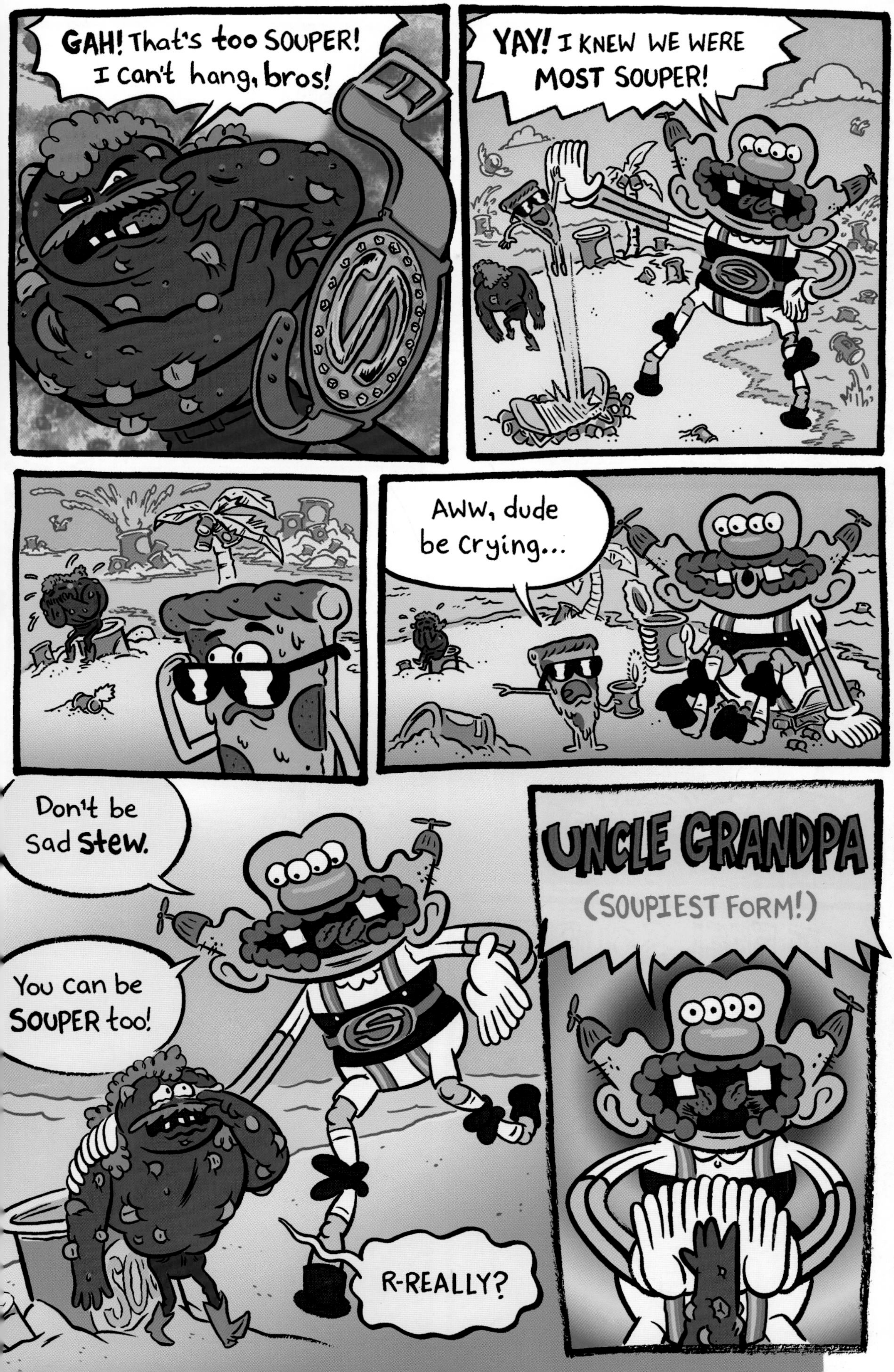

GAH! That's too SOUPER! I can't hang, bros!
YAY! I KNEW WE WERE MOST SOUPER!
AWW, dude be crying...
Don't be sad Stew.
You can be SOUPER too!
R-REALLY?
UNCLE GRANDPA
(SOUPIEST FORM!)

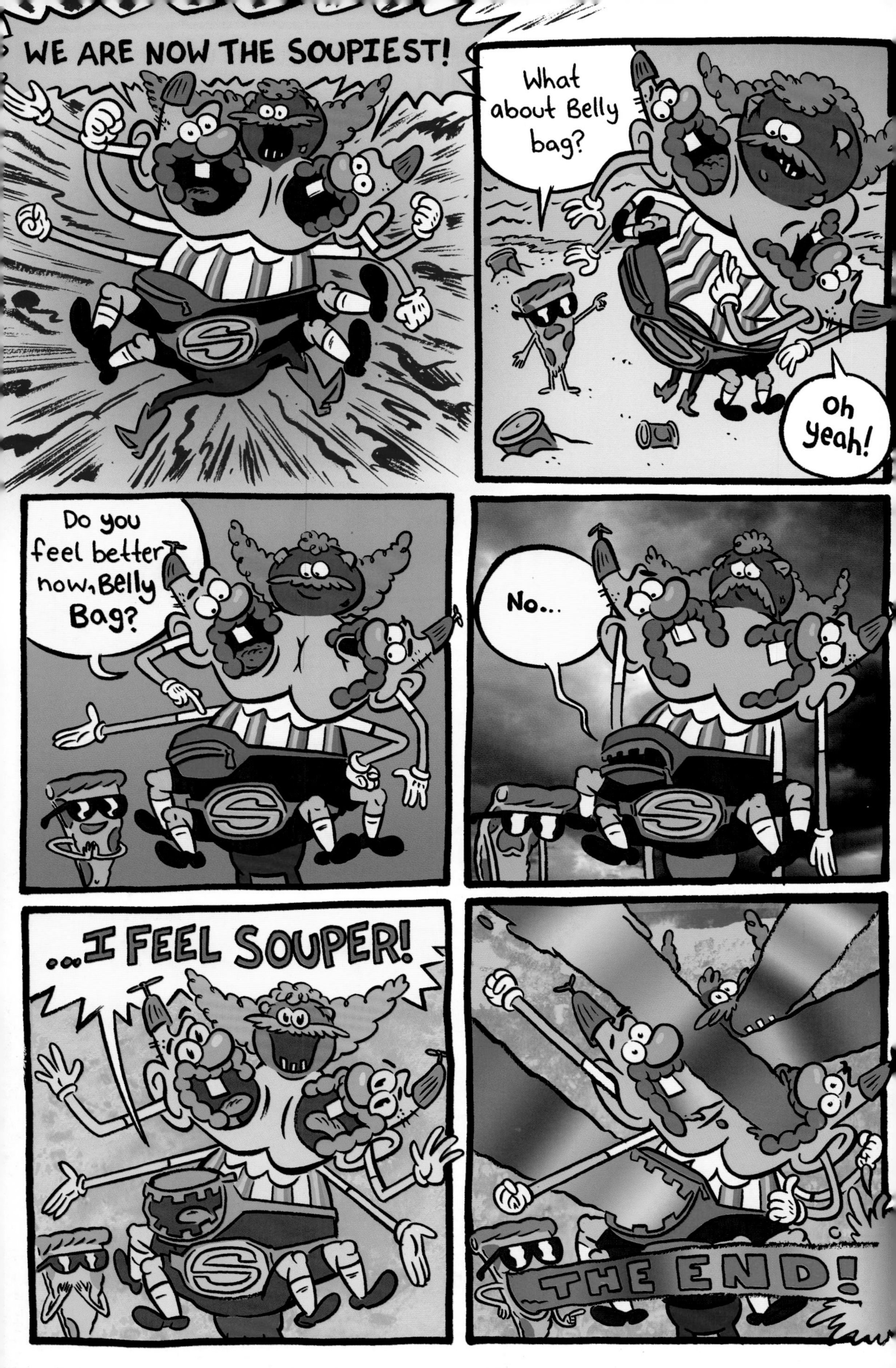
WE ARE NOW THE SOUPIEST!
What about Belly bag?
Oh yeah!
Do you feel better now, Belly Bag?
No...
...I FEEL SOUPER!
THE END!

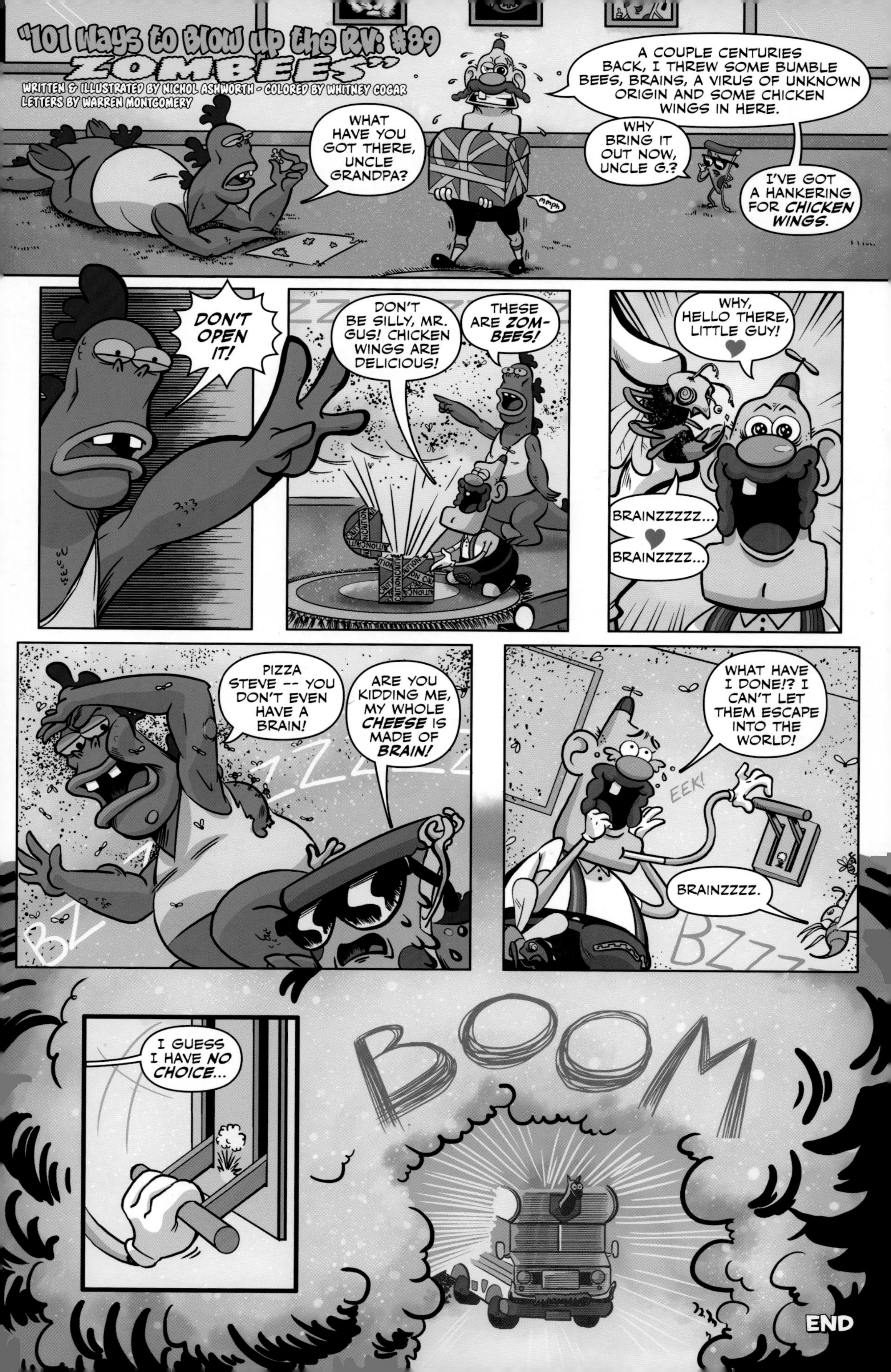
"101 Ways to Blow up the RV: #89
ZOMBEES"
WRITTEN & ILLUSTRATED BY NICHOL ASHWORTH - COLORED BY WHITNEY COGAR
LETTERS BY WARREN MONTGOMERY
WHAT HAVE YOU GOT THERE, UNCLE GRANDPA?
A COUPLE CENTURIES BACK, I THREW SOME BUMBLE BEES, BRAINS, A VIRUS OF UNKNOWN ORIGIN AND SOME CHICKEN WINGS IN HERE.
mmph
WHY BRING IT OUT NOW, UNCLE G.?
I'VE GOT A HANKERING FOR CHICKEN WINGS.
DON'T OPEN IT!
DON'T BE SILLY, MR. GUS! CHICKEN WINGS ARE DELICIOUS!
THESE ARE ZOM-BEES!
WHY, HELLO THERE, LITTLE GUY!
BRAINZZZZZ...
BRAINZZZZ...
PIZZA STEVE -- YOU DON'T EVEN HAVE A BRAIN!
ARE YOU KIDDING ME, MY WHOLE CHEESE IS MADE OF BRAIN!
BZ
WHAT HAVE I DONE!? I CAN'T LET THEM ESCAPE INTO THE WORLD!
EEK!
BRAINZZZZ.
BZZZ
I GUESS I HAVE NO CHOICE...
BOOM
END

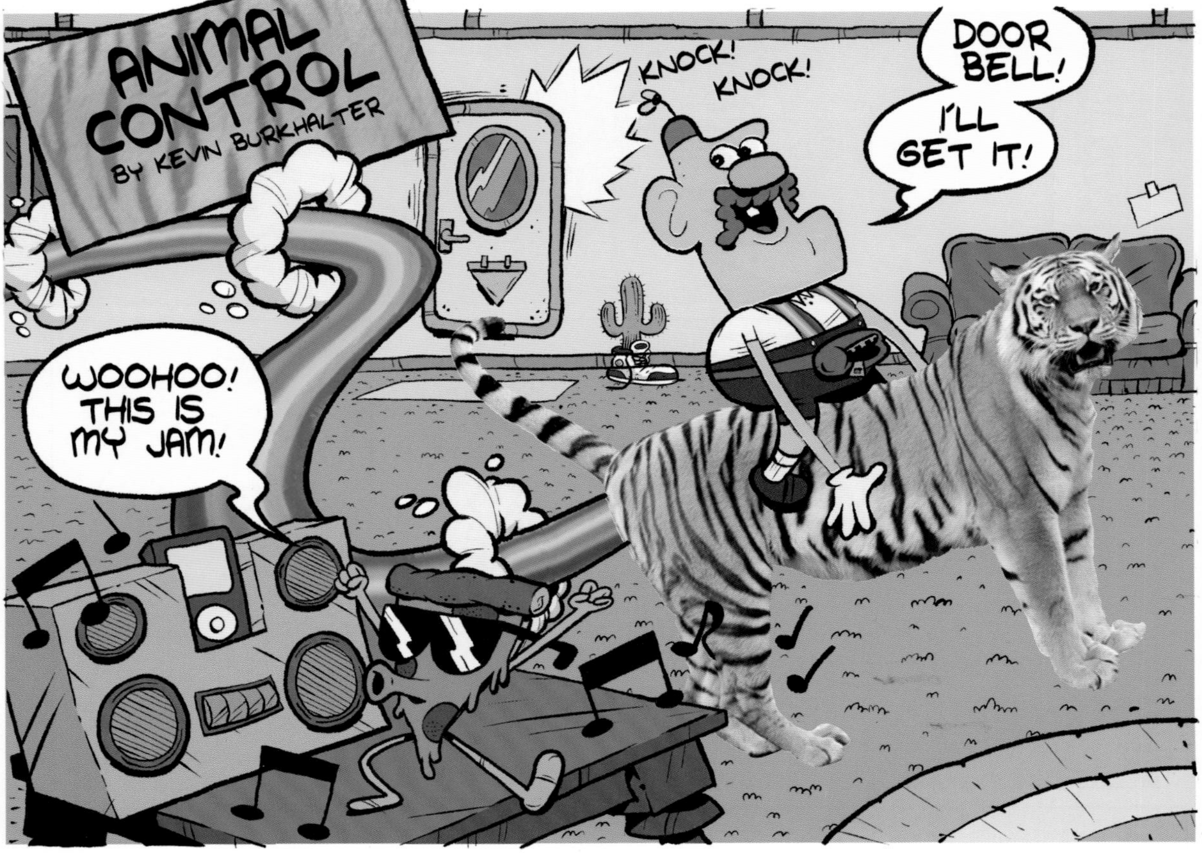
ANIMAL CONTROL
BY KEVIN BURKHALTER
KNOCK! KNOCK!
DOOR BELL!
I'LL GET IT!
WOOHOO! THIS IS MY JAM!

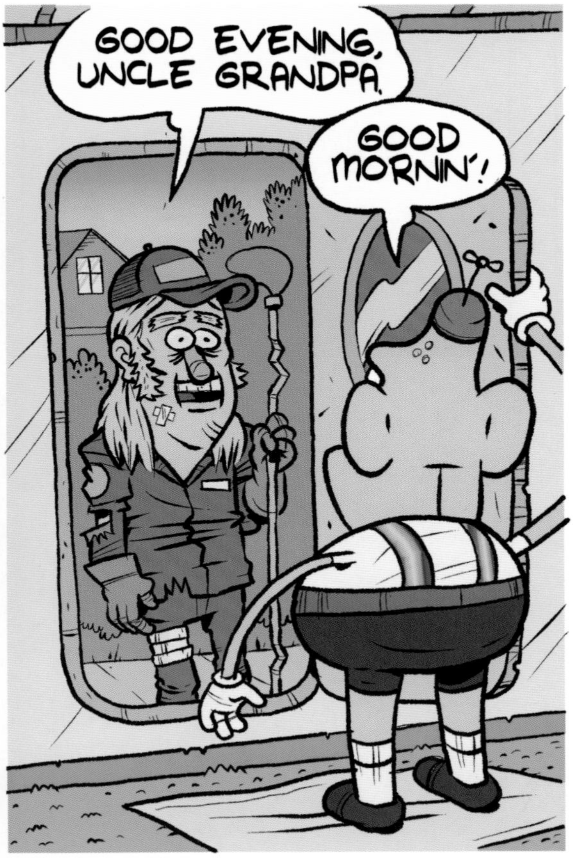
GOOD EVENING, UNCLE GRANDPA.
GOOD MORNIN'!

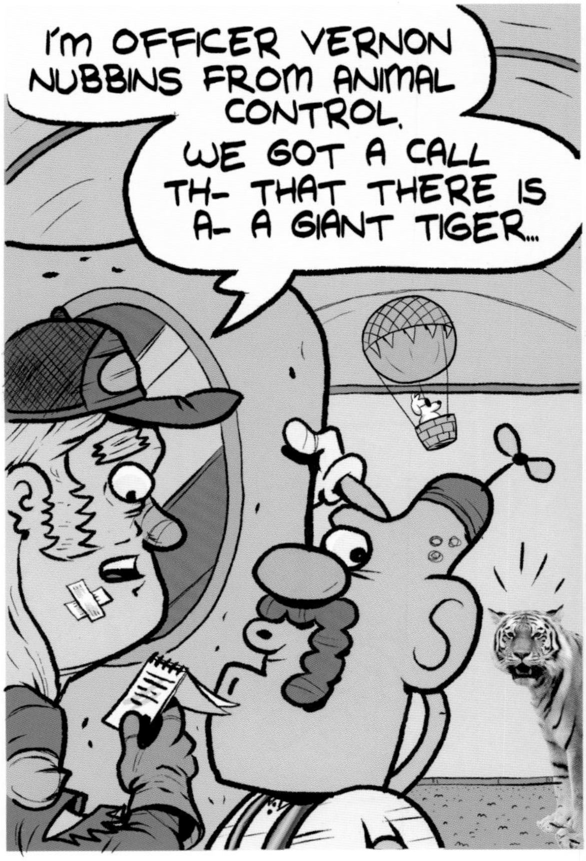
I'M OFFICER VERNON NUBBINS FROM ANIMAL CONTROL.
WE GOT A CALL TH- THAT THERE IS A- A GIANT TIGER...

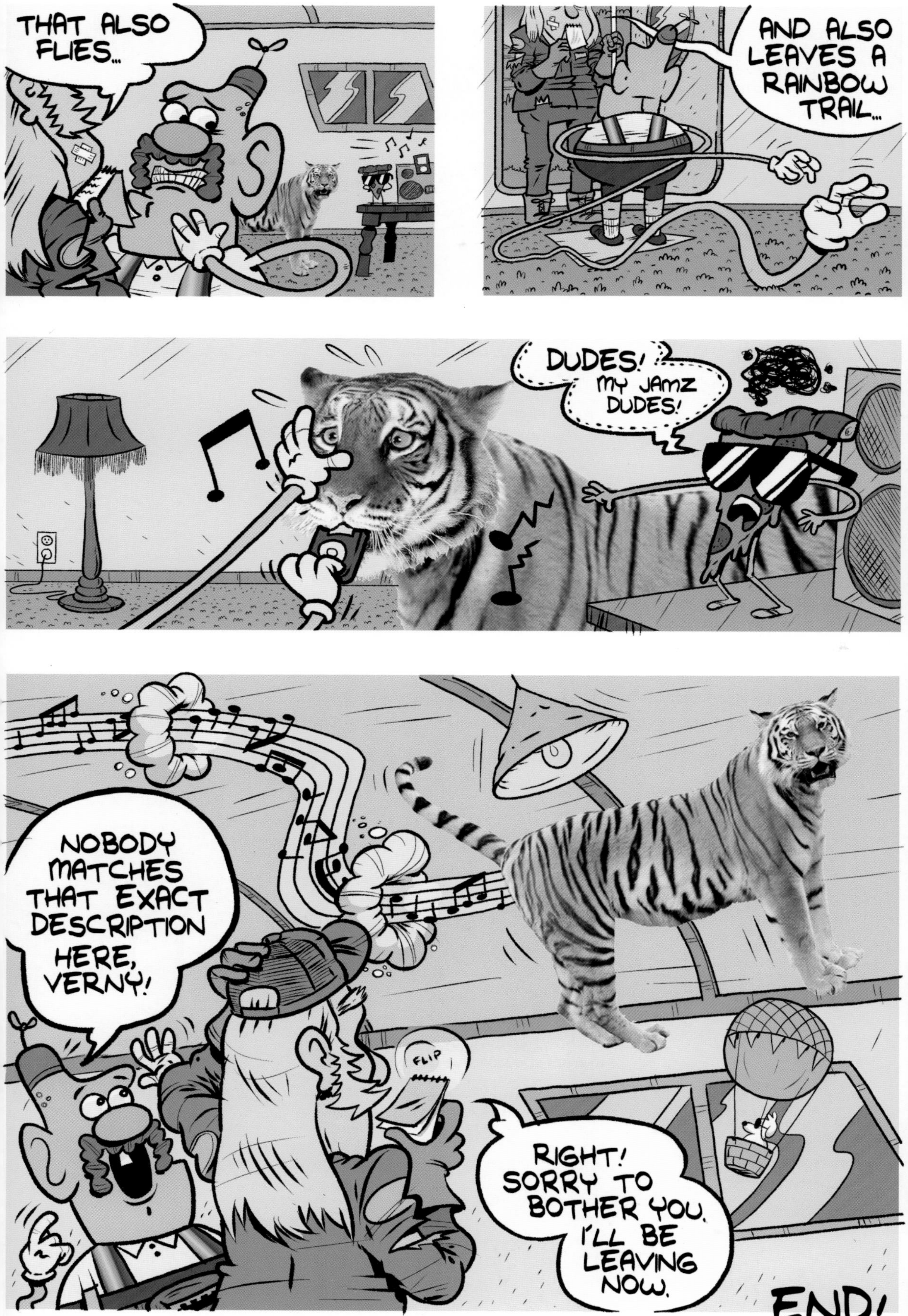
THAT ALSO FLIES...
AND ALSO LEAVES A RAINBOW TRAIL...
DUDES! MY JAMZ DUDES!
NOBODY MATCHES THAT EXACT DESCRIPTION HERE, VERNY!
FLIP
RIGHT! SORRY TO BOTHER YOU. I'LL BE LEAVING NOW.
END!

SOLVE THE PUZZLE TO FREE UNCLE GRANDPA

Pizza Doughnut Burger Game
Tiger Toys Fries Poster
Emperor Laser Radio Television
Candy Ghost Comic Rocket
Grandpa Steve Good Morning
Alien Marshmallow Library

```
N G N G A W H E V R L H T C C
A C L R E O J I M A E E Z I X
D G P A W L N B S P K G M W N
F A E N R L E E J C E O R O L
F M N D E A R F O G C R I U F
R E J P T M H R J T V S O T B
I X R A S H R M O D I C I E G
E A X O O S O Y Z V O I D A R
S T B K P R S W E P I Z Z A I
Y A Z W N A U L Y R A R B I L
T D L I V M E D O U G H N U T
A I N I S T E V E L L Y S P S
M G G A E D O O G P S T R E O
O J T E C N N I K W T D W A H
T V V F R J N J B Q S F P E G
```

BLAST! FOILED AGAIN
I WILL GET YOU NEXT TIME UNCLE GRANDPA.

THANKS FOR ALL THE HELP NOW WE
BETTER GET OUT OF HERE.

ANSWER KEY

```
T V V F R J N J B Q S F P E G
O J T E C N N I K W T D W A H
M G G A E D O O G P S T R E O
A I N I S T E V E L L Y S P S
T D L I V M E D O U G H N U T
Y A Z W N A U L Y R A R B I L
S T B K P R S W E P I Z Z A I
E A X O O S O Y Z V O I D A R
I X R A S H R M O D I C I E G
R E J P T M H R J T V S O T B
F M N D E A R F O G C R I U F
F A E N R L E E J C E O R O L
D G P A W L N B S P K G M W N
A C L R E O J I M A E E Z I X
N G N G A W H E V R L H T C C
```

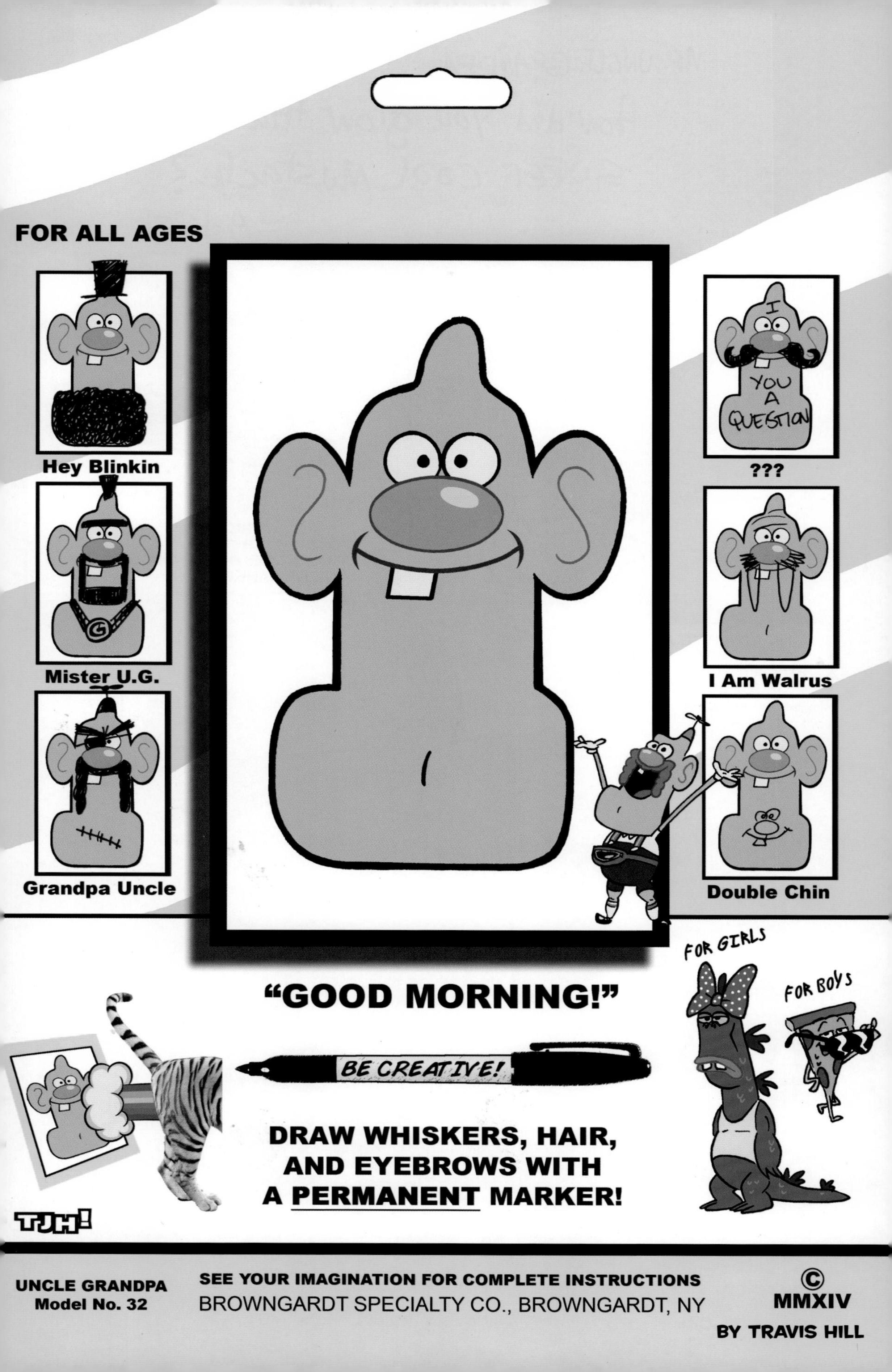

FOR ALL AGES
Hey Blinkin
Mister U.G.
Grandpa Uncle
I
YOU
A
QUESTION
???
I Am Walrus
Double Chin
"GOOD MORNING!"
BE CREATIVE!
FOR GIRLS
FOR BOYS
DRAW WHISKERS, HAIR, AND EYEBROWS WITH A PERMANENT MARKER!
TJH!
UNCLE GRANDPA
Model No. 32
SEE YOUR IMAGINATION FOR COMPLETE INSTRUCTIONS
BROWNGARDT SPECIALTY CO., BROWNGARDT, NY
©
MMXIV
BY TRAVIS HILL

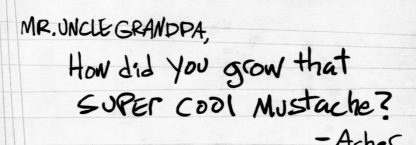

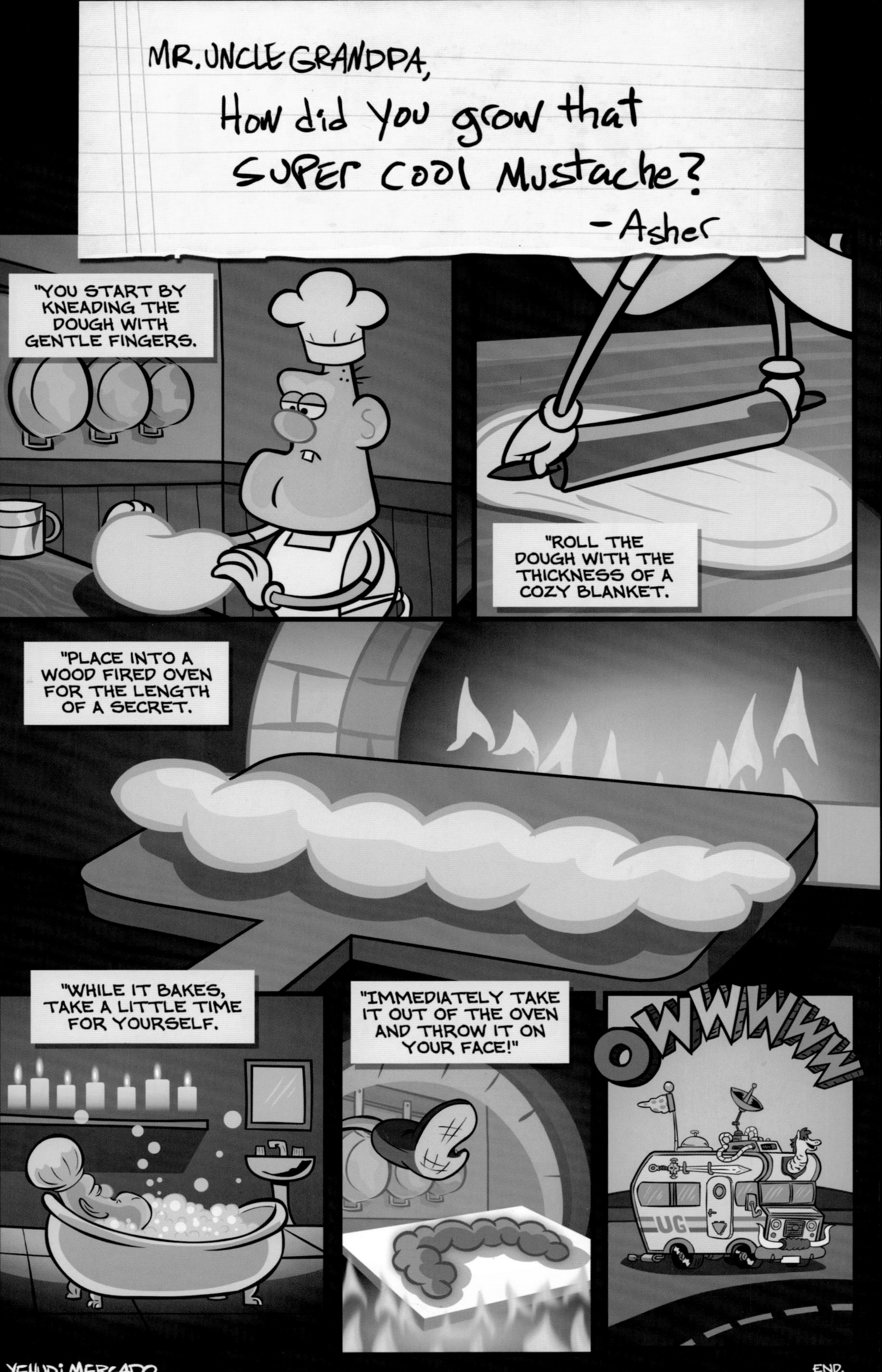

MR. UNCLE GRANDPA,
How did you grow that
SUPER COOL Mustache?
— Asher

"YOU START BY KNEADING THE DOUGH WITH GENTLE FINGERS.

"ROLL THE DOUGH WITH THE THICKNESS OF A COZY BLANKET.

"PLACE INTO A WOOD FIRED OVEN FOR THE LENGTH OF A SECRET.

"WHILE IT BAKES, TAKE A LITTLE TIME FOR YOURSELF.

"IMMEDIATELY TAKE IT OUT OF THE OVEN AND THROW IT ON YOUR FACE!"

YEHUDI MERCADO

END.

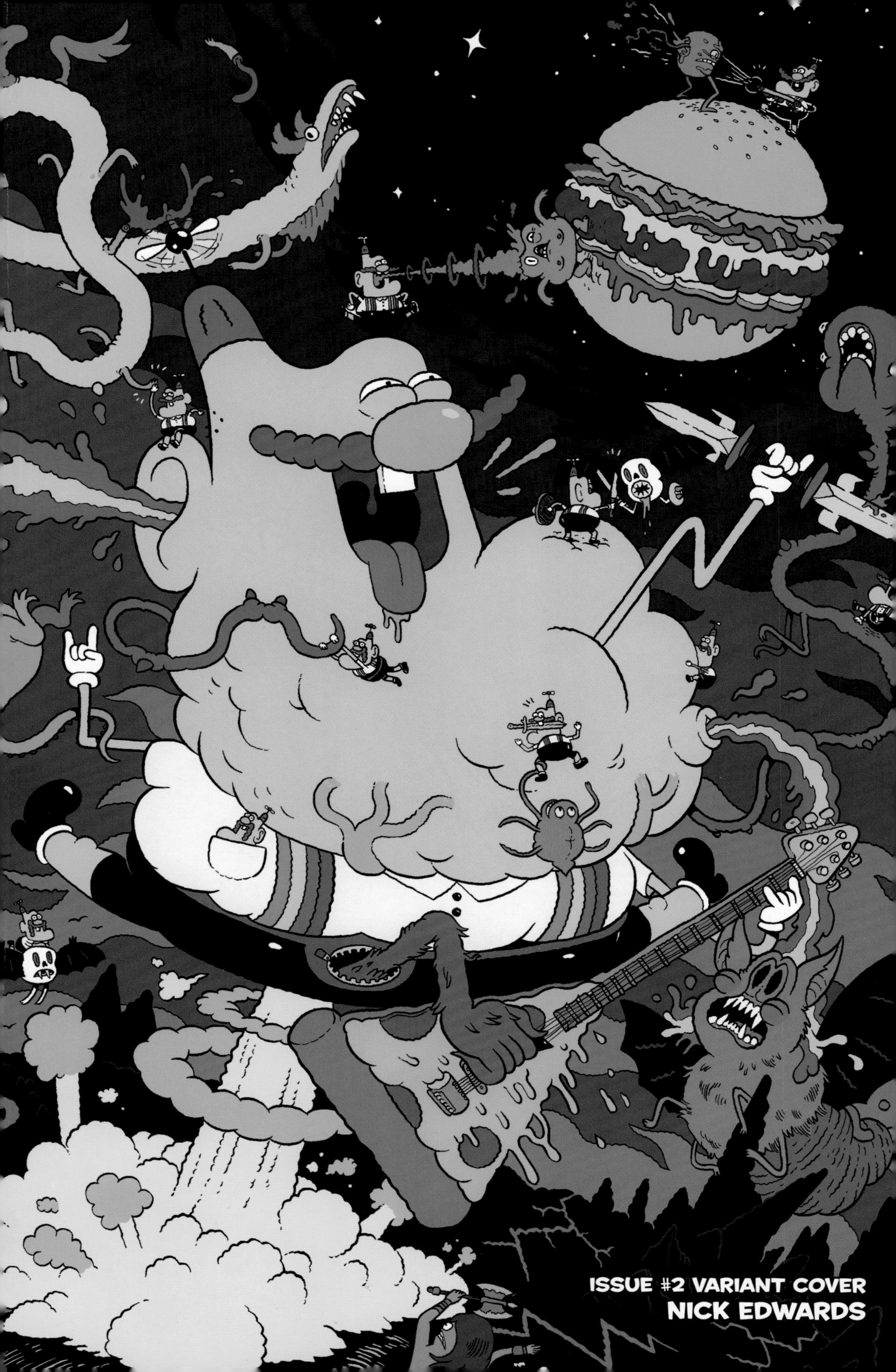

ISSUE #2 VARIANT COVER
NICK EDWARDS

ISSUE #3 COVER
ALEXIS ZIRITT

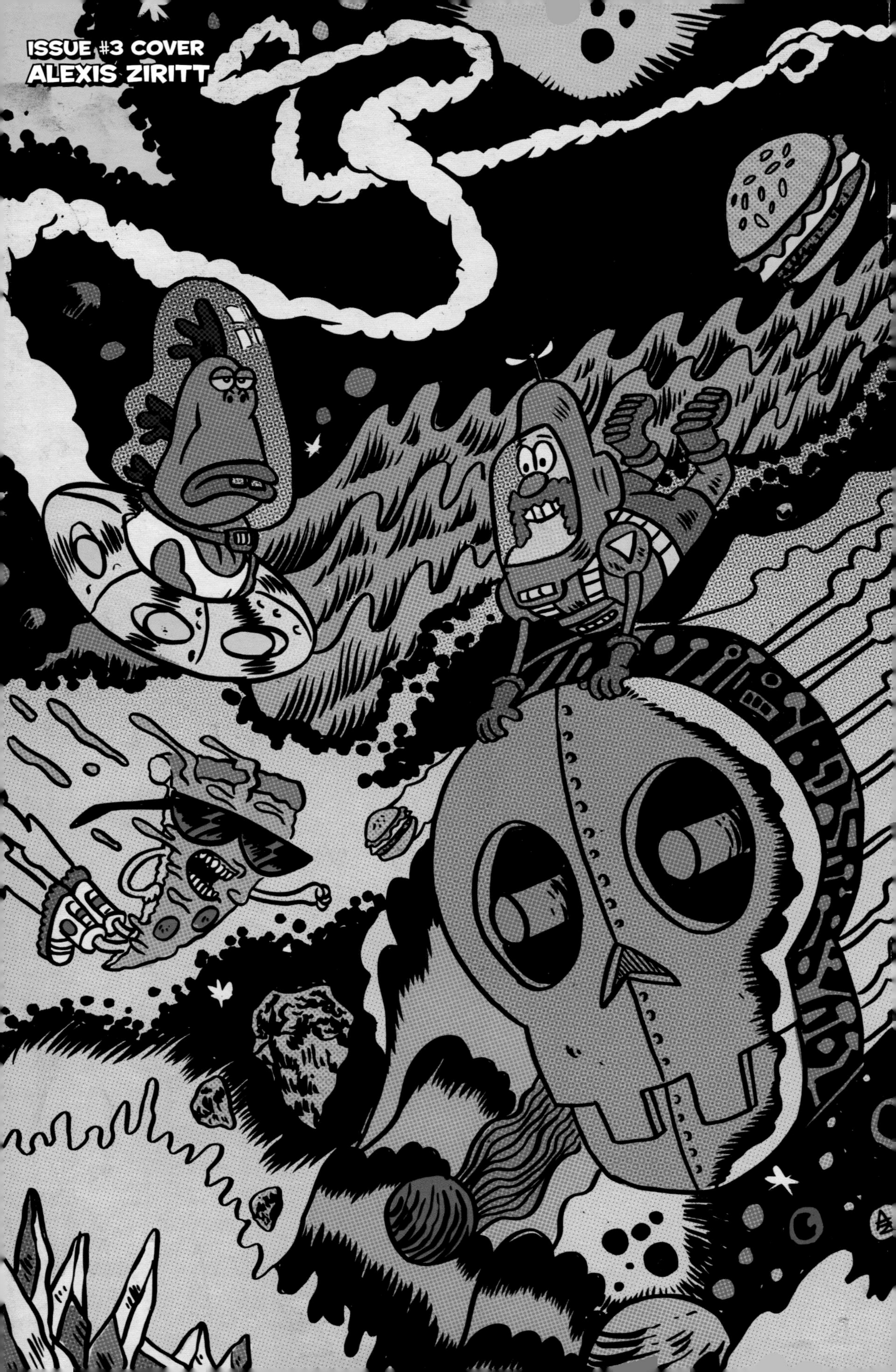

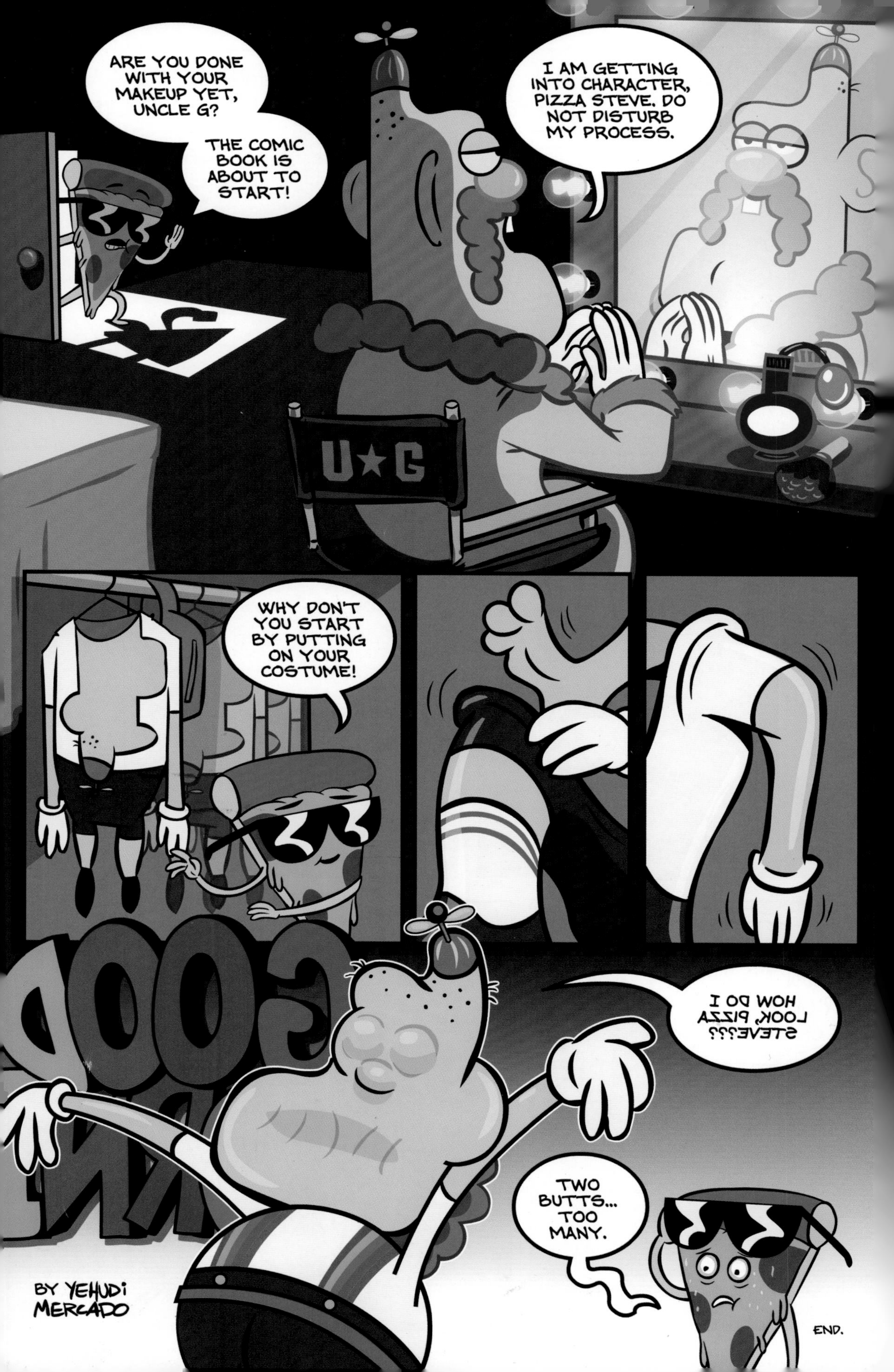
ARE YOU DONE WITH YOUR MAKEUP YET, UNCLE G?
THE COMIC BOOK IS ABOUT TO START!
I AM GETTING INTO CHARACTER, PIZZA STEVE. DO NOT DISTURB MY PROCESS.
U★G
WHY DON'T YOU START BY PUTTING ON YOUR COSTUME!
GOOD
HOW DO I LOOK, PIZZA STEVE???
TWO BUTTS... TOO MANY.
BY YEHUDI MERCADO
END.

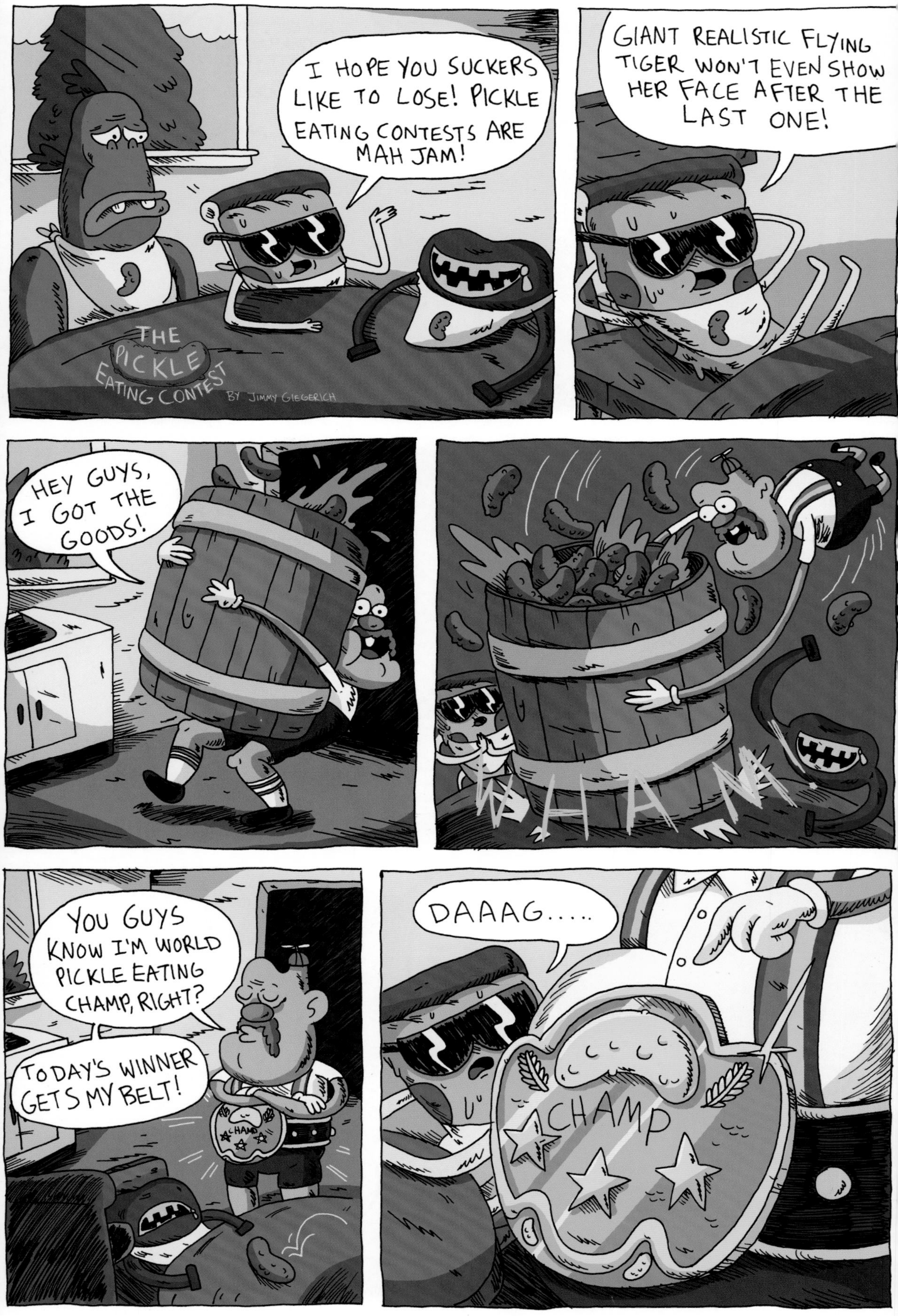
THE PICKLE EATING CONTEST
BY JIMMY GIEGERICH
I HOPE YOU SUCKERS LIKE TO LOSE! PICKLE EATING CONTESTS ARE MAH JAM!
GIANT REALISTIC FLYING TIGER WON'T EVEN SHOW HER FACE AFTER THE LAST ONE!
HEY GUYS, I GOT THE GOODS!
WHAM
YOU GUYS KNOW I'M WORLD PICKLE EATING CHAMP, RIGHT?
TODAY'S WINNER GETS MY BELT!
DAAAG.....
CHAMP

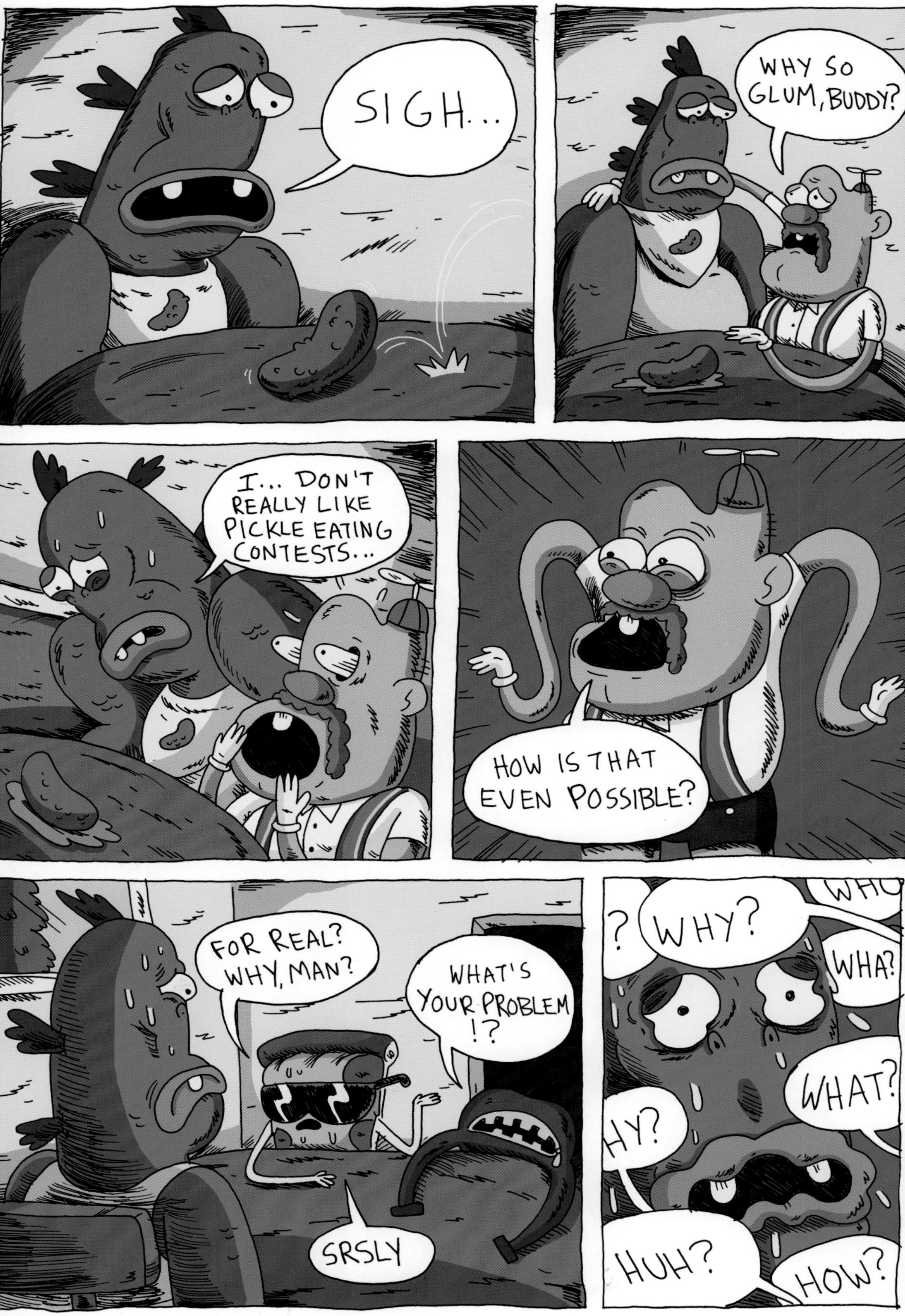
SIGH...
WHY SO GLUM, BUDDY?
I... DON'T REALLY LIKE PICKLE EATING CONTESTS...
HOW IS THAT EVEN POSSIBLE?
FOR REAL? WHY, MAN?
WHAT'S YOUR PROBLEM !?
SRSLY
WHY?
WHA?
WHAT?
HUH?
HOW?

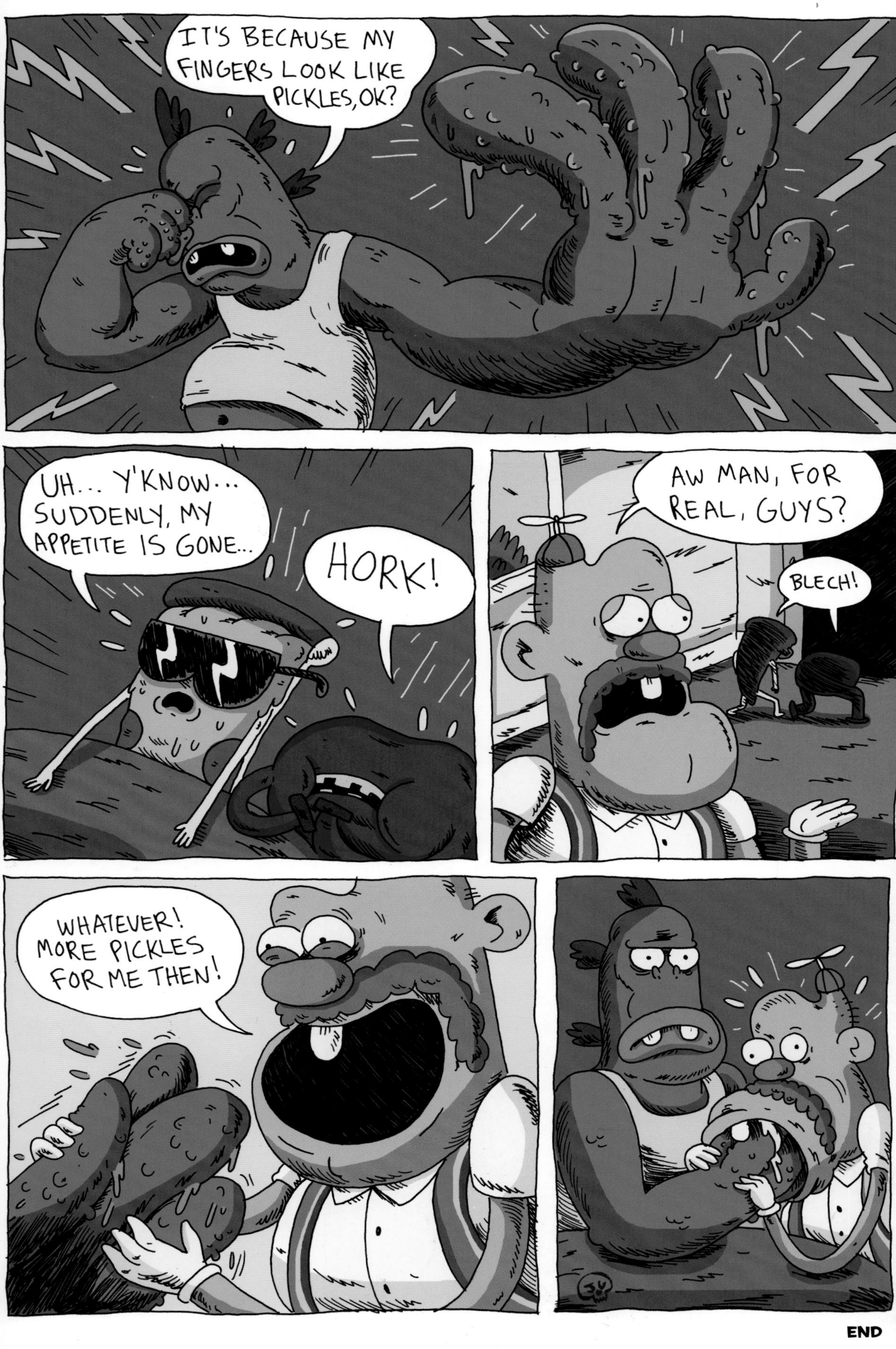
IT'S BECAUSE MY FINGERS LOOK LIKE PICKLES, OK?
UH... Y'KNOW... SUDDENLY, MY APPETITE IS GONE...
HORK!
AW MAN, FOR REAL, GUYS?
BLECH!
WHATEVER! MORE PICKLES FOR ME THEN!

END

A Tangle of Torso Dangles

BY NICHOL ASHWORTH
COLORS BY WHITNEY COGAR

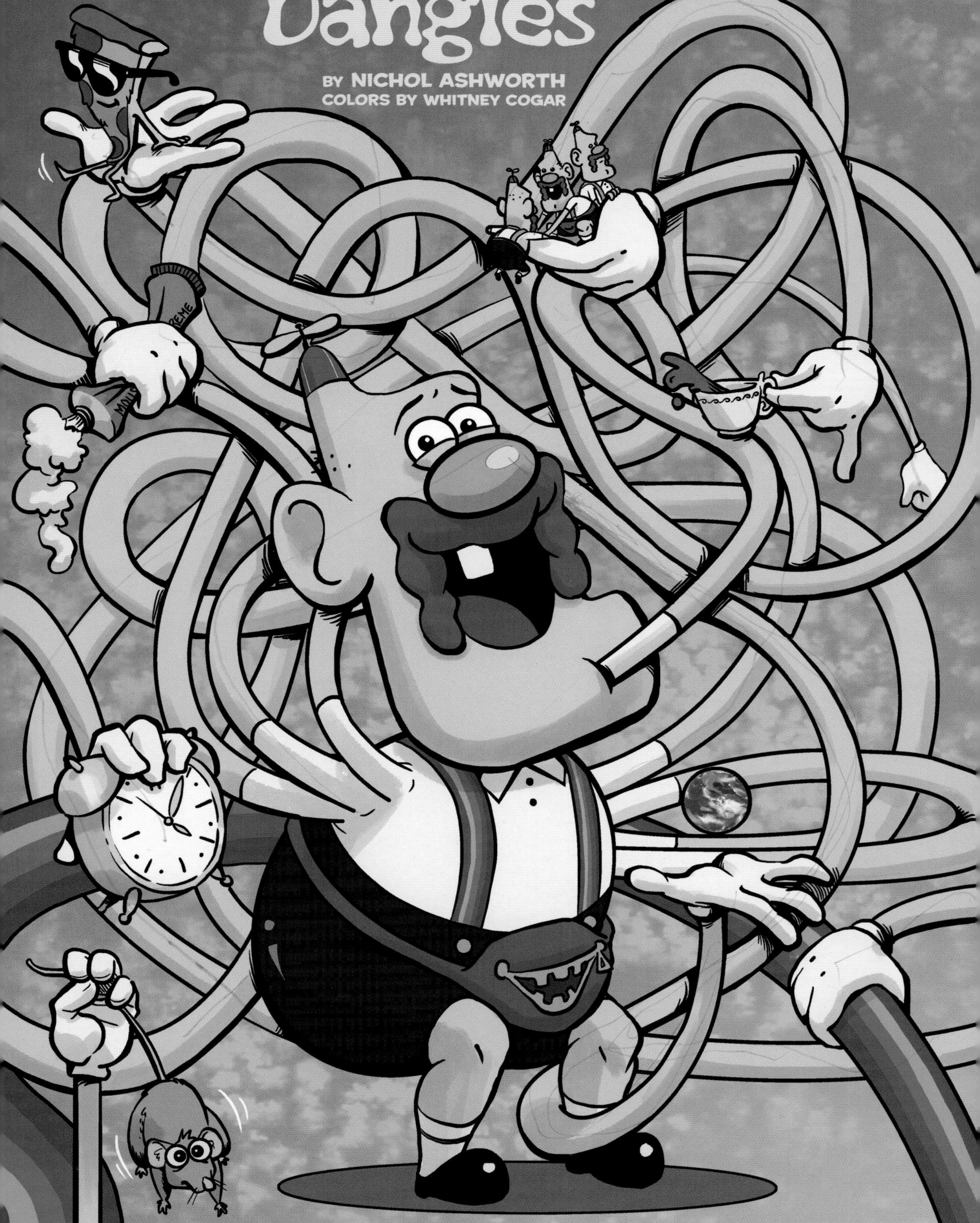

UNCLE GRANDPA HAS, LIKE, A BAJILLION ARMS AND THEY'RE ALL TANGLED UP! GO THROUGH THE MAZE AND FIGURE OUT WHICH HAND AND ARM ARE ATTACHED TO THE CLEFT IN HIS CHIN!

The correct answer is: the hand with the globe.

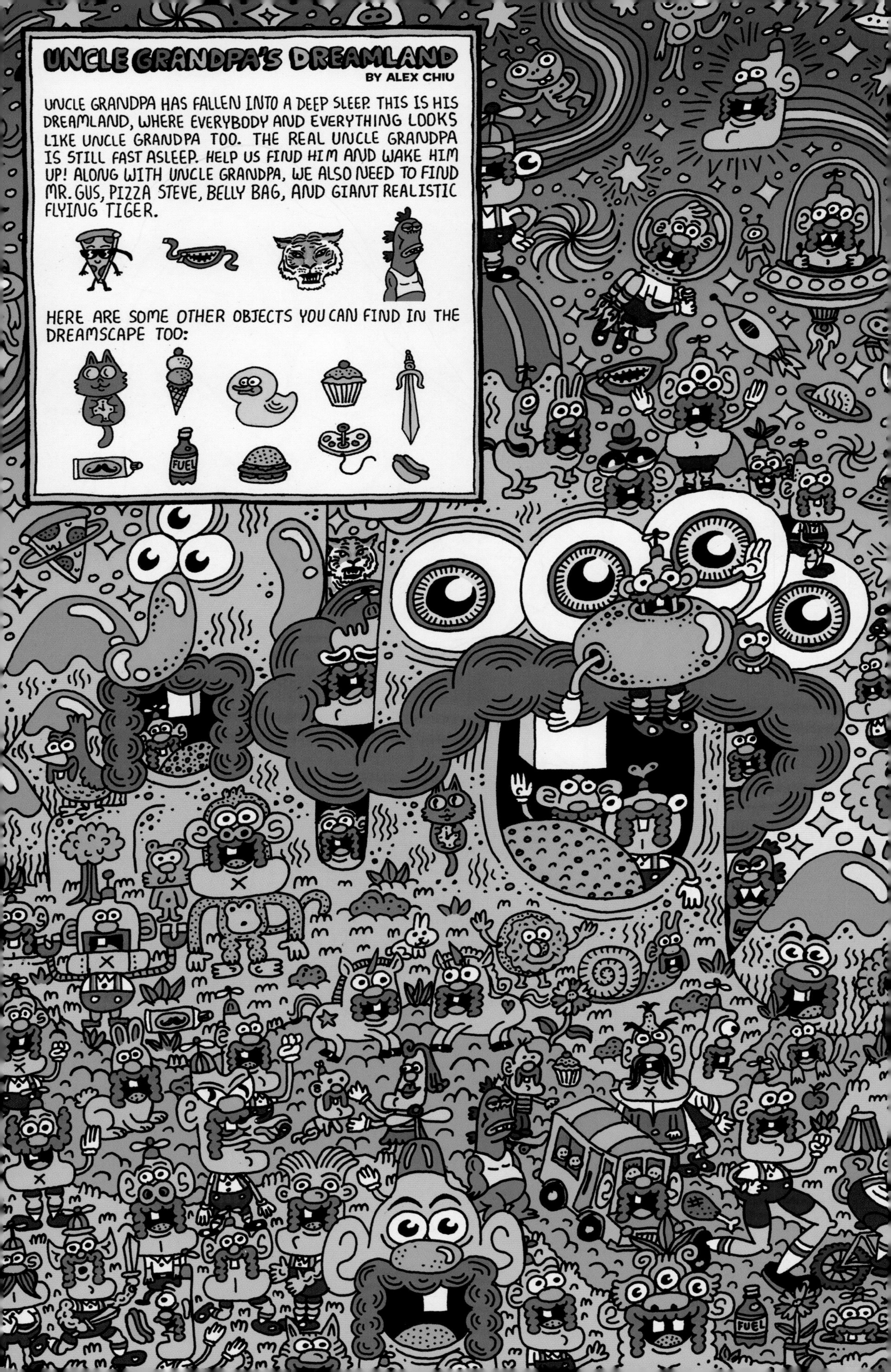
UNCLE GRANDPA'S DREAMLAND
BY ALEX CHIU
UNCLE GRANDPA HAS FALLEN INTO A DEEP SLEEP. THIS IS HIS DREAMLAND, WHERE EVERYBODY AND EVERYTHING LOOKS LIKE UNCLE GRANDPA TOO. THE REAL UNCLE GRANDPA IS STILL FAST ASLEEP. HELP US FIND HIM AND WAKE HIM UP! ALONG WITH UNCLE GRANDPA, WE ALSO NEED TO FIND MR. GUS, PIZZA STEVE, BELLY BAG, AND GIANT REALISTIC FLYING TIGER.
HERE ARE SOME OTHER OBJECTS YOU CAN FIND IN THE DREAMSCAPE TOO:

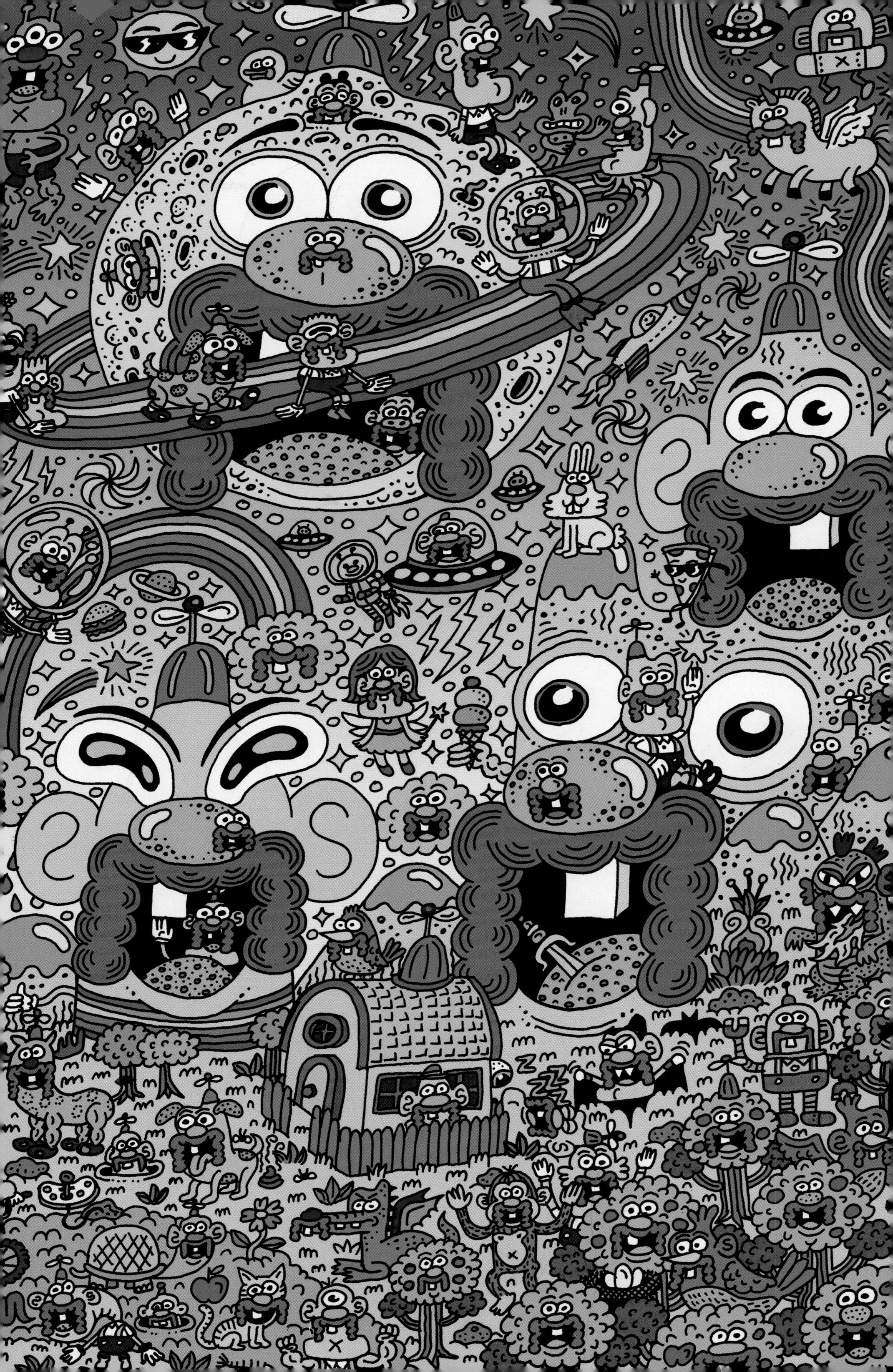

UNCLE GRANDPA GETS THE SPINS! BY KEVIN BURKHALTER

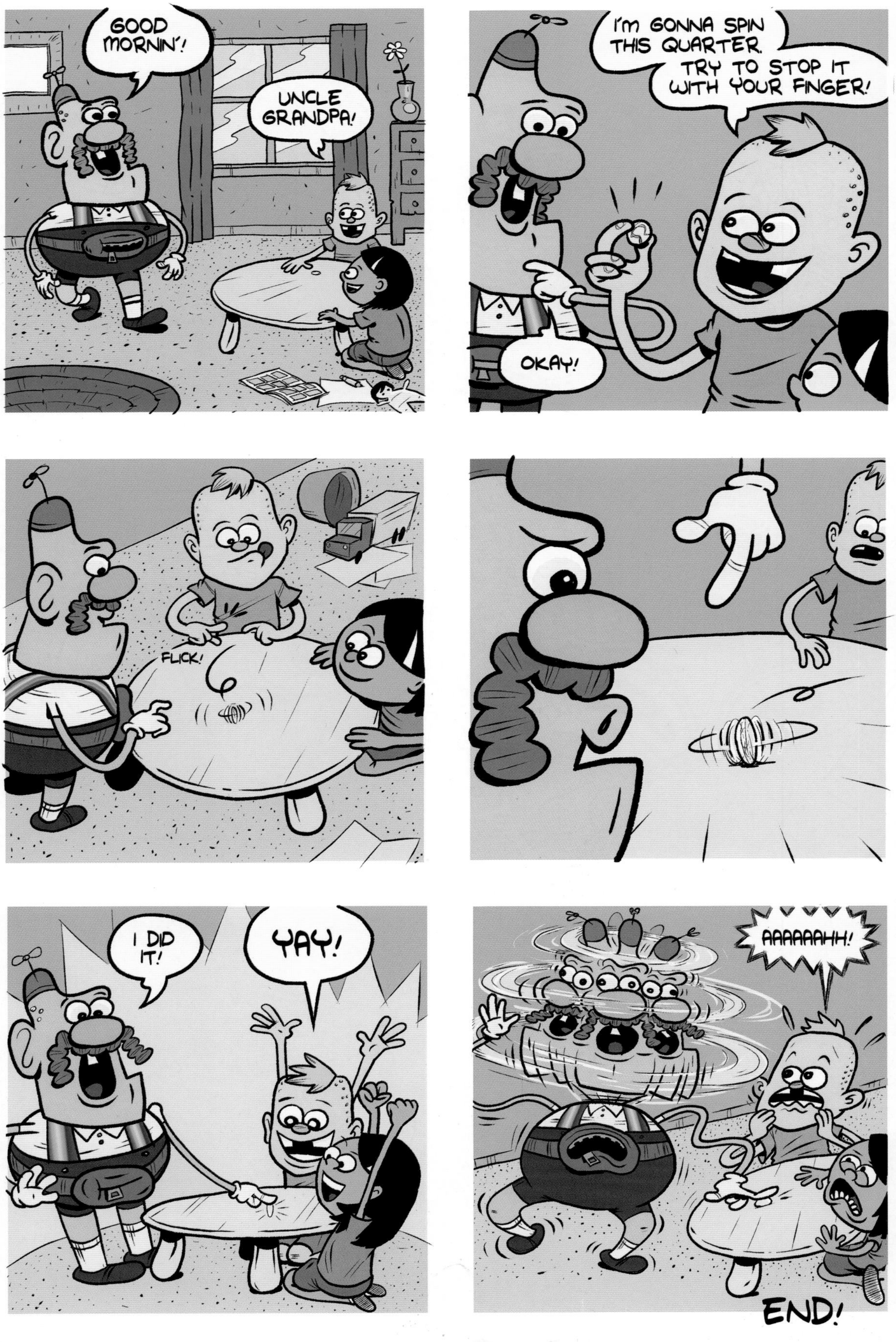
GOOD MORNIN'!
UNCLE GRANDPA!
I'M GONNA SPIN THIS QUARTER.
TRY TO STOP IT WITH YOUR FINGER!
OKAY!
FLICK!
I DID IT!
YAY!
AAAAAAHH!
END!

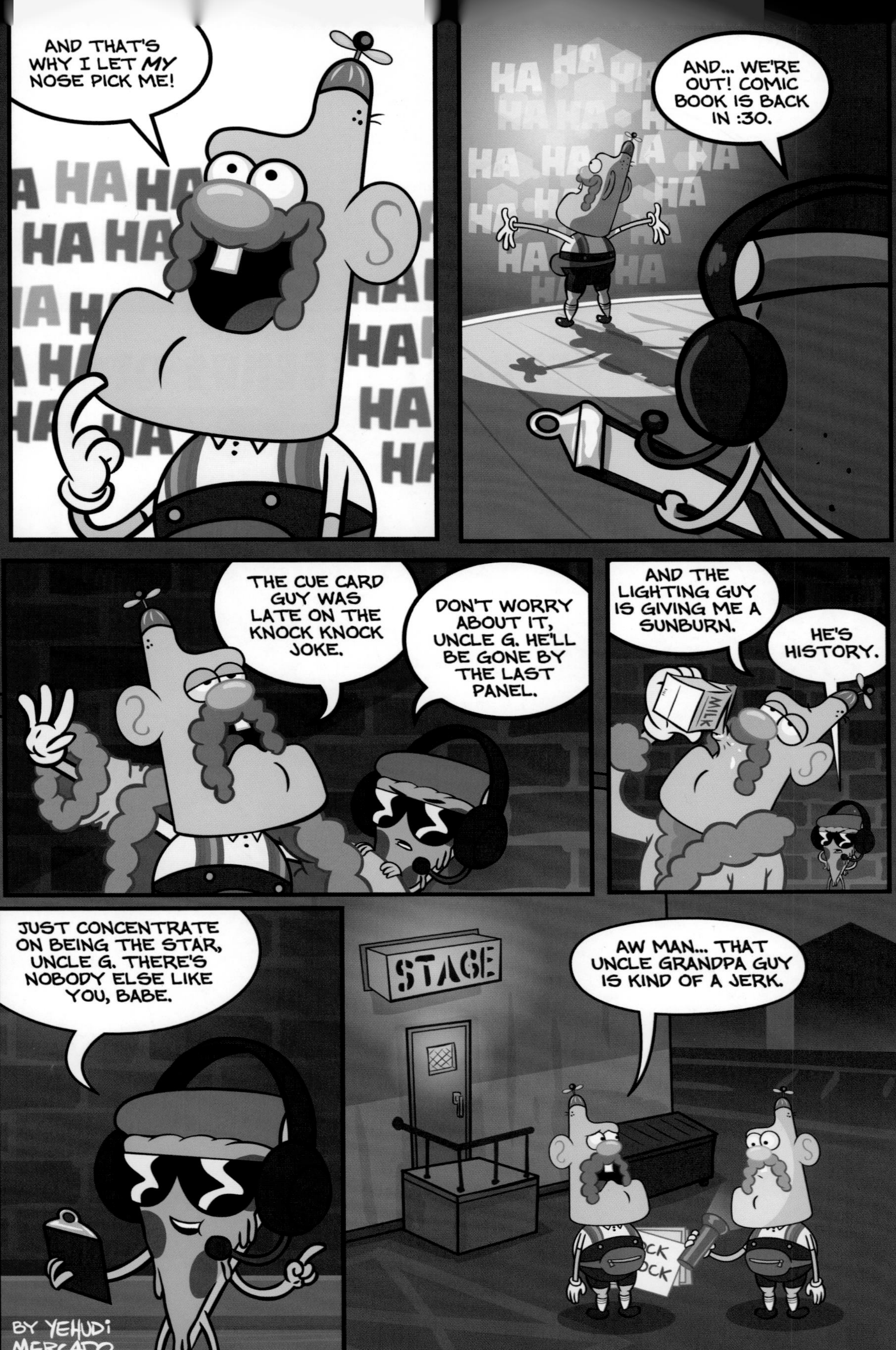
AND THAT'S WHY I LET MY NOSE PICK ME!
HA HA HA HA HA HA HA HA HA HA HA HA
AND... WE'RE OUT! COMIC BOOK IS BACK IN :30.
THE CUE CARD GUY WAS LATE ON THE KNOCK KNOCK JOKE.
DON'T WORRY ABOUT IT, UNCLE G. HE'LL BE GONE BY THE LAST PANEL.
AND THE LIGHTING GUY IS GIVING ME A SUNBURN.
MILK
HE'S HISTORY.
JUST CONCENTRATE ON BEING THE STAR, UNCLE G. THERE'S NOBODY ELSE LIKE YOU, BABE.
STAGE
AW MAN... THAT UNCLE GRANDPA GUY IS KIND OF A JERK.
BY YEHUDI MERCADO
END.

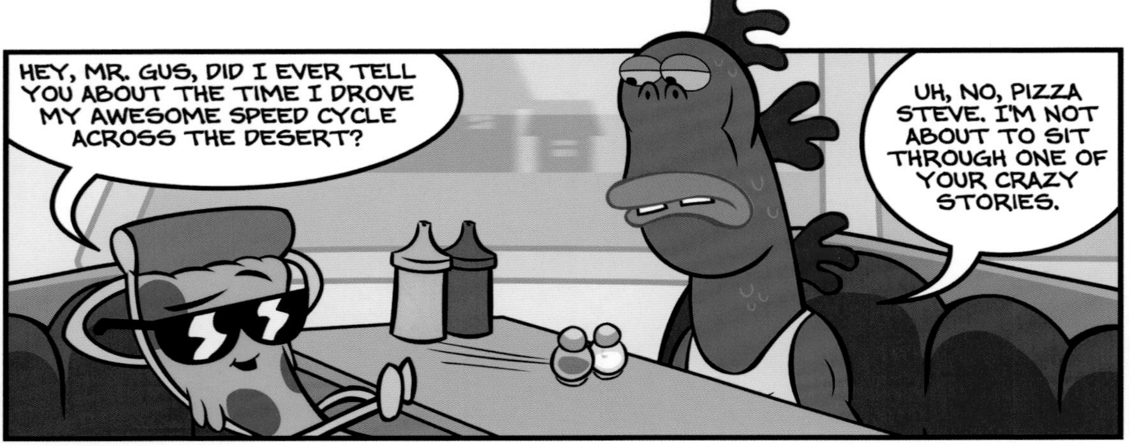
HEY, MR. GUS, DID I EVER TELL YOU ABOUT THE TIME I DROVE MY AWESOME SPEED CYCLE ACROSS THE DESERT?
UH, NO, PIZZA STEVE. I'M NOT ABOUT TO SIT THROUGH ONE OF YOUR CRAZY STORIES.

IT'S NOT A STORY, IT'S...

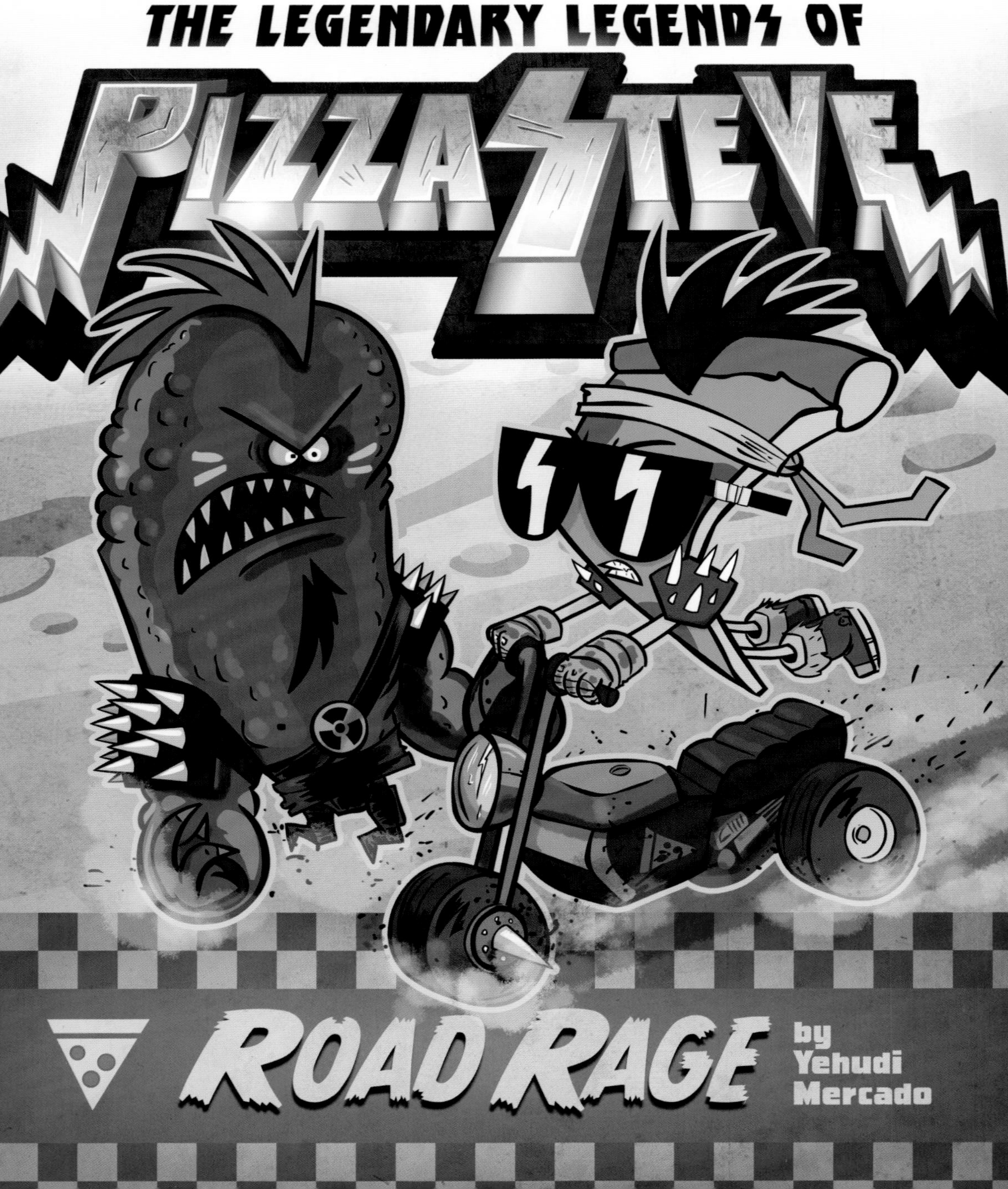
THE LEGENDARY LEGENDS OF
PIZZA STEVE
ROAD RAGE
by
Yehudi
Mercado

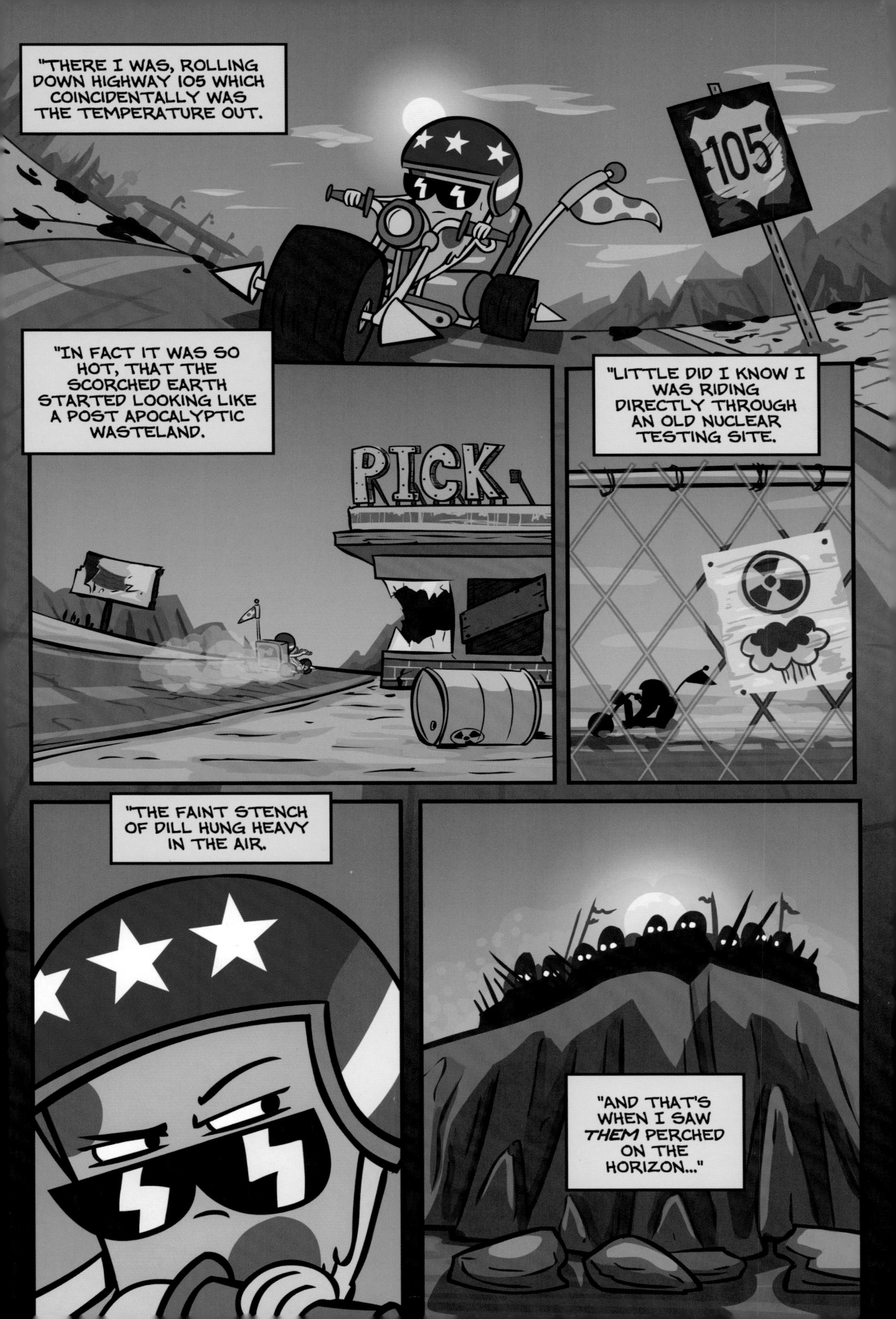
"THERE I WAS, ROLLING DOWN HIGHWAY 105 WHICH COINCIDENTALLY WAS THE TEMPERATURE OUT.
105
"IN FACT IT WAS SO HOT, THAT THE SCORCHED EARTH STARTED LOOKING LIKE A POST APOCALYPTIC WASTELAND.
PICK
"LITTLE DID I KNOW I WAS RIDING DIRECTLY THROUGH AN OLD NUCLEAR TESTING SITE.
"THE FAINT STENCH OF DILL HUNG HEAVY IN THE AIR.
"AND THAT'S WHEN I SAW *THEM* PERCHED ON THE HORIZON..."

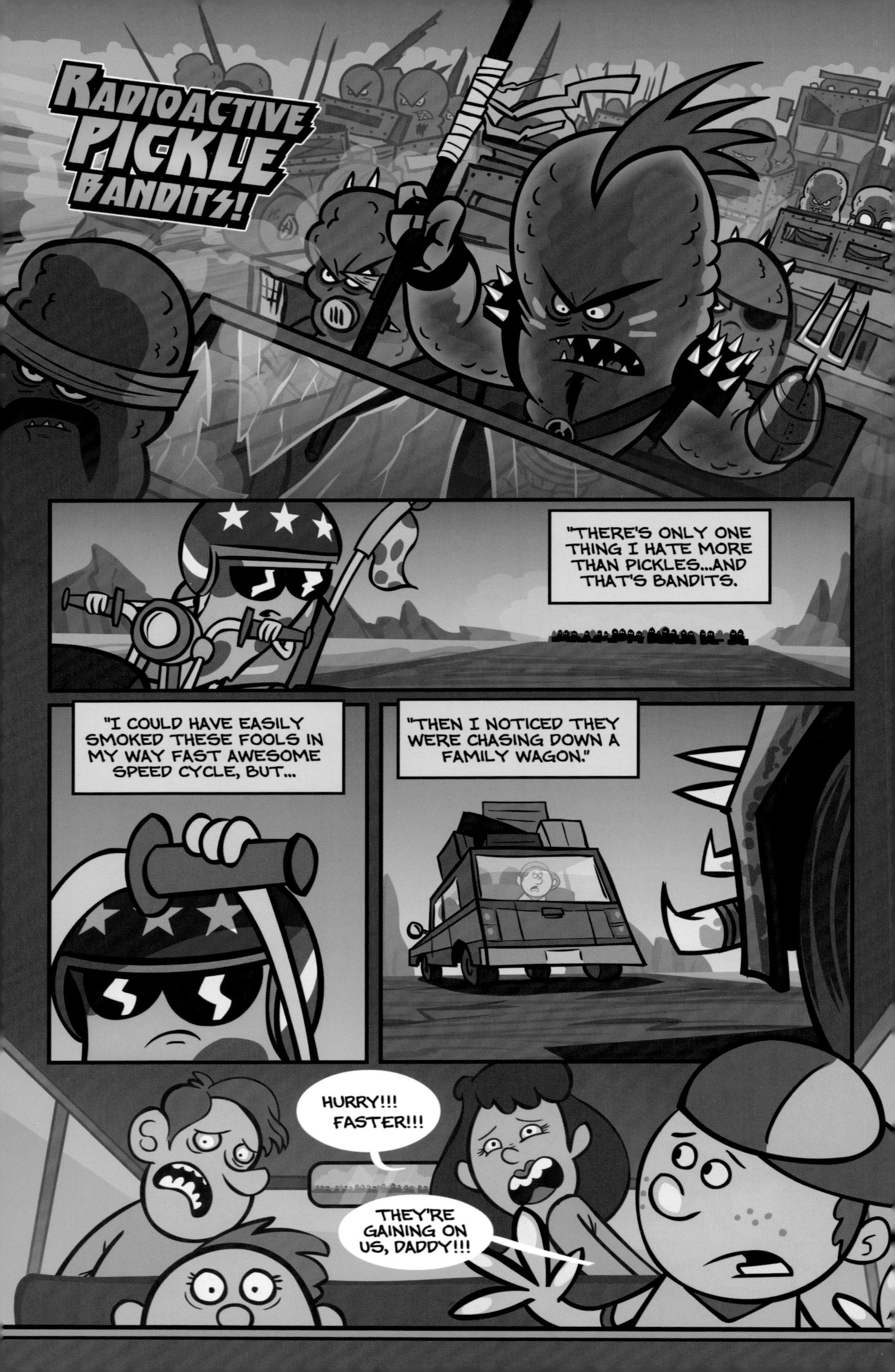
RADIOACTIVE PICKLE BANDITS!
"THERE'S ONLY ONE THING I HATE MORE THAN PICKLES...AND THAT'S BANDITS.
"I COULD HAVE EASILY SMOKED THESE FOOLS IN MY WAY FAST AWESOME SPEED CYCLE, BUT...
"THEN I NOTICED THEY WERE CHASING DOWN A FAMILY WAGON."
HURRY!!! FASTER!!!
THEY'RE GAINING ON US, DADDY!!!

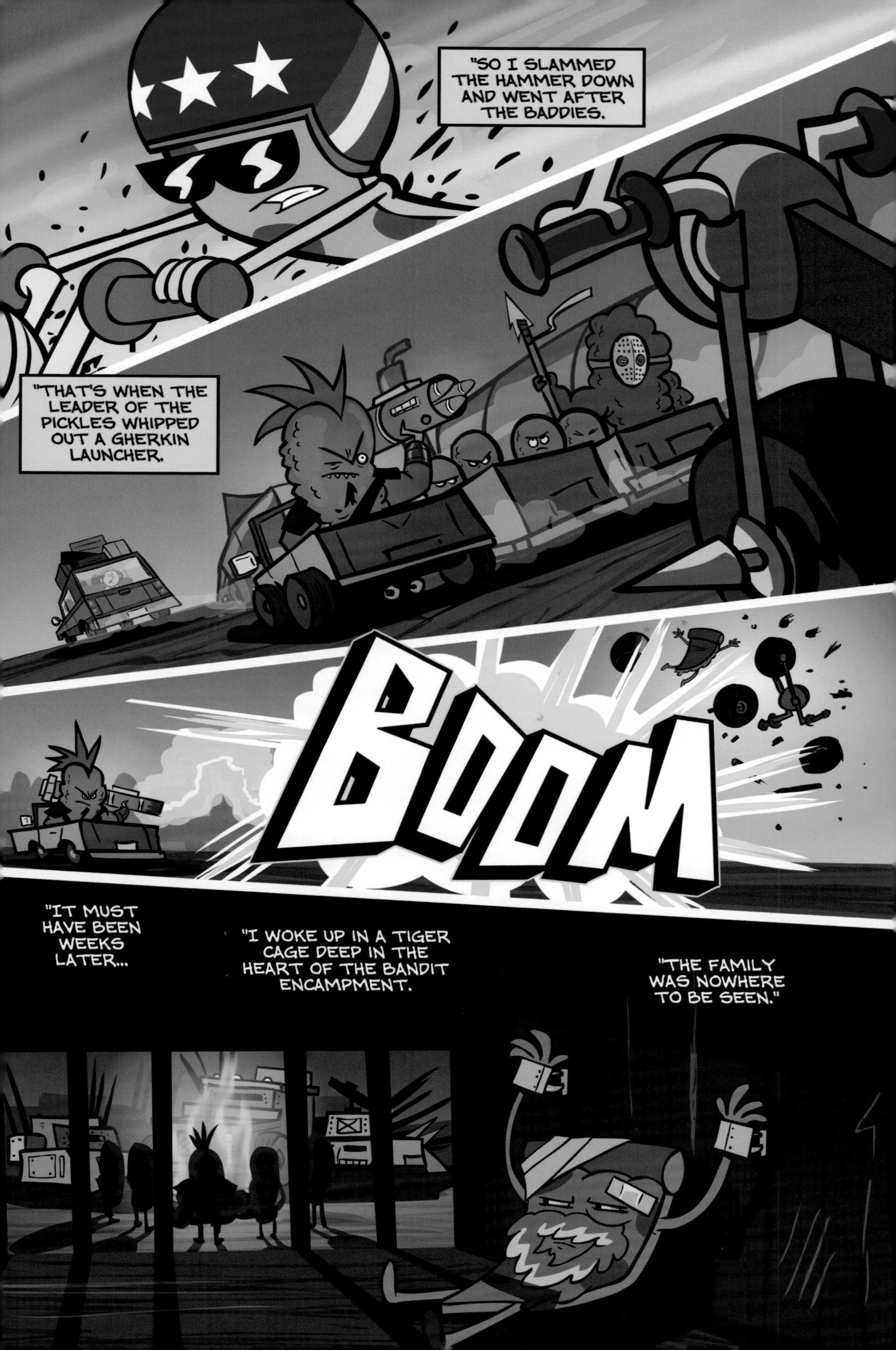
"SO I SLAMMED THE HAMMER DOWN AND WENT AFTER THE BADDIES.
"THAT'S WHEN THE LEADER OF THE PICKLES WHIPPED OUT A GHERKIN LAUNCHER.
BOOM
"IT MUST HAVE BEEN WEEKS LATER...
"I WOKE UP IN A TIGER CAGE DEEP IN THE HEART OF THE BANDIT ENCAMPMENT.
"THE FAMILY WAS NOWHERE TO BE SEEN."

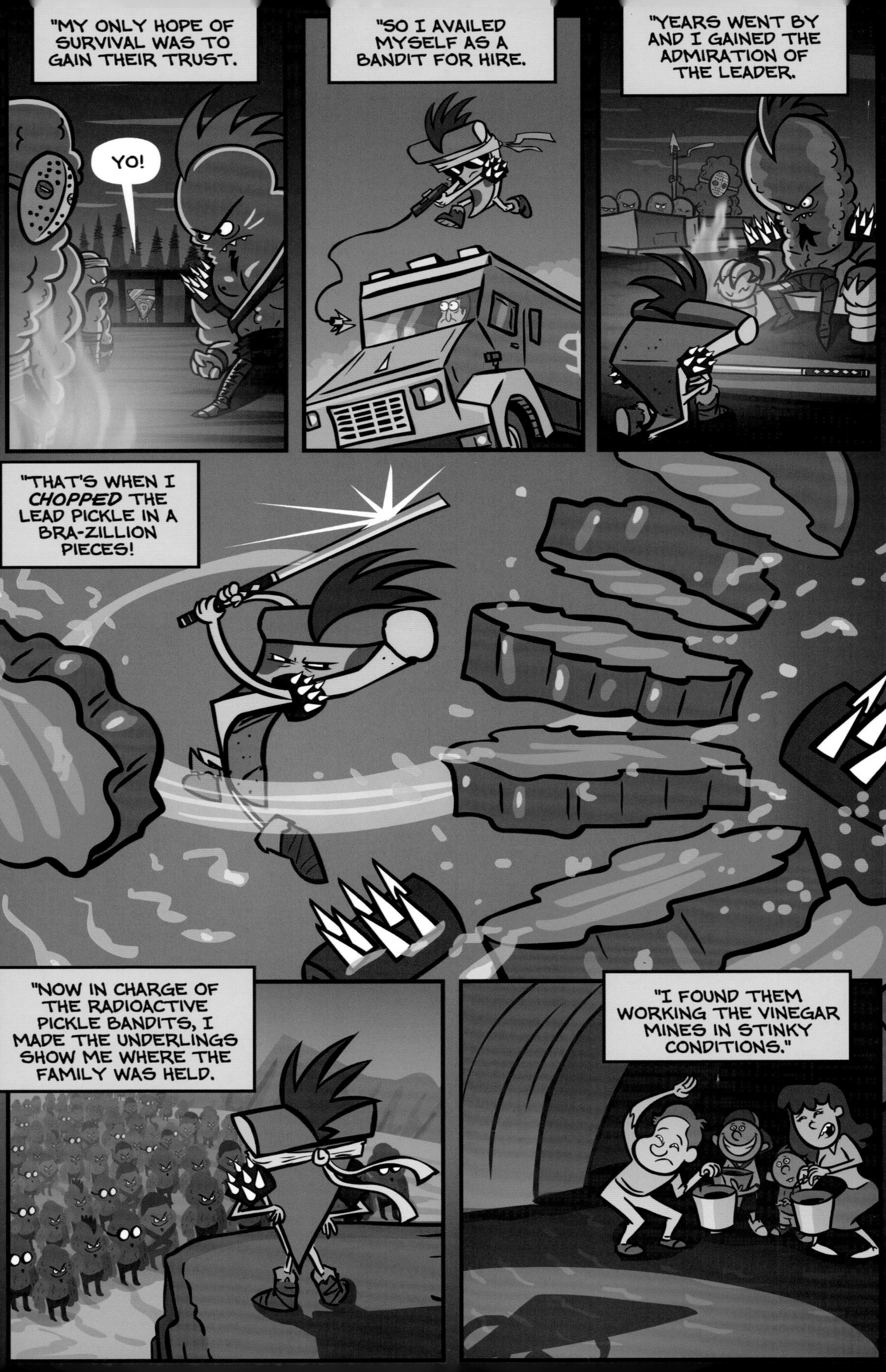
"MY ONLY HOPE OF SURVIVAL WAS TO GAIN THEIR TRUST.
YO!
"SO I AVAILED MYSELF AS A BANDIT FOR HIRE.
"YEARS WENT BY AND I GAINED THE ADMIRATION OF THE LEADER.
"THAT'S WHEN I *CHOPPED* THE LEAD PICKLE IN A BRA-ZILLION PIECES!
"NOW IN CHARGE OF THE RADIOACTIVE PICKLE BANDITS, I MADE THE UNDERLINGS SHOW ME WHERE THE FAMILY WAS HELD.
"I FOUND THEM WORKING THE VINEGAR MINES IN STINKY CONDITIONS."

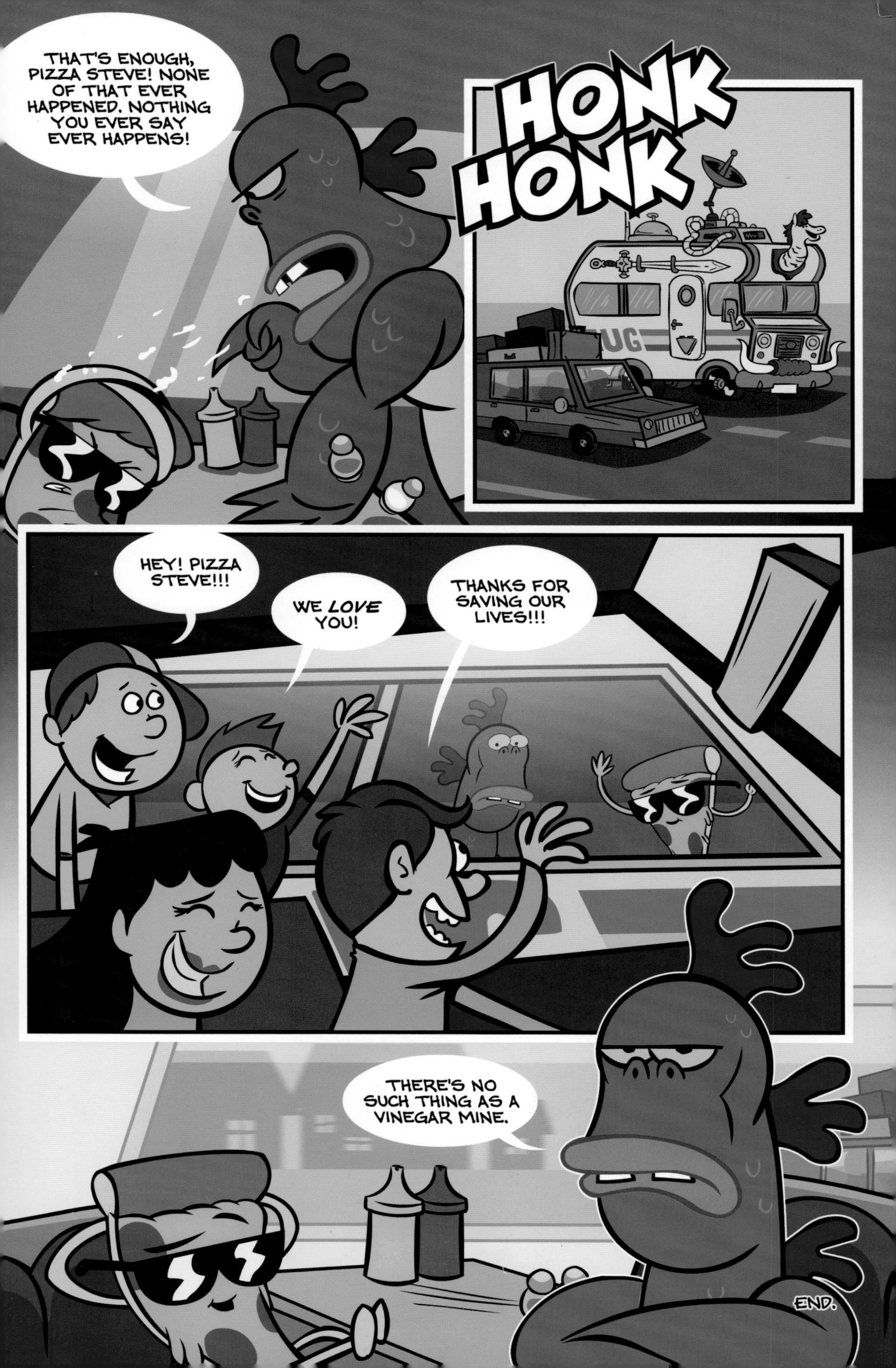
THAT'S ENOUGH, PIZZA STEVE! NONE OF THAT EVER HAPPENED. NOTHING YOU EVER SAY EVER HAPPENS!
HONK HONK
UG
HEY! PIZZA STEVE!!!
WE LOVE YOU!
THANKS FOR SAVING OUR LIVES!!!
THERE'S NO SUCH THING AS A VINEGAR MINE.
END.

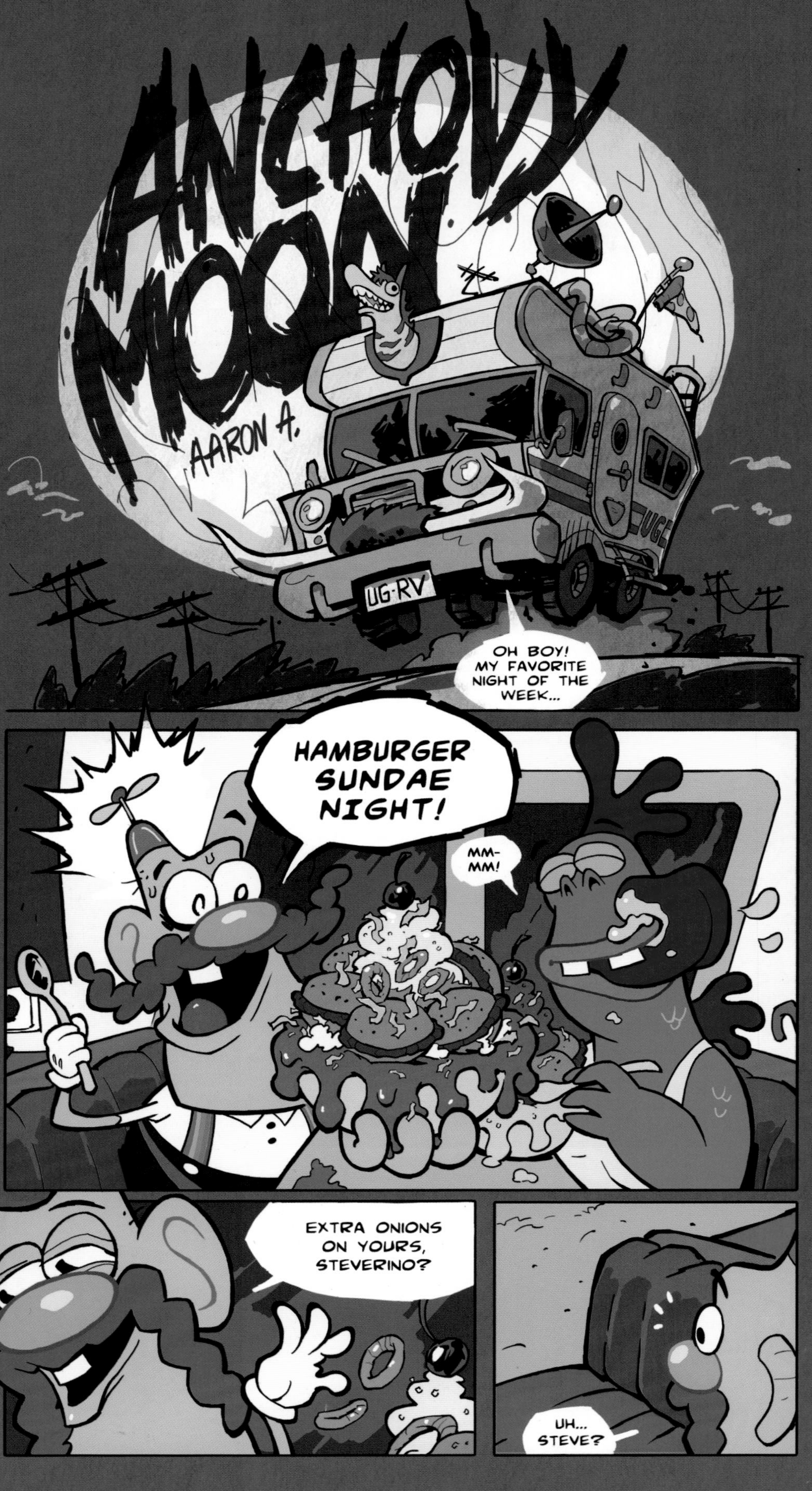
ANCHOVY MOON
AARON A.
UG-RV
OH BOY! MY FAVORITE NIGHT OF THE WEEK...
HAMBURGER SUNDAE NIGHT!
MM-MM!
EXTRA ONIONS ON YOURS, STEVERINO?
UH... STEVE?

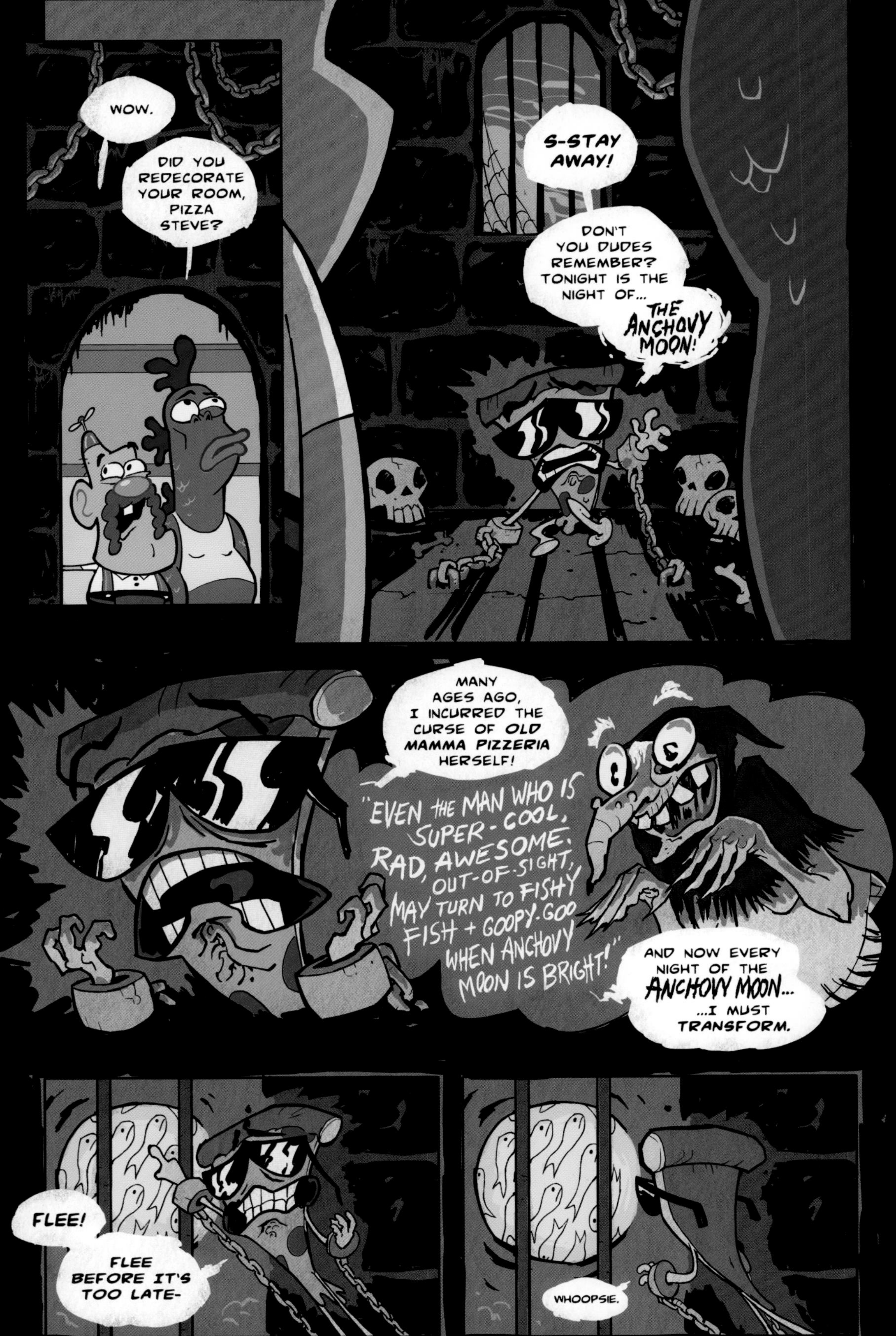
WOW.
DID YOU REDECORATE YOUR ROOM, PIZZA STEVE?
S-STAY AWAY!
DON'T YOU DUDES REMEMBER? TONIGHT IS THE NIGHT OF...
THE ANCHOVY MOON!
MANY AGES AGO, I INCURRED THE CURSE OF OLD MAMMA PIZZERIA HERSELF!
"EVEN THE MAN WHO IS SUPER-COOL, RAD, AWESOME, OUT-OF-SIGHT, MAY TURN TO FISHY FISH + GOOPY-GOO WHEN ANCHOVY MOON IS BRIGHT!"
AND NOW EVERY NIGHT OF THE ANCHOVY MOON...
...I MUST TRANSFORM.
FLEE!
FLEE BEFORE IT'S TOO LATE-
WHOOPSIE.

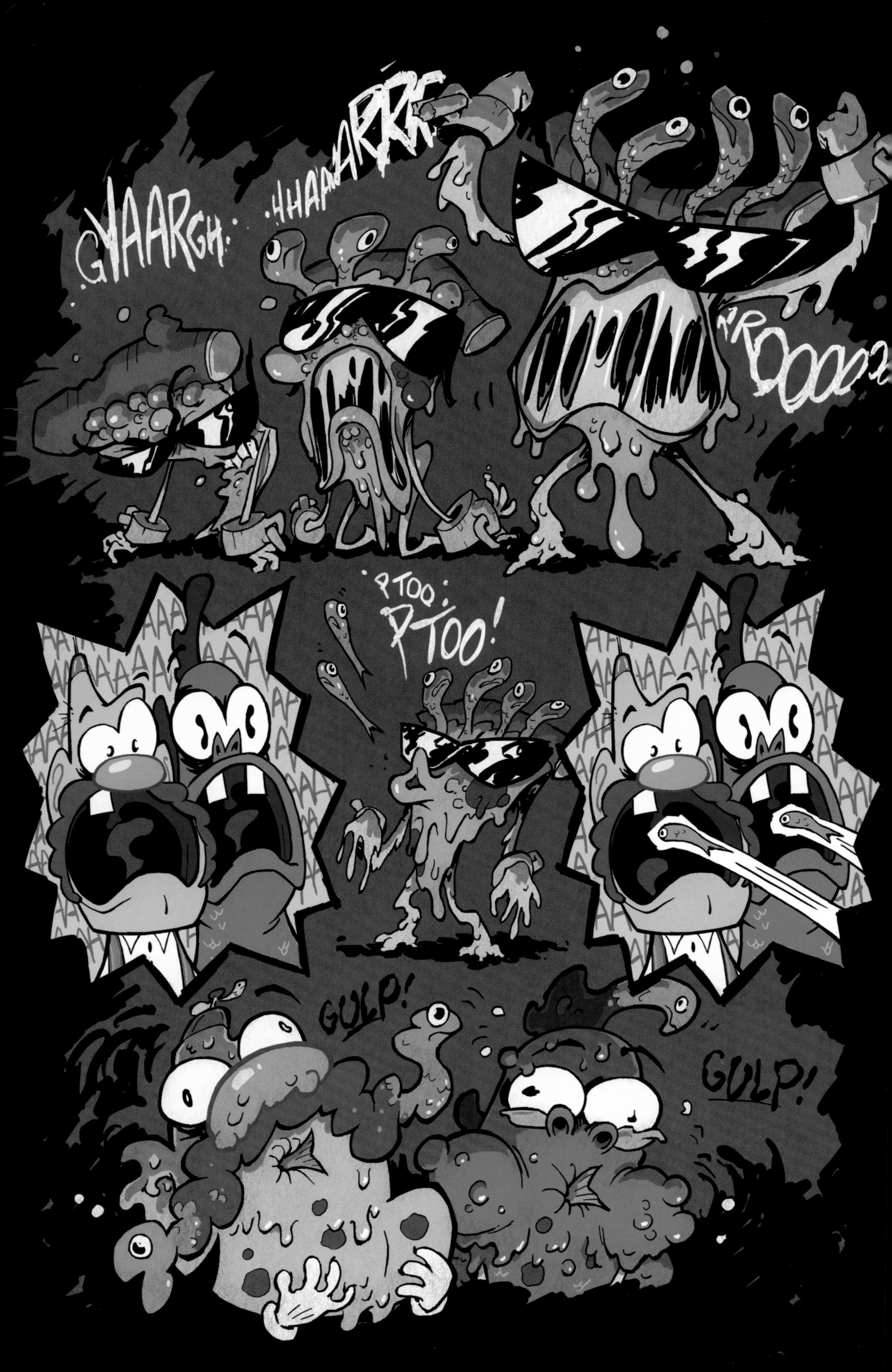

GYAARGH
HHAAAARRR
ROOOOO
P TOO
P TOO!
GULP!
GULP!

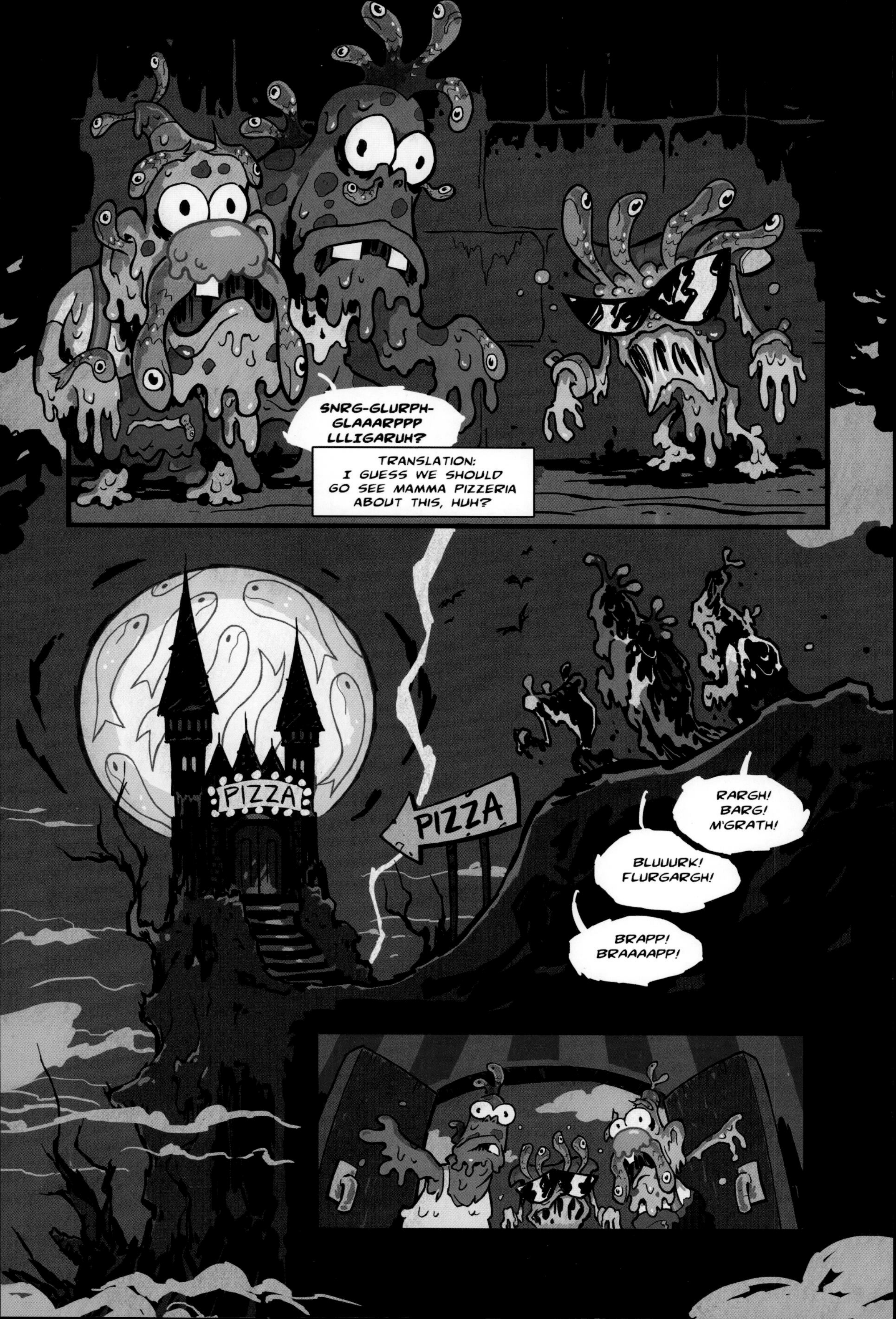
SNRG-GLURPH-GLAAARPPP LLLIGARUH?
TRANSLATION: I GUESS WE SHOULD GO SEE MAMMA PIZZERIA ABOUT THIS, HUH?
PIZZA
PIZZA
RARGH! BARG! M'GRATH!
BLUUURK! FLURGARGH!
BRAPP! BRAAAAPP!

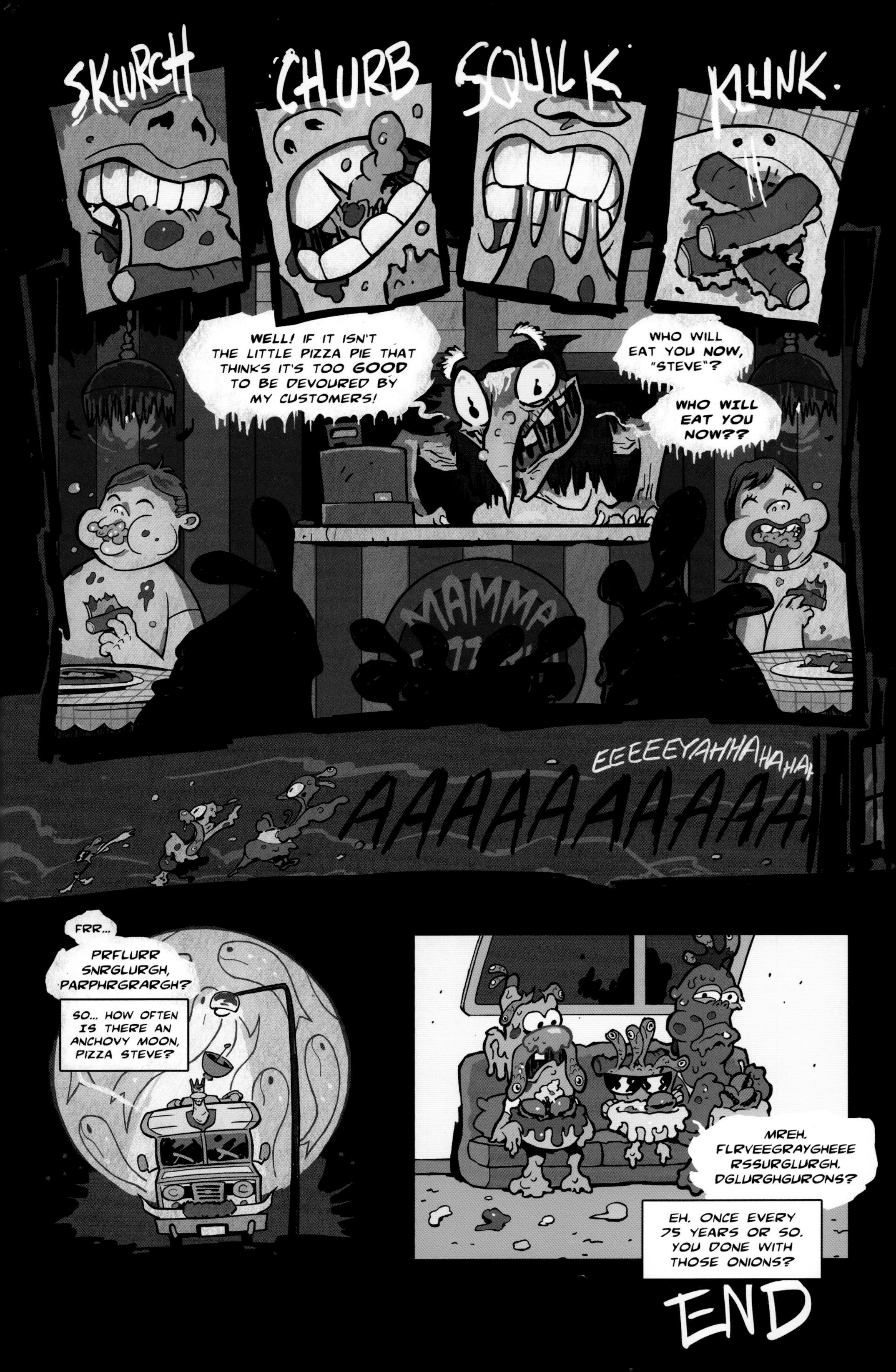
SKLURCH
CHURB
SQUILK
KLUNK.
WELL! IF IT ISN'T THE LITTLE PIZZA PIE THAT THINKS IT'S TOO GOOD TO BE DEVOURED BY MY CUSTOMERS!
WHO WILL EAT YOU NOW, "STEVE"?
WHO WILL EAT YOU NOW??
MAMMA
EEEEEYAHHAHAHAH
AAAAAAAAAAA
FRR...
PRFLURR SNRGLURGH, PARPHRGRARGH?
SO... HOW OFTEN IS THERE AN ANCHOVY MOON, PIZZA STEVE?
MREH. FLRVEEGRAYGHEEE RSSURGLURGH. DGLURGHGURONS?
EH. ONCE EVERY 75 YEARS OR SO. YOU DONE WITH THOSE ONIONS?
END

UNCLE GRANDPA in "FROWN TOWN"

BY DAVID DEGRAND

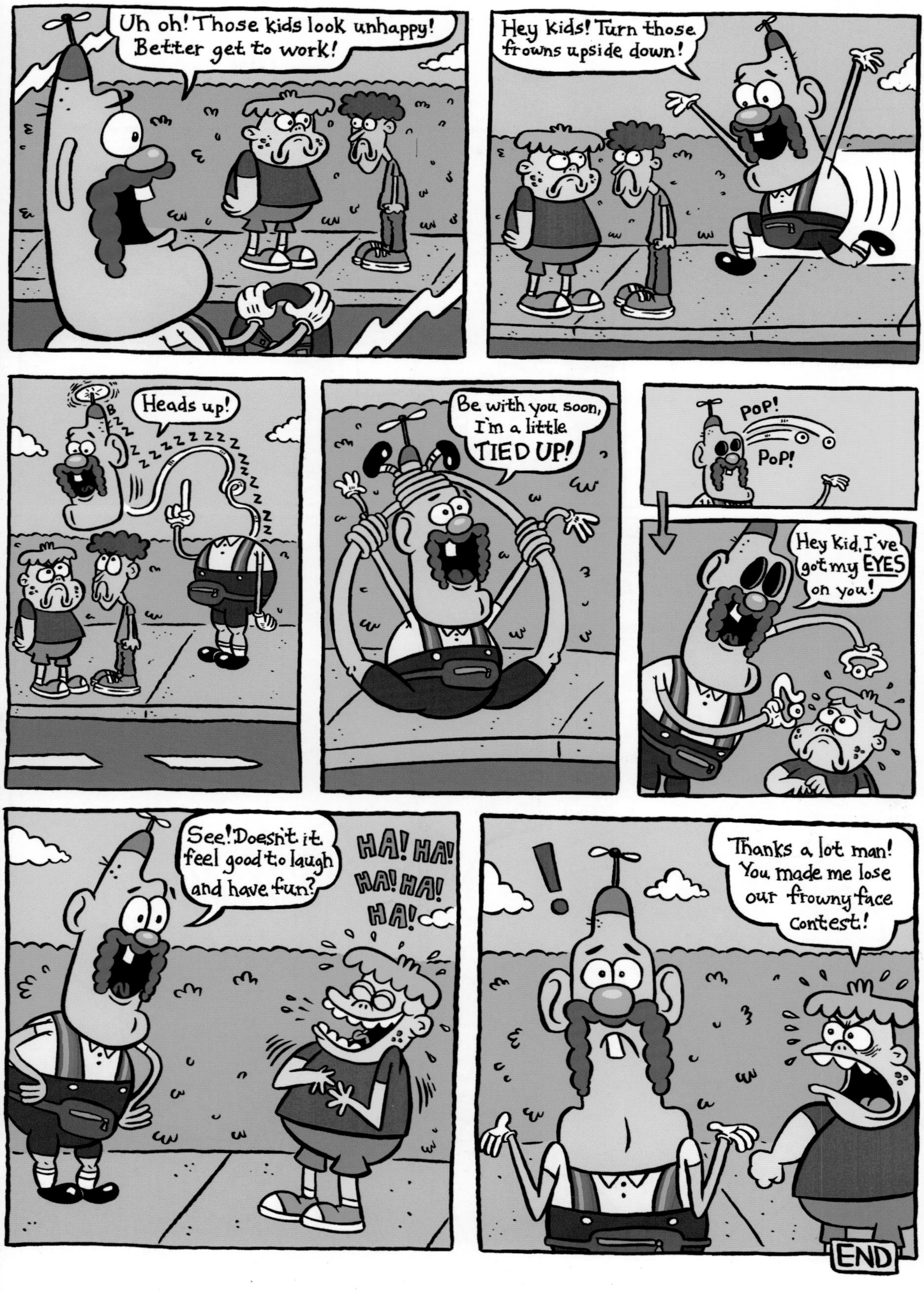
Uh oh! Those kids look unhappy! Better get to work!
Hey kids! Turn those frowns upside down!
Heads up!
Be with you soon, I'm a little TIED UP!
POP!
POP!
Hey kid, I've got my EYES on you!
See! Doesn't it feel good to laugh and have fun?
HA! HA! HA! HA! HA!
!
Thanks a lot man! You made me lose our frowny face contest!
END

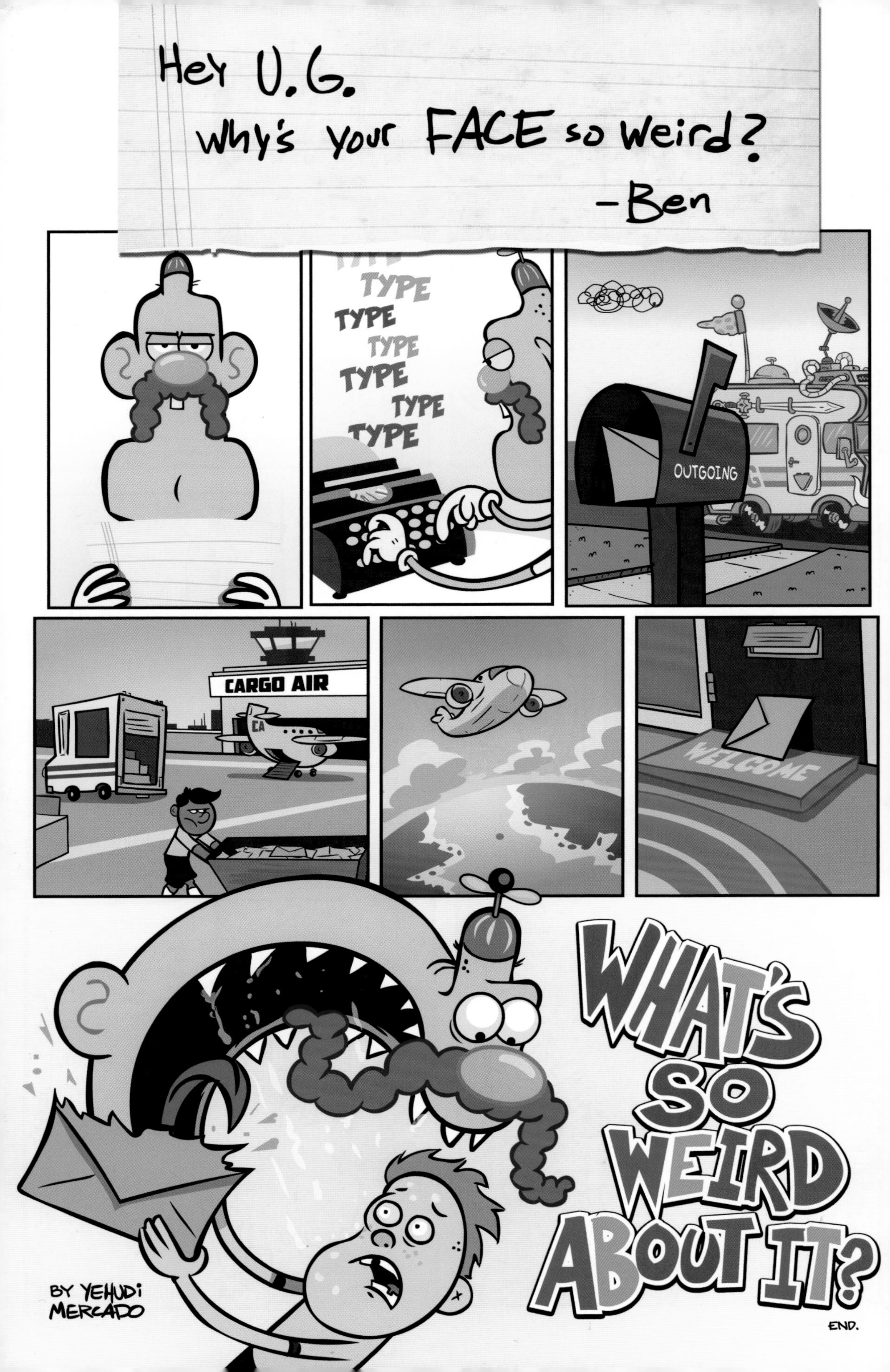
Hey U.G.
Why's your FACE so Weird?
-Ben
TYPE
TYPE
TYPE
TYPE
TYPE
TYPE
OUTGOING
CARGO AIR
CA
WELCOME
WHAT'S SO WEIRD ABOUT IT?
BY YEHUDI MERCADO
END.

ISSUE #3 VARIANT COVER
BRANDON REESE

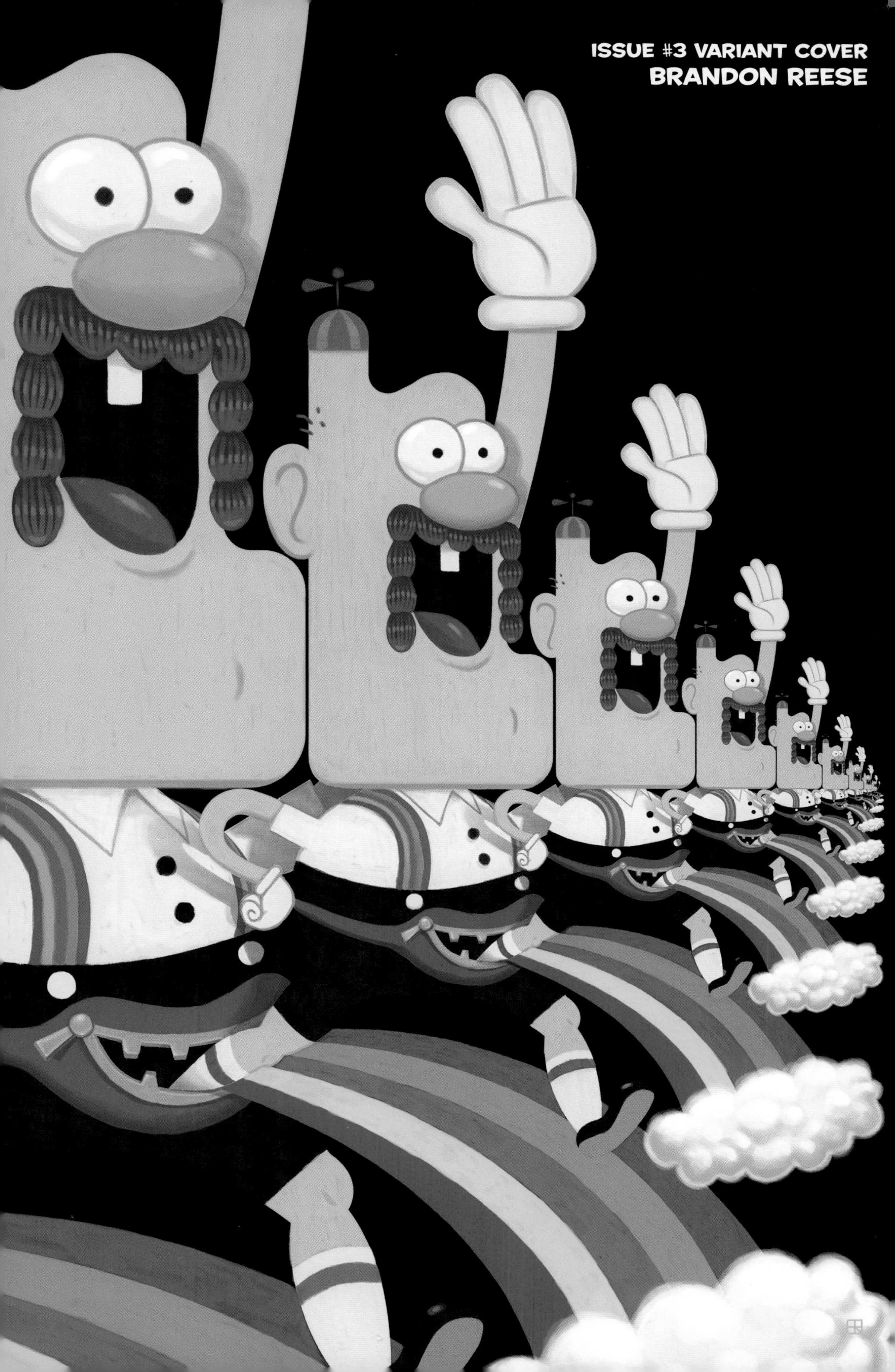

ISSUE #4 COVER
ZÉ BURNAY

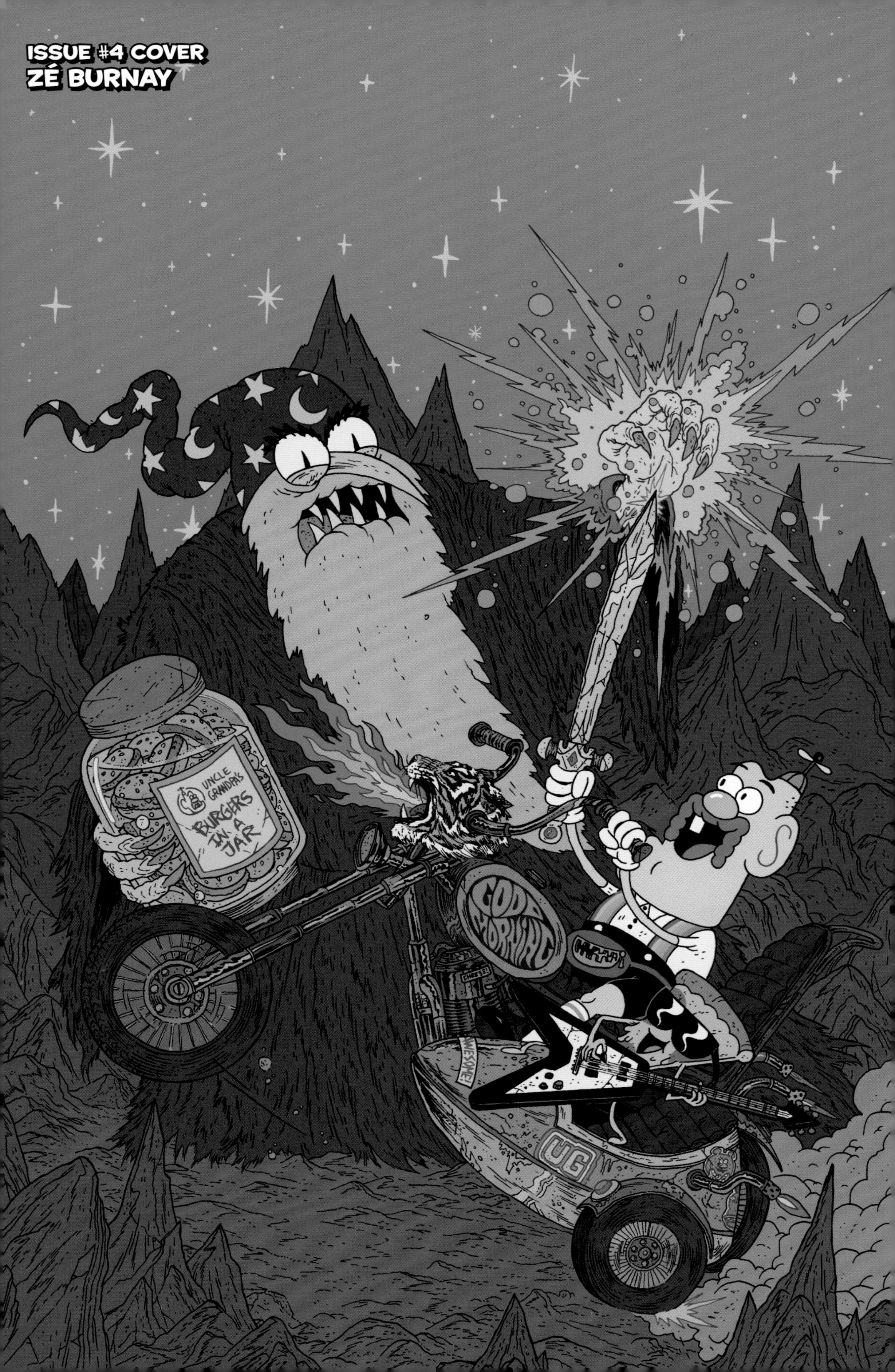
UNCLE GRANDPA'S
BURGERS IN A JAR
UG

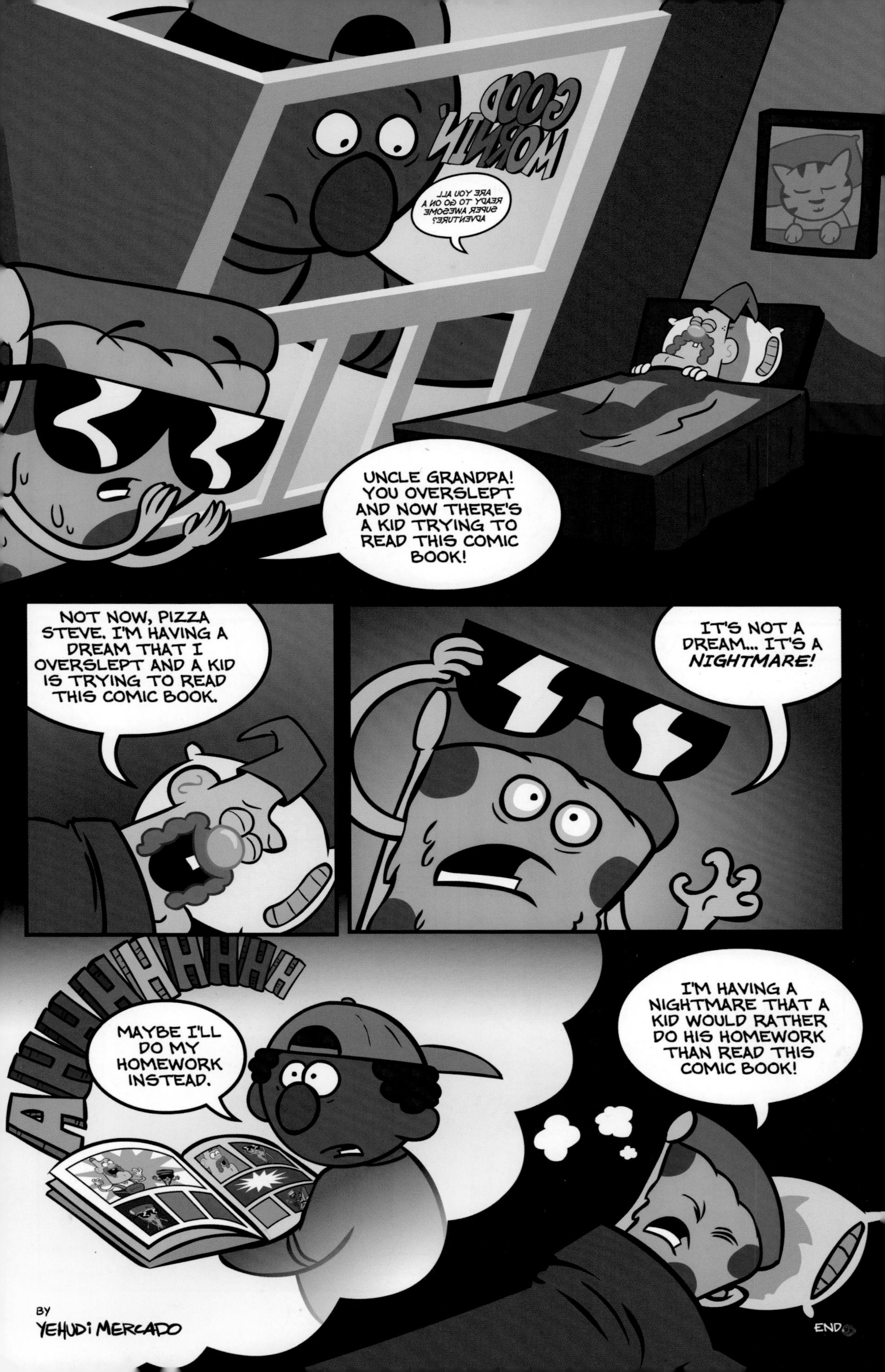
GOOD MORNIN'
ARE YOU ALL READY TO GO ON A SUPER AWESOME ADVENTURE?
UNCLE GRANDPA! YOU OVERSLEPT AND NOW THERE'S A KID TRYING TO READ THIS COMIC BOOK!
NOT NOW, PIZZA STEVE. I'M HAVING A DREAM THAT I OVERSLEPT AND A KID IS TRYING TO READ THIS COMIC BOOK.
IT'S NOT A DREAM... IT'S A NIGHTMARE!
AHHHHHHHHHH
MAYBE I'LL DO MY HOMEWORK INSTEAD.
I'M HAVING A NIGHTMARE THAT A KID WOULD RATHER DO HIS HOMEWORK THAN READ THIS COMIC BOOK!
BY YEHUDI MERCADO
END

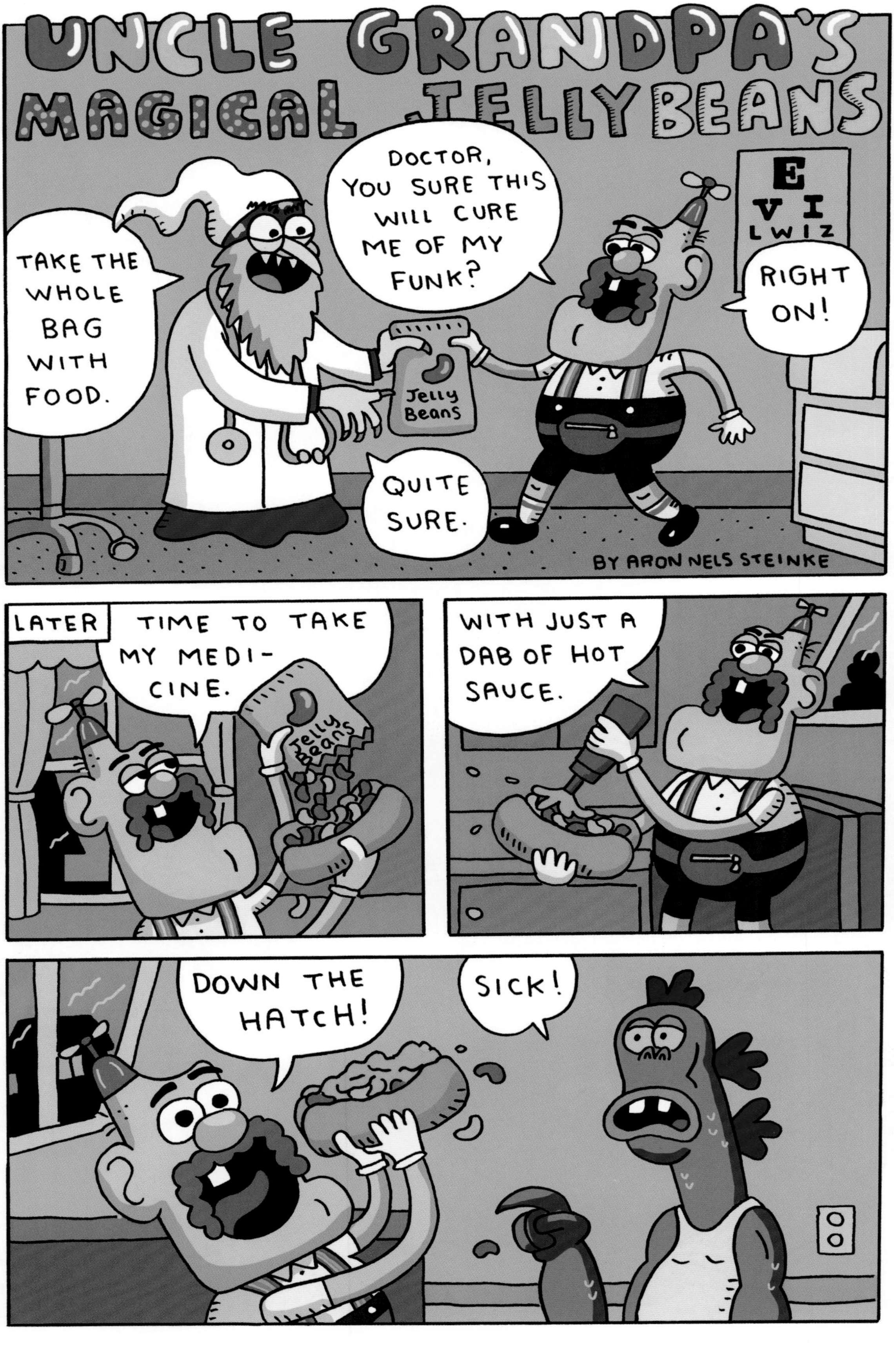
UNCLE GRANDPA'S MAGICAL JELLY BEANS
TAKE THE WHOLE BAG WITH FOOD.
DOCTOR, YOU SURE THIS WILL CURE ME OF MY FUNK?
QUITE SURE.
RIGHT ON!
E
V I
L W I Z
Jelly Beans
BY ARON NELS STEINKE
LATER
TIME TO TAKE MY MEDICINE.
Jelly Beans
WITH JUST A DAB OF HOT SAUCE.
DOWN THE HATCH!
SICK!

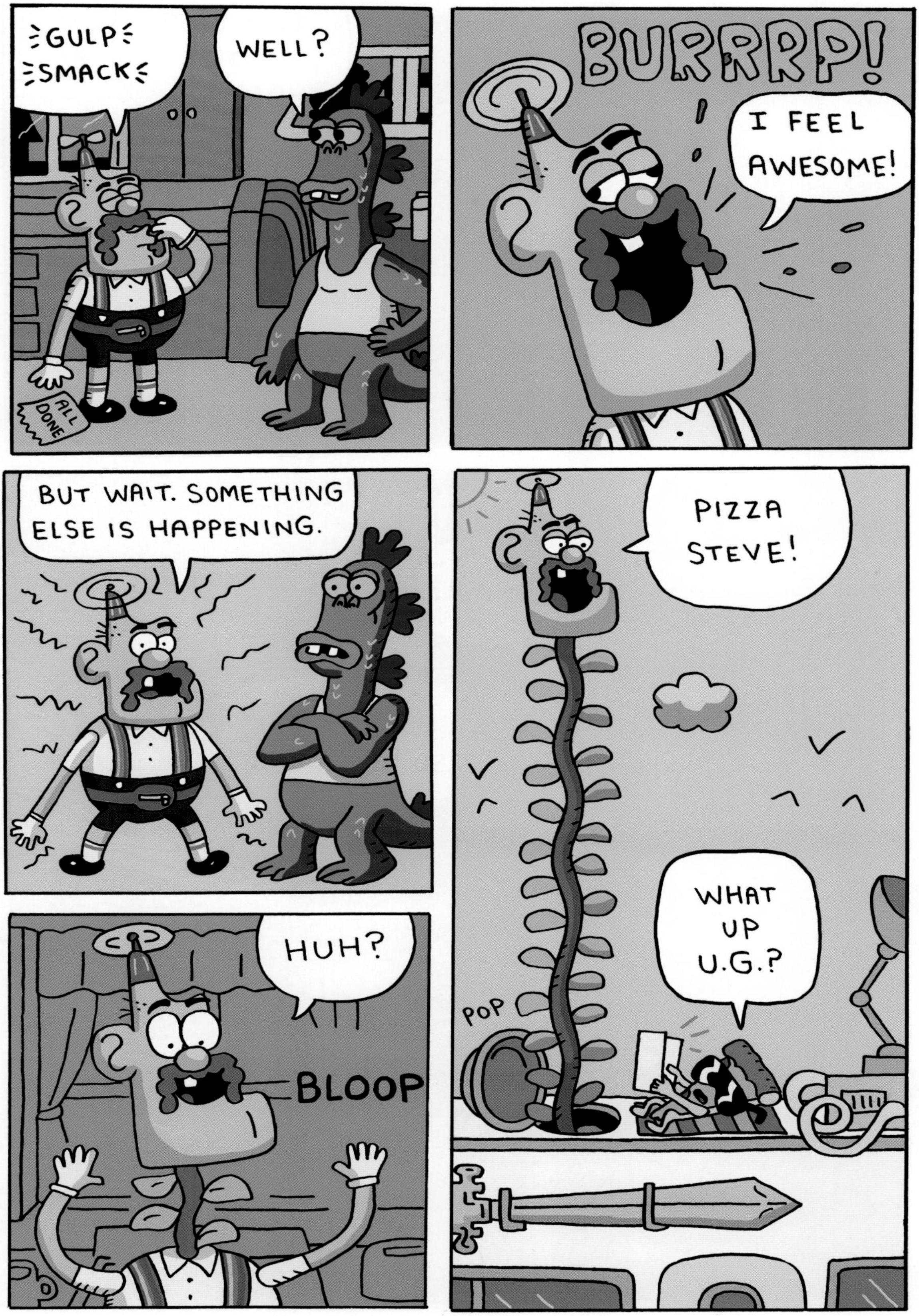
GULP
SMACK
ALL DONE
WELL?
BURRRP!
I FEEL AWESOME!
BUT WAIT. SOMETHING ELSE IS HAPPENING.
HUH?
BLOOP
PIZZA STEVE!
WHAT UP U.G.?
POP

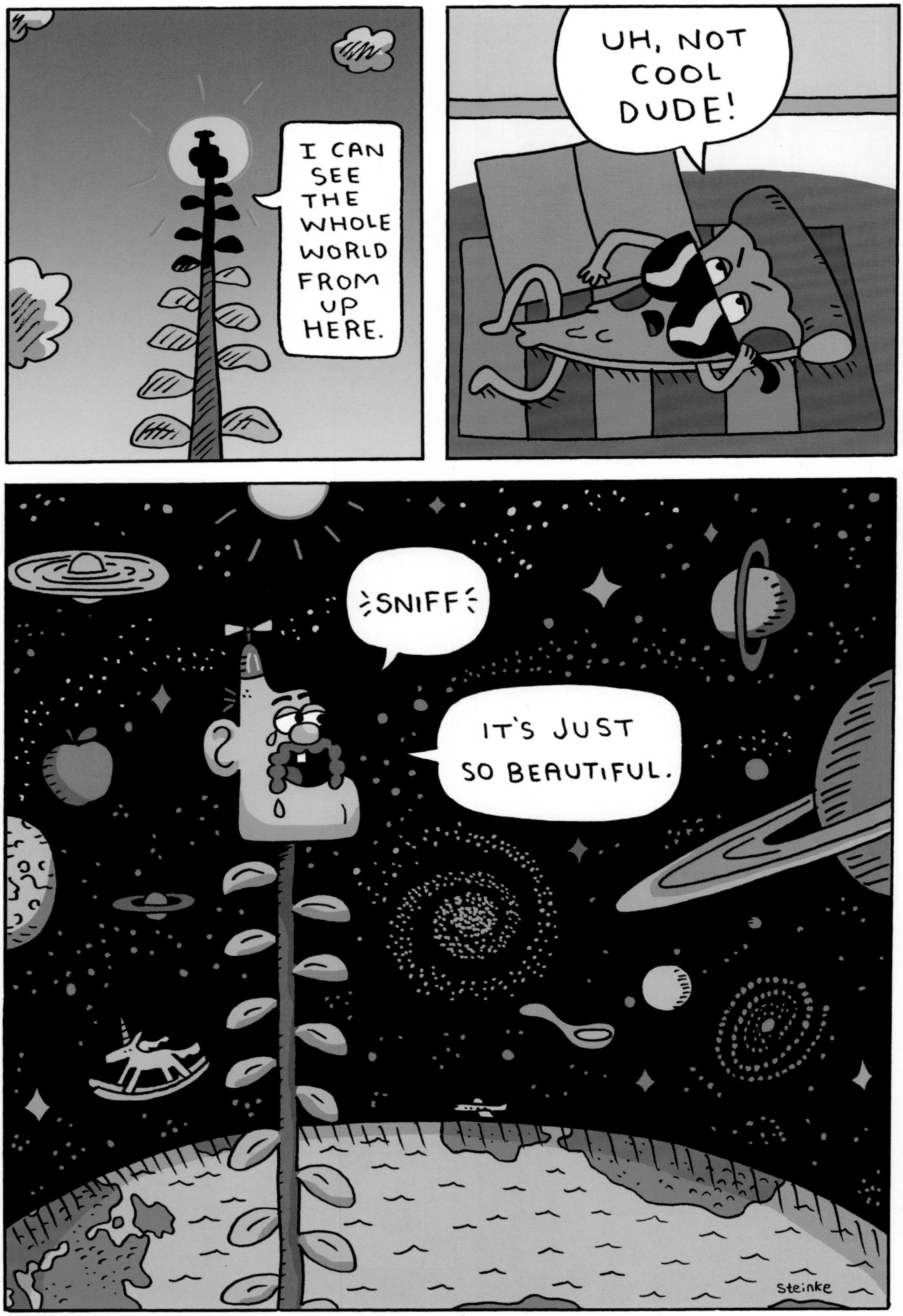
I CAN SEE THE WHOLE WORLD FROM UP HERE.
UH, NOT COOL DUDE!
SNIFF
IT'S JUST SO BEAUTIFUL.
steinke

END

Ballroom Dancing Search-and-Find
by Nichol Ashworth

5 Uncle Grandpas	6 Roses	2 Ice-skating Rinks
2 Tutus	1 Dimensional Rift	2 Christmas Trees
3 Pairs of Dancers	1 Theft in-progress	1 Cake
7 Gifts	2 Top Hats	1 Unicorn

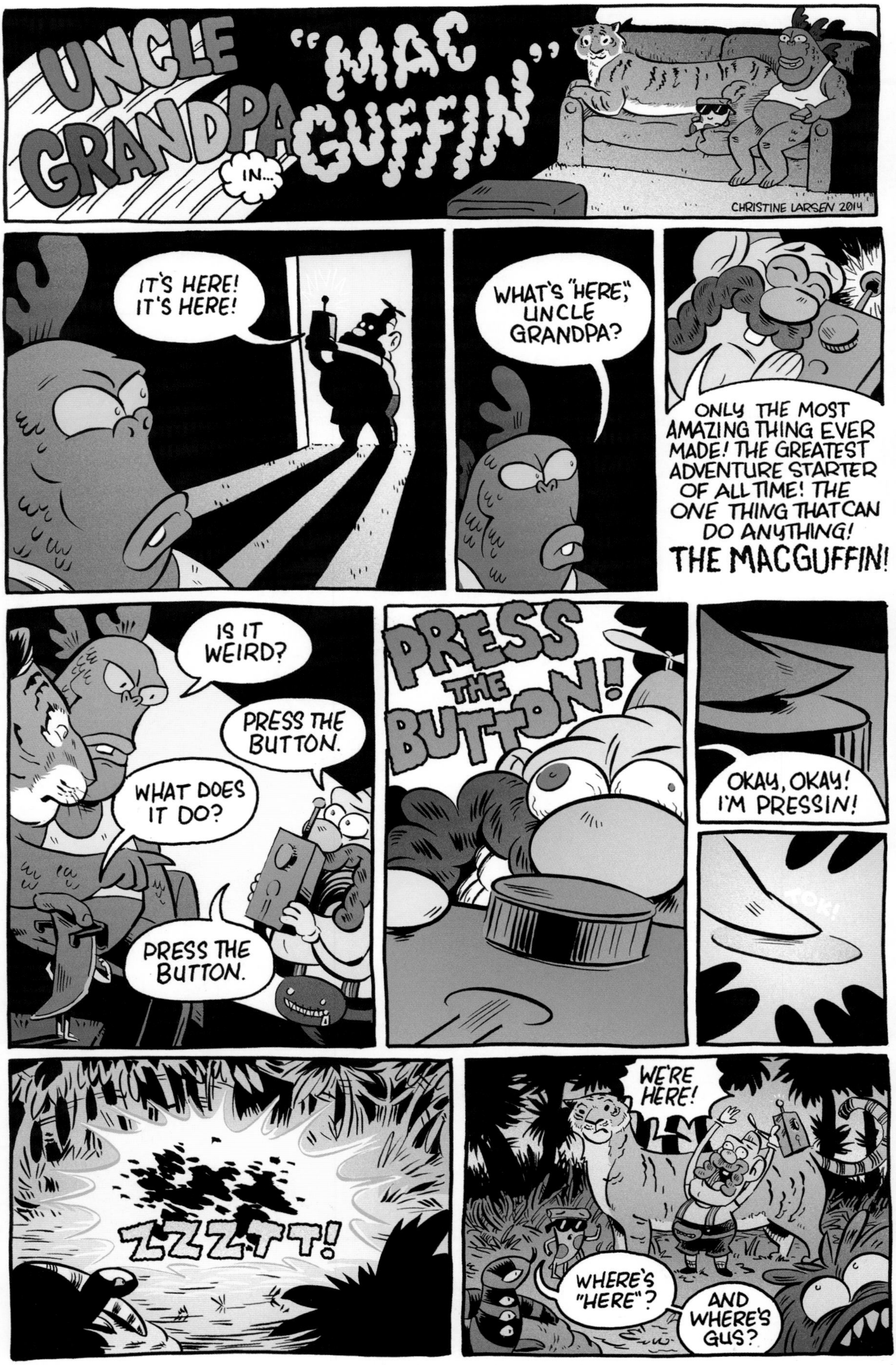
UNCLE GRANDPA IN... "MAC GUFFIN"
CHRISTINE LARSEN 2014
IT'S HERE! IT'S HERE!
WHAT'S "HERE," UNCLE GRANDPA?
ONLY THE MOST AMAZING THING EVER MADE! THE GREATEST ADVENTURE STARTER OF ALL TIME! THE ONE THING THAT CAN DO ANYTHING!
THE MACGUFFIN!
IS IT WEIRD?
PRESS THE BUTTON.
WHAT DOES IT DO?
PRESS THE BUTTON.
PRESS THE BUTTON!
OKAY, OKAY! I'M PRESSIN!
TOK!
ZZZTTT!
WE'RE HERE!
WHERE'S "HERE"?
AND WHERE'S GUS?

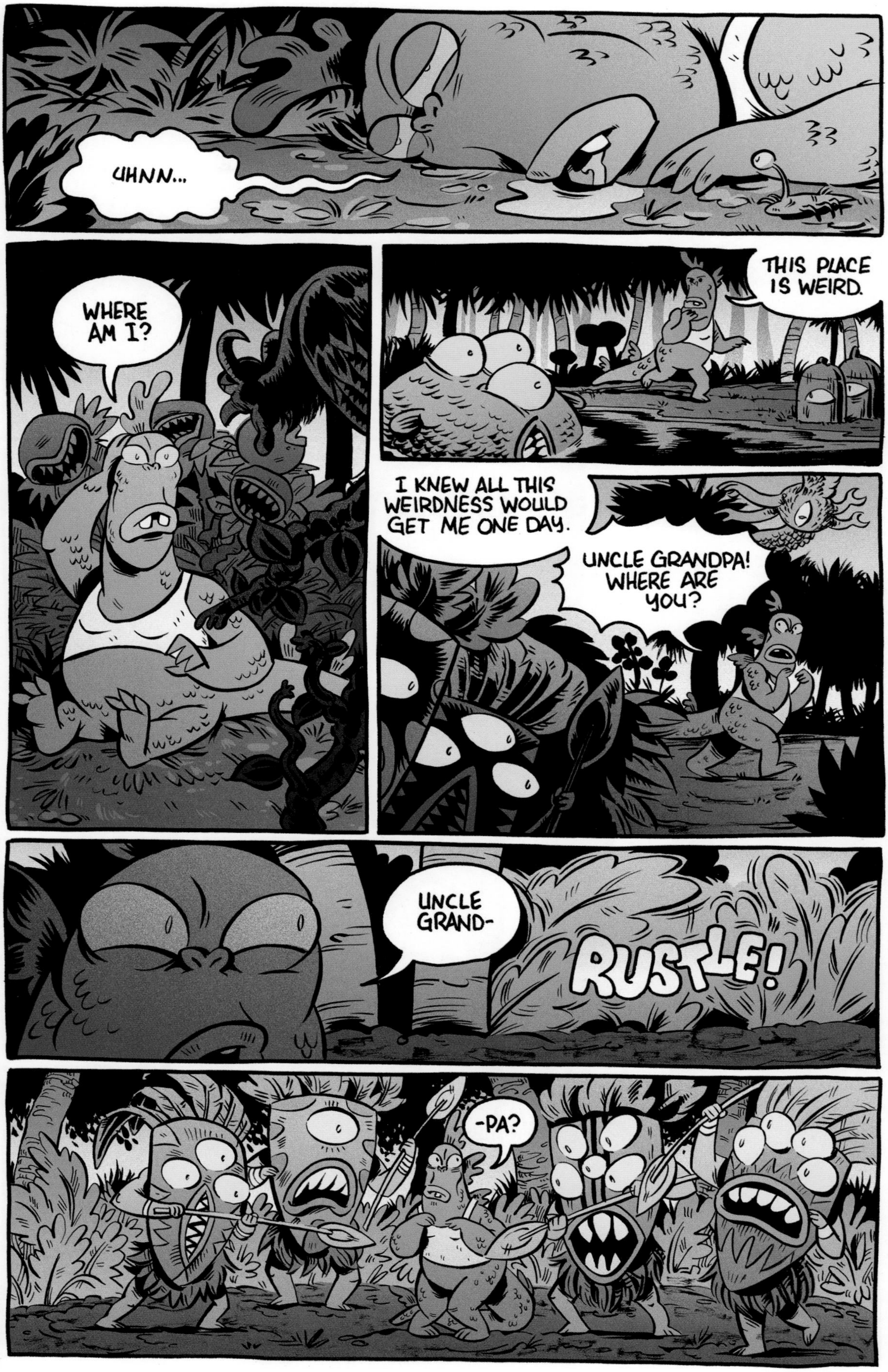
UHNN...
WHERE AM I?
THIS PLACE IS WEIRD.
I KNEW ALL THIS WEIRDNESS WOULD GET ME ONE DAY.
UNCLE GRANDPA! WHERE ARE YOU?
UNCLE GRAND-
RUSTLE!
-PA?

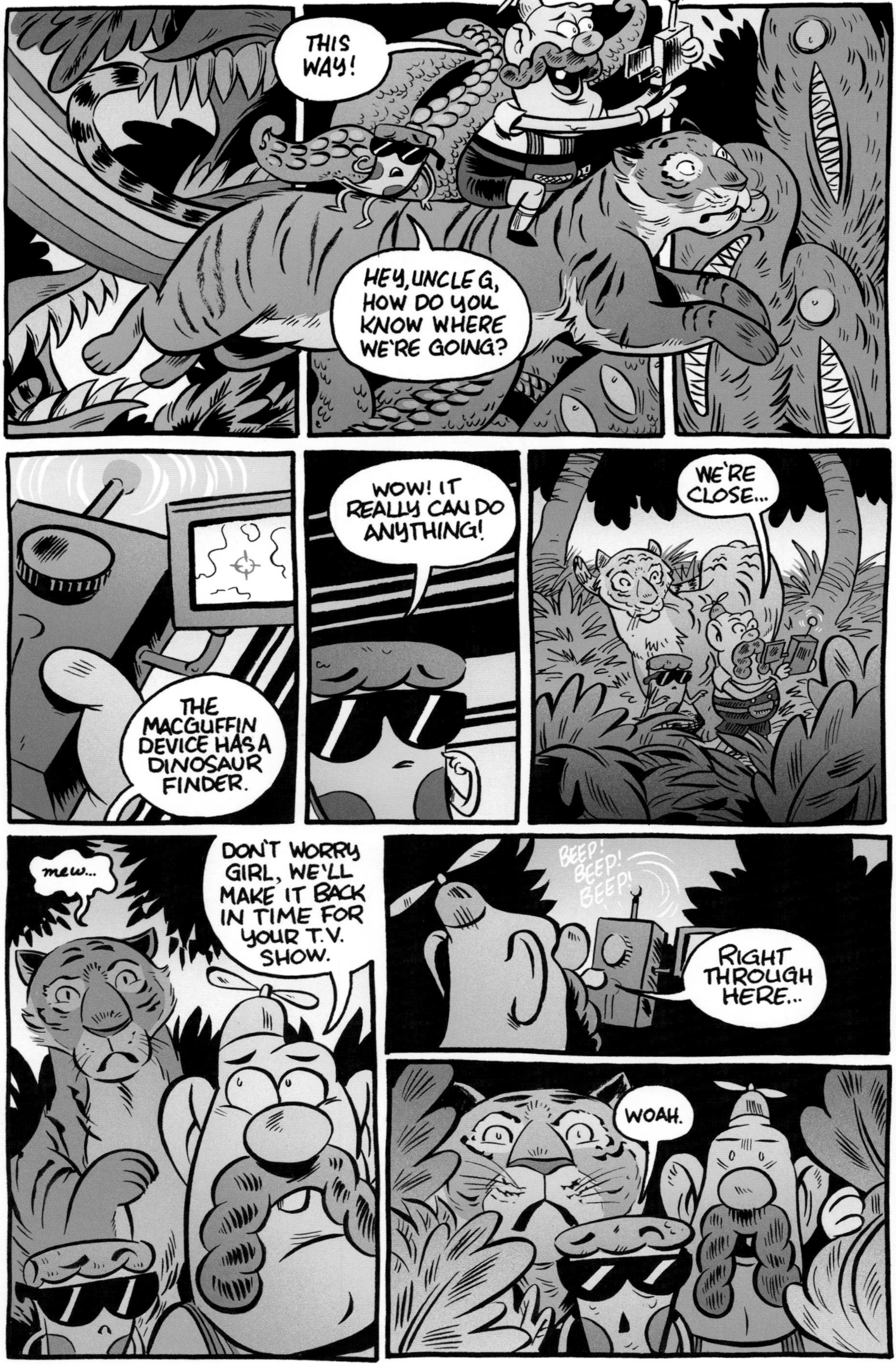
THIS WAY!
HEY, UNCLE G, HOW DO YOU KNOW WHERE WE'RE GOING?
THE MACGUFFIN DEVICE HAS A DINOSAUR FINDER.
WOW! IT REALLY CAN DO ANYTHING!
WE'RE CLOSE...
mew...
DON'T WORRY GIRL, WE'LL MAKE IT BACK IN TIME FOR YOUR T.V. SHOW.
BEEP! BEEP! BEEP!
RIGHT THROUGH HERE...
WOAH.

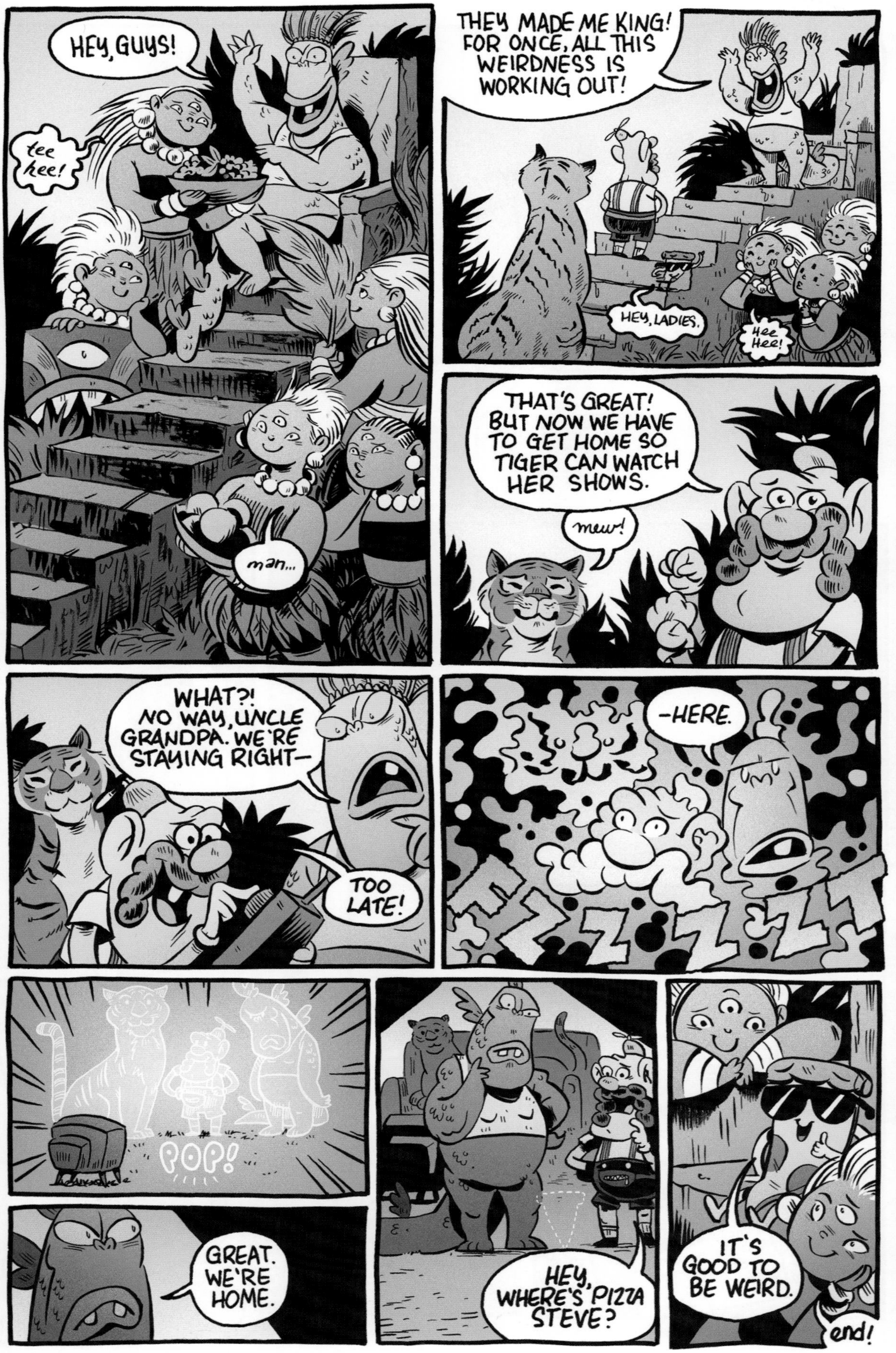
HEY, GUYS!
tee hee!
man...
THEY MADE ME KING! FOR ONCE, ALL THIS WEIRDNESS IS WORKING OUT!
HEY, LADIES.
Hee Hee!
THAT'S GREAT! BUT NOW WE HAVE TO GET HOME SO TIGER CAN WATCH HER SHOWS.
mew!
WHAT?! NO WAY, UNCLE GRANDPA. WE'RE STAYING RIGHT—
TOO LATE!
-HERE.
FZZZZT
POP!
GREAT. WE'RE HOME.
HEY, WHERE'S PIZZA STEVE?
IT'S GOOD TO BE WEIRD.
end!

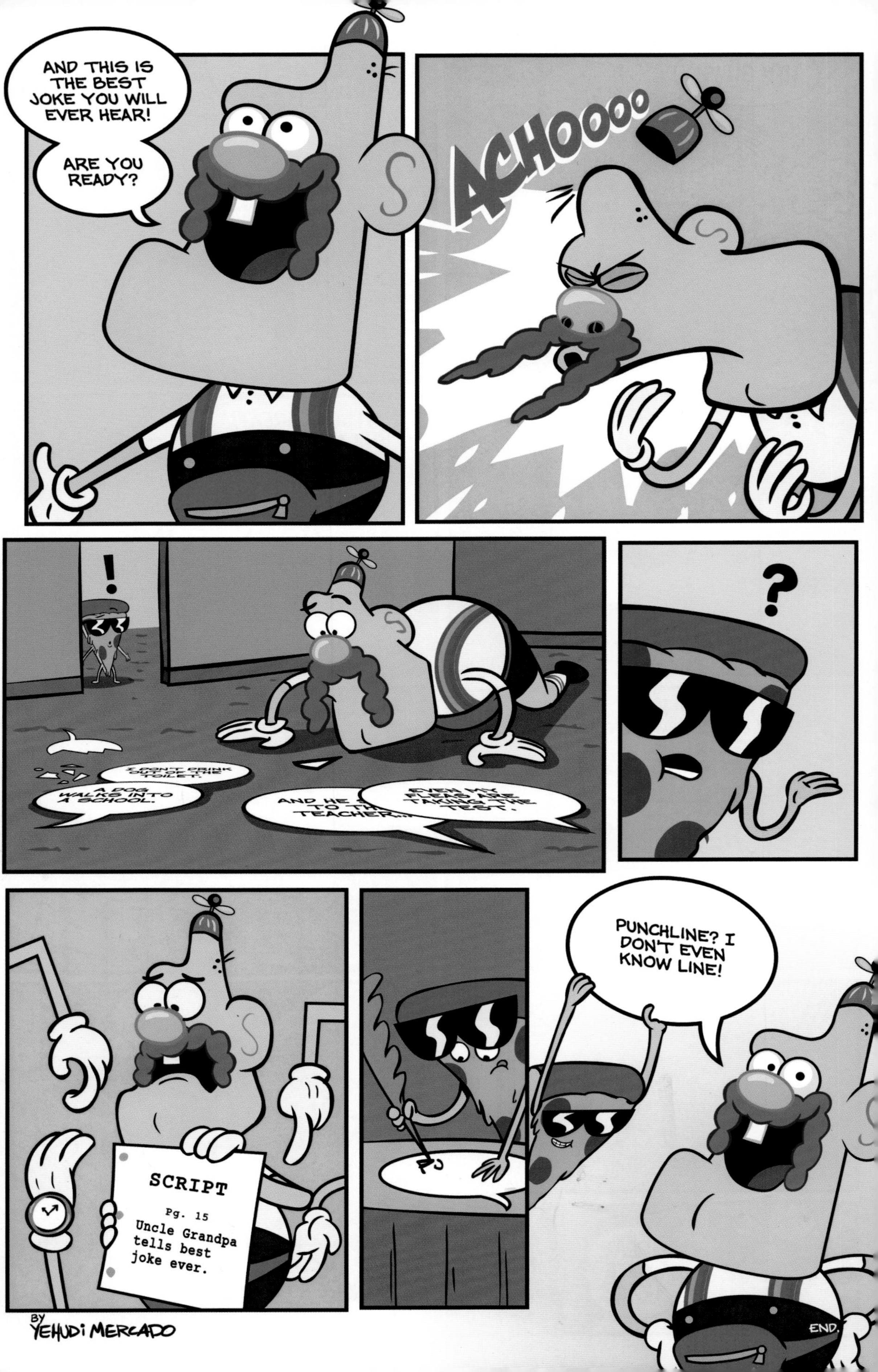

AND THIS IS THE BEST JOKE YOU WILL EVER HEAR!
ARE YOU READY?
ACHOOOO
!
I DON'T DRINK OUT OF THE TOILET.
A DOG WALKS INTO A SCHOOL.
AND HE S TO TH TEACHER...
EVEN MY FLEAS ARE TAKING THE TEST.
?
SCRIPT
Pg. 15
Uncle Grandpa tells best joke ever.
PUNCHLINE? I DON'T EVEN KNOW LINE!
END.
BY YEHUDI MERCADO

LEMON MOO

EVGENY YAKOVLEV

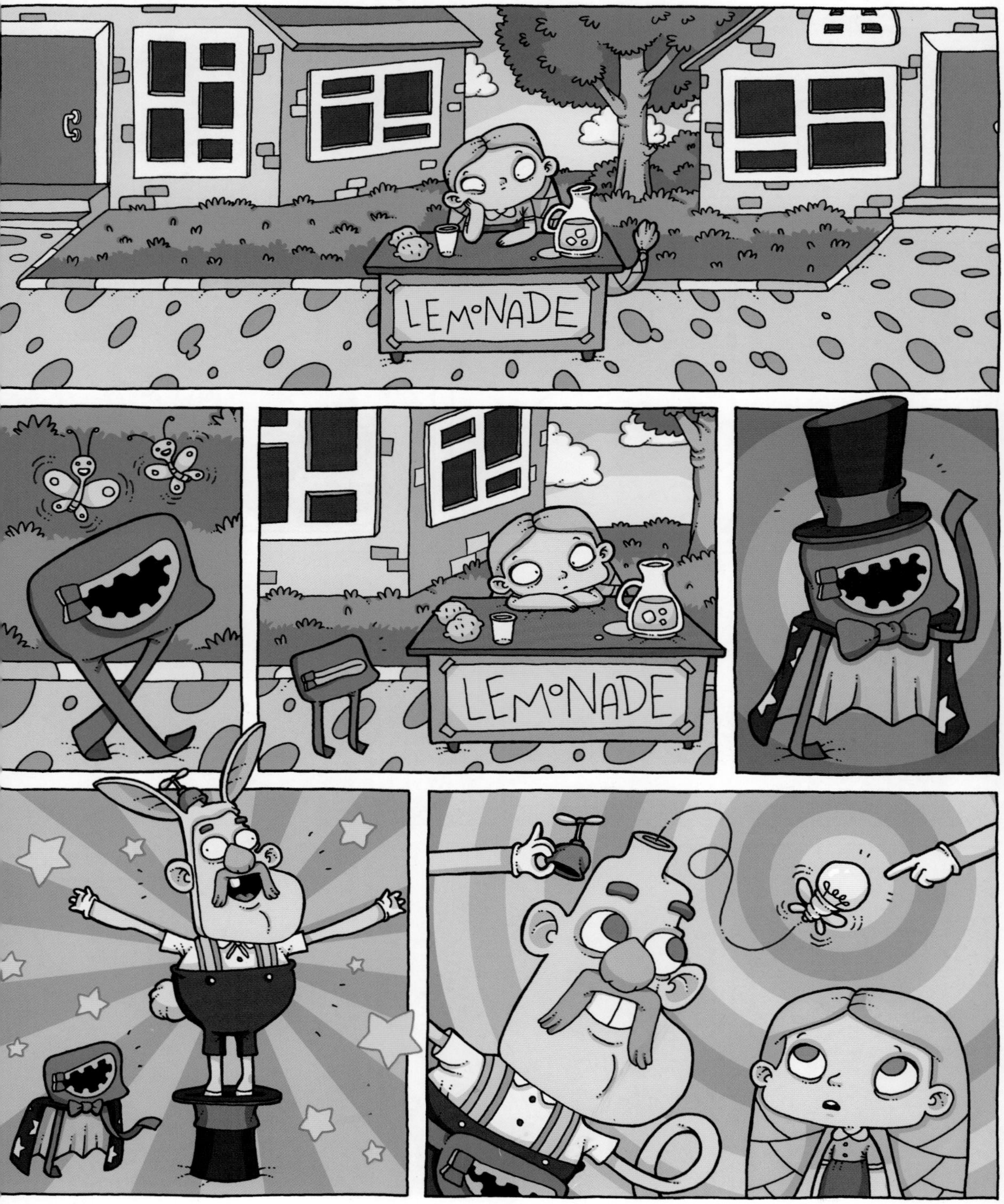
LEMONADE
LEMONADE

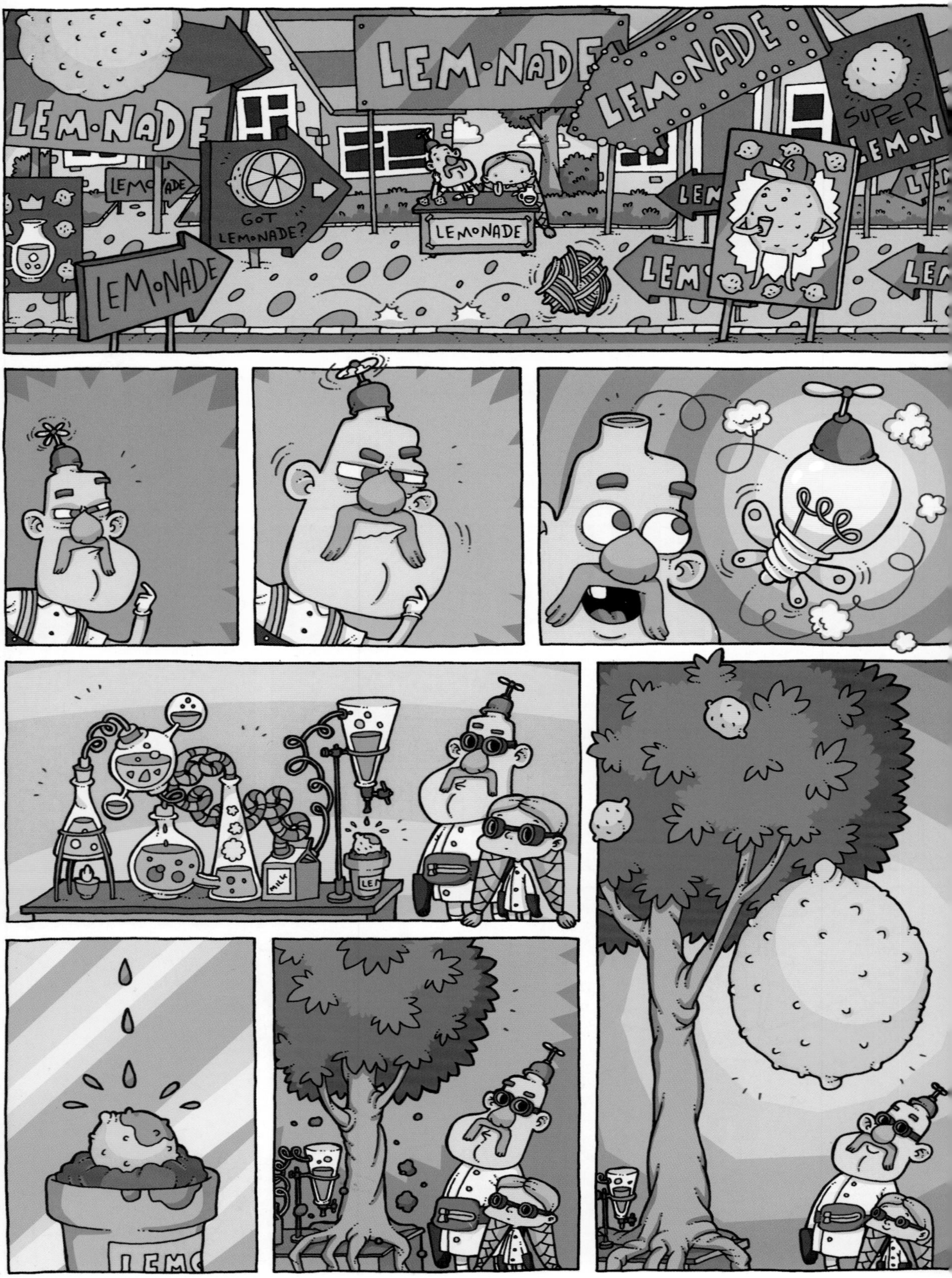
LEM•NADE
LEM•NADE
LEM•NADE
LEMONADE
GOT LEMONADE?
LEMONADE
SUPER LEMON
LEMONADE
MILK

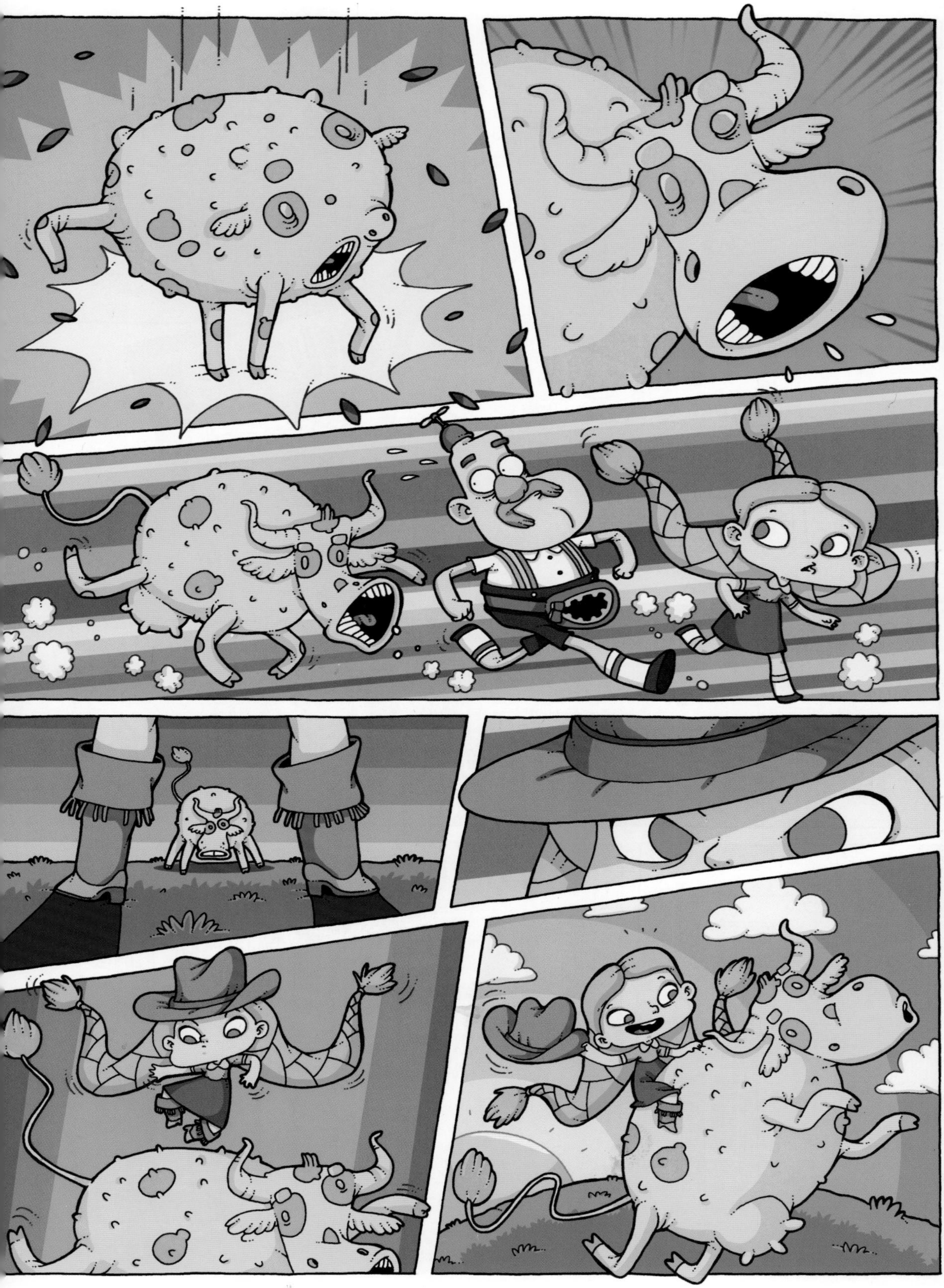

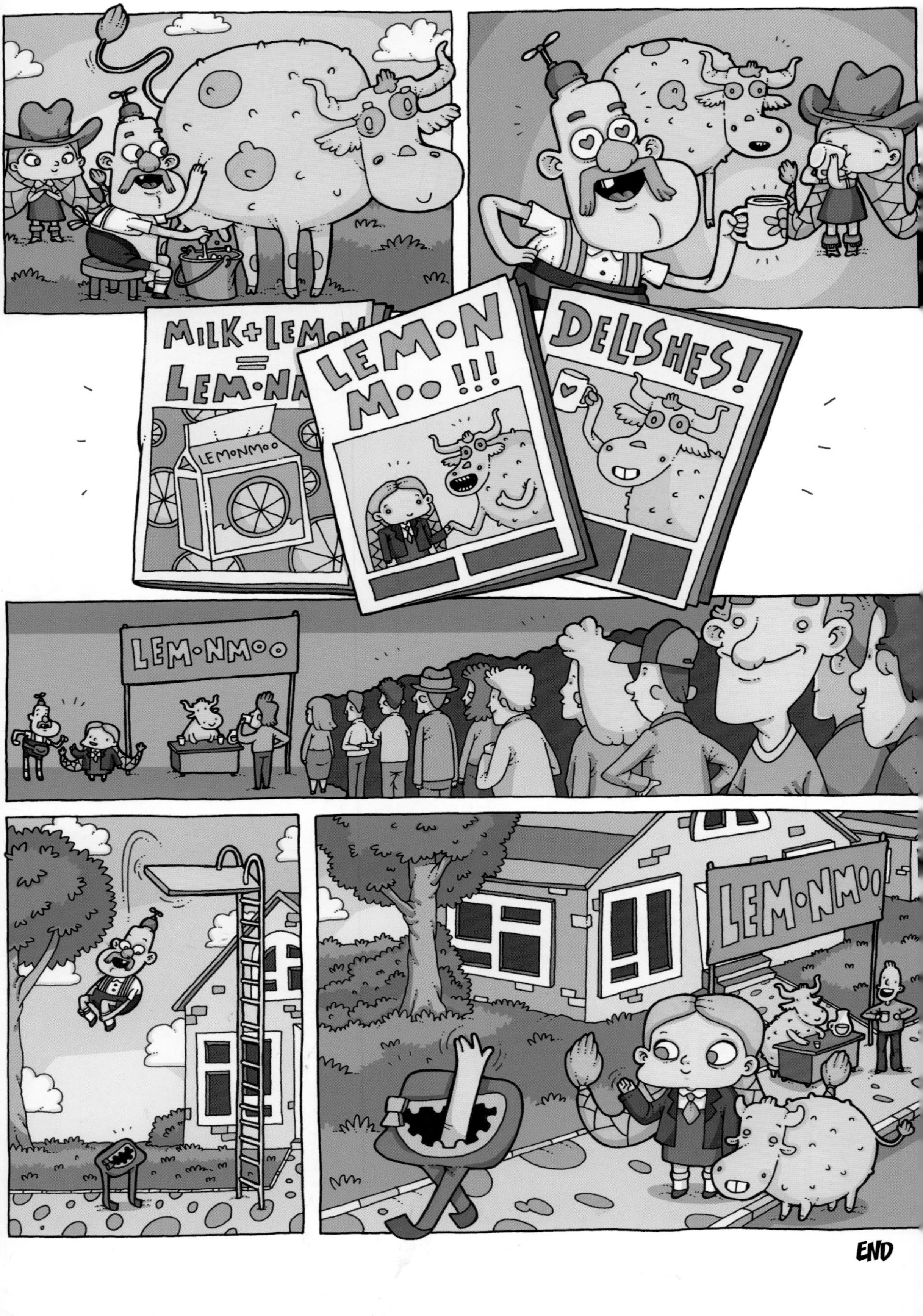

MILK+LEM•N
=
LEM•N
LEMONMOO
LEM•N
M•• !!!
DELISHES!
LEM•NM••
LEM•NM••
END

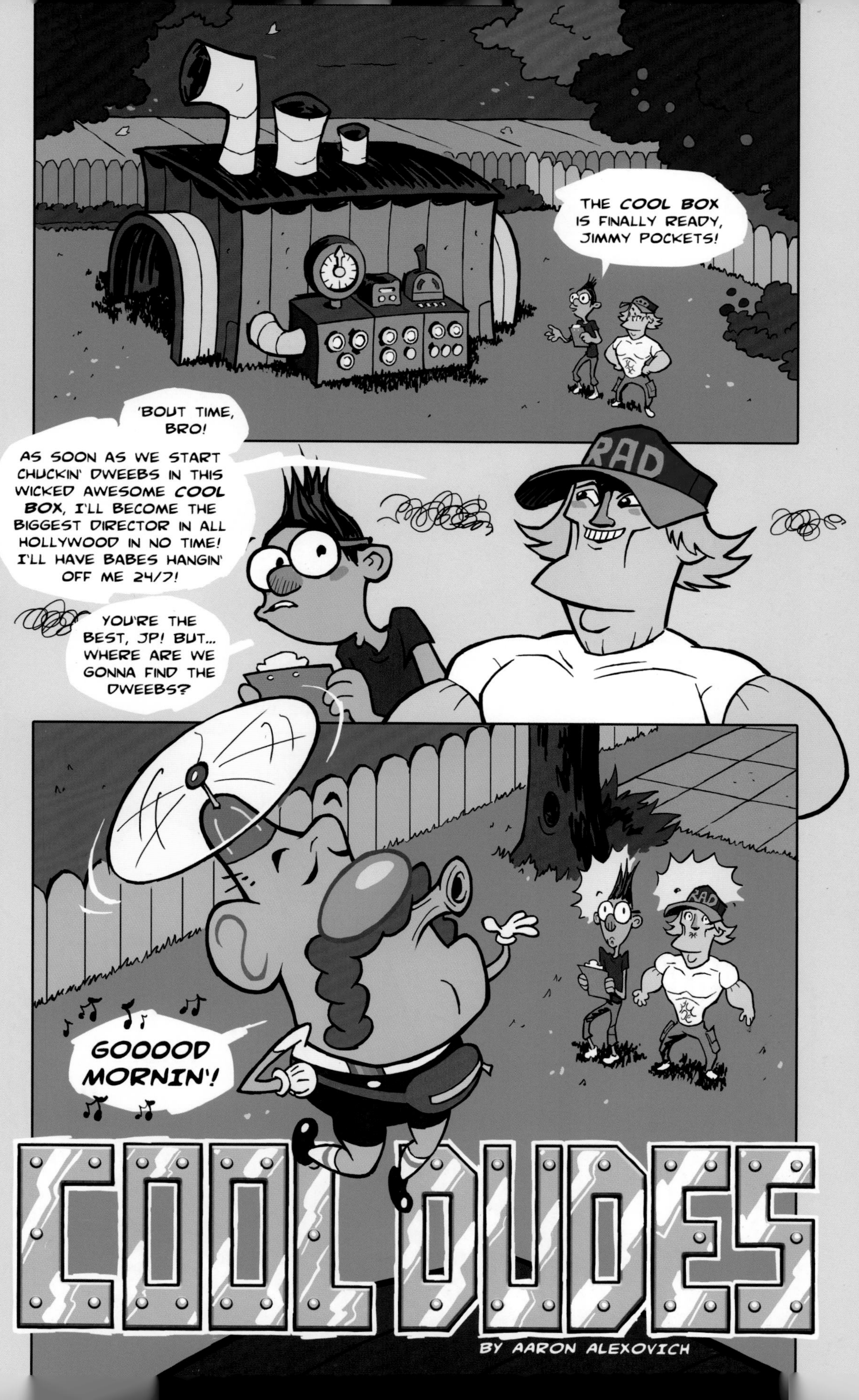
THE COOL BOX IS FINALLY READY, JIMMY POCKETS!
'BOUT TIME, BRO!
AS SOON AS WE START CHUCKIN' DWEEBS IN THIS WICKED AWESOME COOL BOX, I'LL BECOME THE BIGGEST DIRECTOR IN ALL HOLLYWOOD IN NO TIME! I'LL HAVE BABES HANGIN' OFF ME 24/7!
RAD
YOU'RE THE BEST, JP! BUT... WHERE ARE WE GONNA FIND THE DWEEBS?
RAD
GOOOOD MORNIN'!
COOL DUDES
BY AARON ALEXOVICH

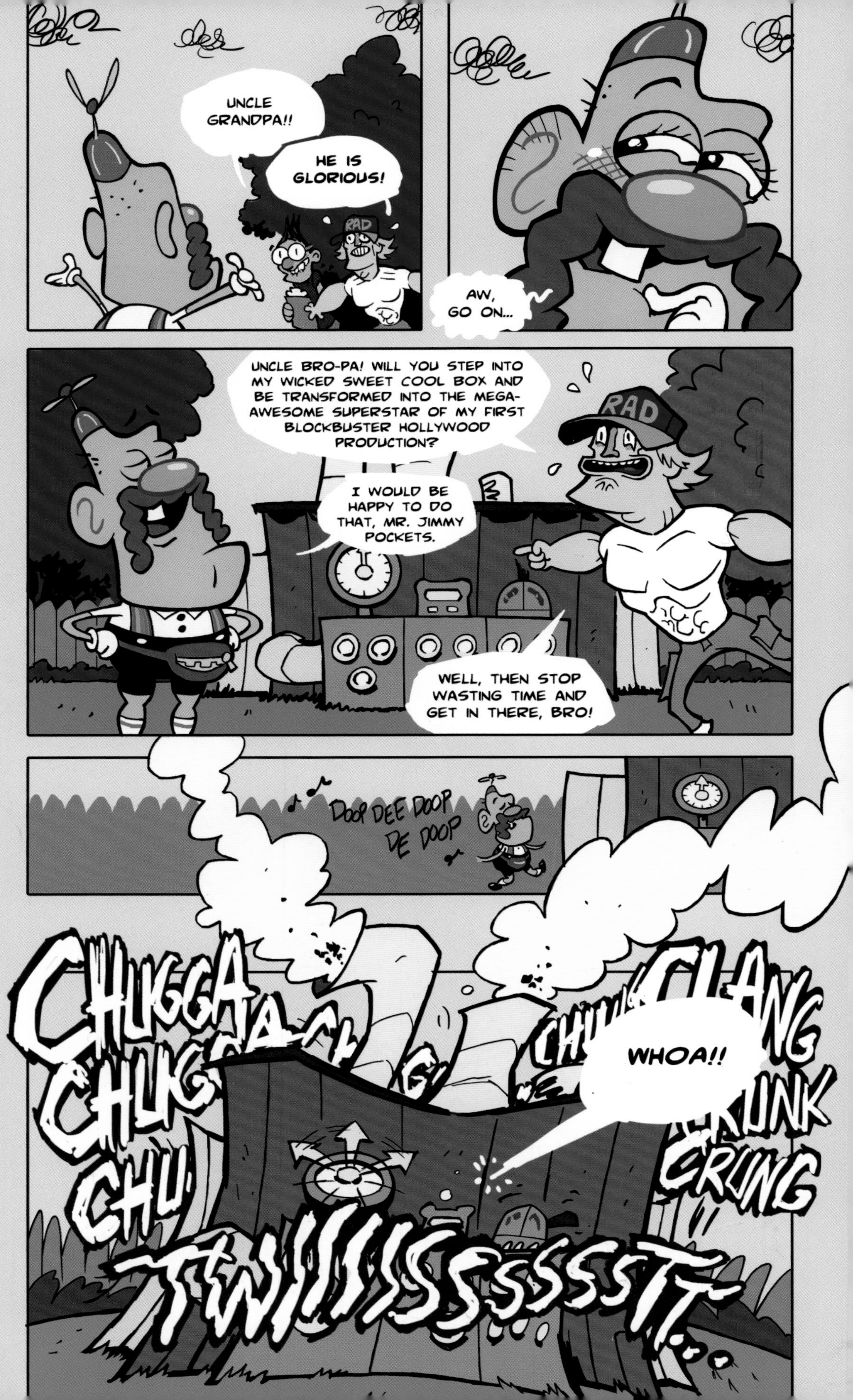
UNCLE GRANDPA!!
HE IS GLORIOUS!
AW, GO ON...
UNCLE BRO-PA! WILL YOU STEP INTO MY WICKED SWEET COOL BOX AND BE TRANSFORMED INTO THE MEGA-AWESOME SUPERSTAR OF MY FIRST BLOCKBUSTER HOLLYWOOD PRODUCTION?
RAD
I WOULD BE HAPPY TO DO THAT, MR. JIMMY POCKETS.
WELL, THEN STOP WASTING TIME AND GET IN THERE, BRO!
DOOP DEE DOOP DE DOOP
CHUGGA
CLANG
WHOA!!
KRUNK
CRUNG
TWIIIISSSSSST...

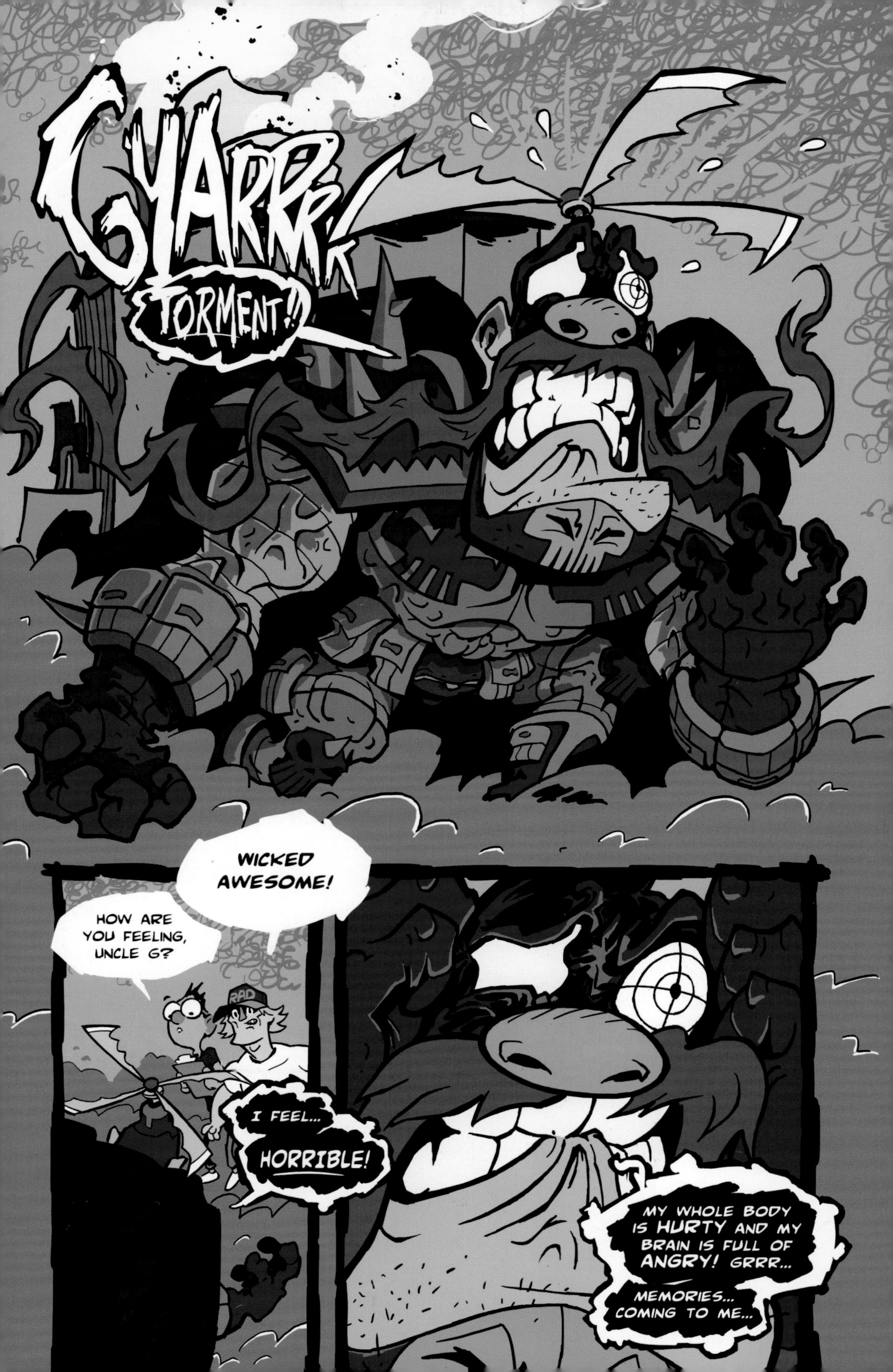
GYARRRK
TORMENT!!
WICKED AWESOME!
HOW ARE YOU FEELING, UNCLE G?
RAD
I FEEL... HORRIBLE!
MY WHOLE BODY IS HURTY AND MY BRAIN IS FULL OF ANGRY! GRRR...
MEMORIES... COMING TO ME...

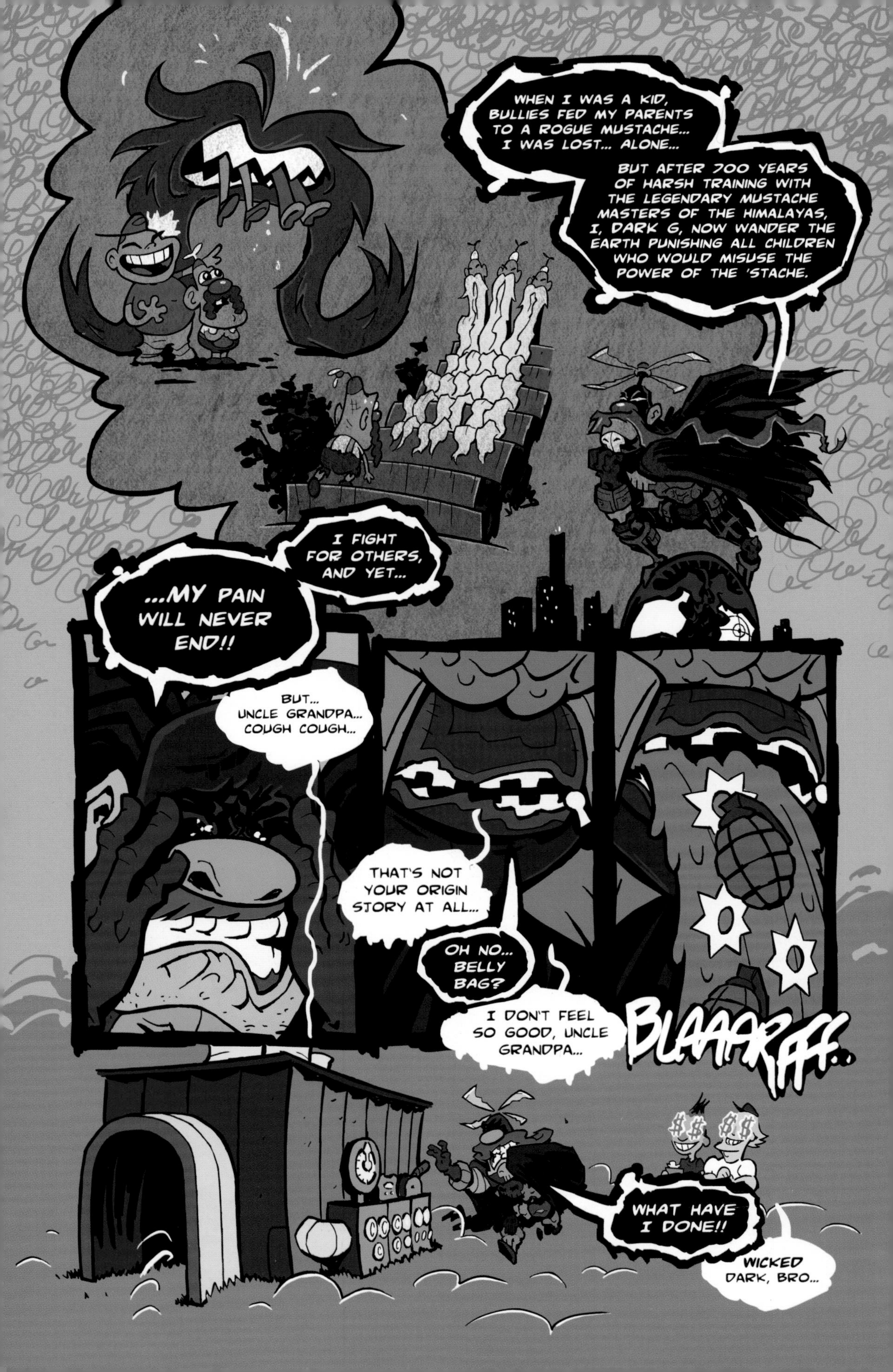
WHEN I WAS A KID, BULLIES FED MY PARENTS TO A ROGUE MUSTACHE... I WAS LOST... ALONE...
BUT AFTER 700 YEARS OF HARSH TRAINING WITH THE LEGENDARY MUSTACHE MASTERS OF THE HIMALAYAS, I, DARK G, NOW WANDER THE EARTH PUNISHING ALL CHILDREN WHO WOULD MISUSE THE POWER OF THE 'STACHE.
I FIGHT FOR OTHERS, AND YET...
...MY PAIN WILL NEVER END!!
BUT... UNCLE GRANDPA... COUGH COUGH...
THAT'S NOT YOUR ORIGIN STORY AT ALL...
OH NO... BELLY BAG?
I DON'T FEEL SO GOOD, UNCLE GRANDPA...
BLAAARFF...
WHAT HAVE I DONE!!
WICKED DARK, BRO...

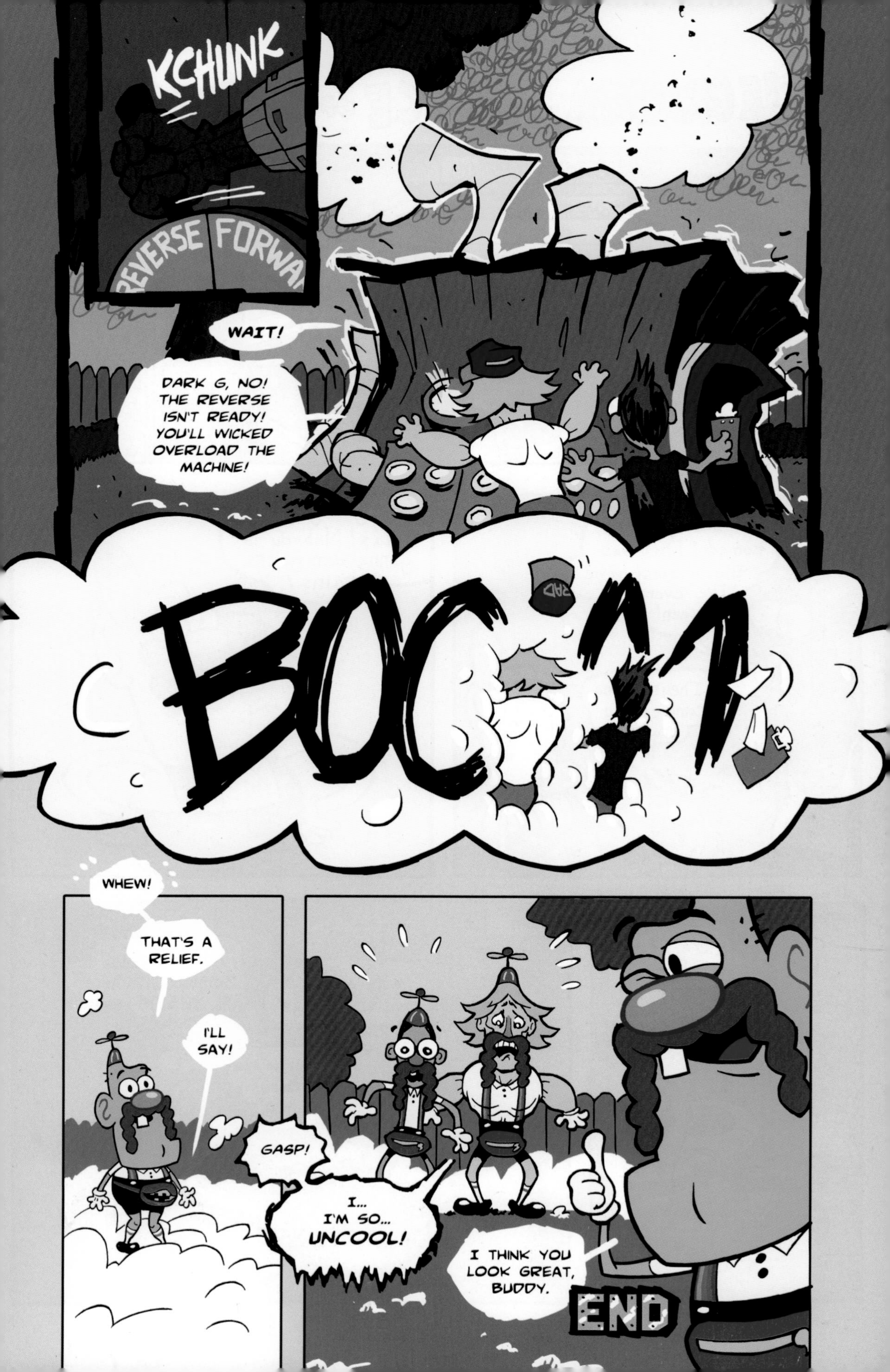
KCHUNK
REVERSE FORWA
WAIT!
DARK G, NO! THE REVERSE ISN'T READY! YOU'LL WICKED OVERLOAD THE MACHINE!
BOOM
WHEW!
THAT'S A RELIEF.
I'LL SAY!
GASP!
I... I'M SO... UNCOOL!
I THINK YOU LOOK GREAT, BUDDY.
END

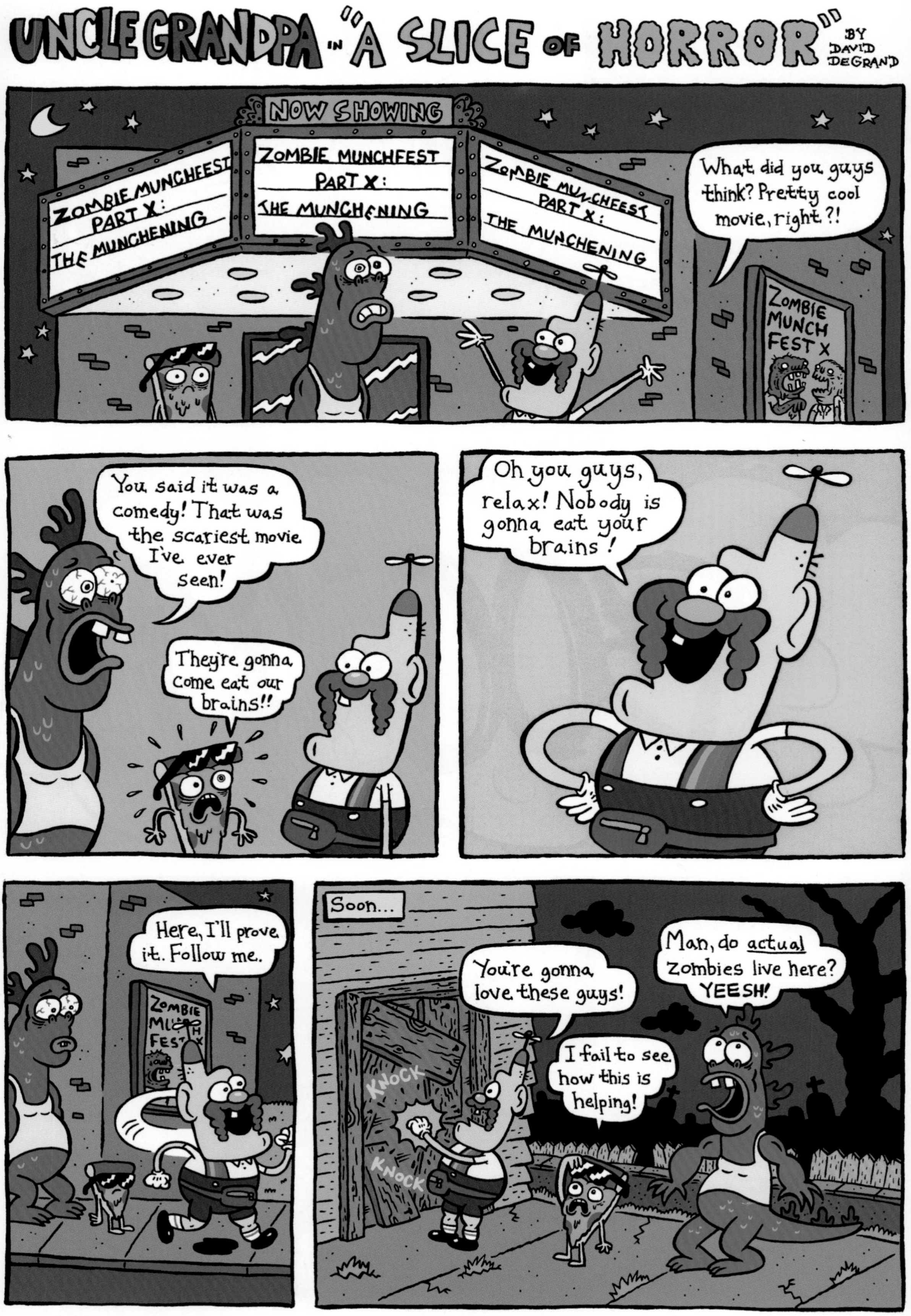
UNCLE GRANDPA in "A SLICE of HORROR" BY DAVID DEGRAND
NOW SHOWING
ZOMBIE MUNCHFEST PART X: THE MUNCHENING
ZOMBIE MUNCHFEST PART X: THE MUNCHENING
ZOMBIE MUNCHFEST PART X: THE MUNCHENING
What did you guys think? Pretty cool movie, right?!
ZOMBIE MUNCH FEST X
You said it was a comedy! That was the scariest movie I've ever seen!
They're gonna come eat our brains!!
Oh you guys, relax! Nobody is gonna eat your brains!
Here, I'll prove it. Follow me.
Soon...
You're gonna love these guys!
Man, do actual zombies live here? YEESH!
I fail to see how this is helping!
KNOCK
KNOCK

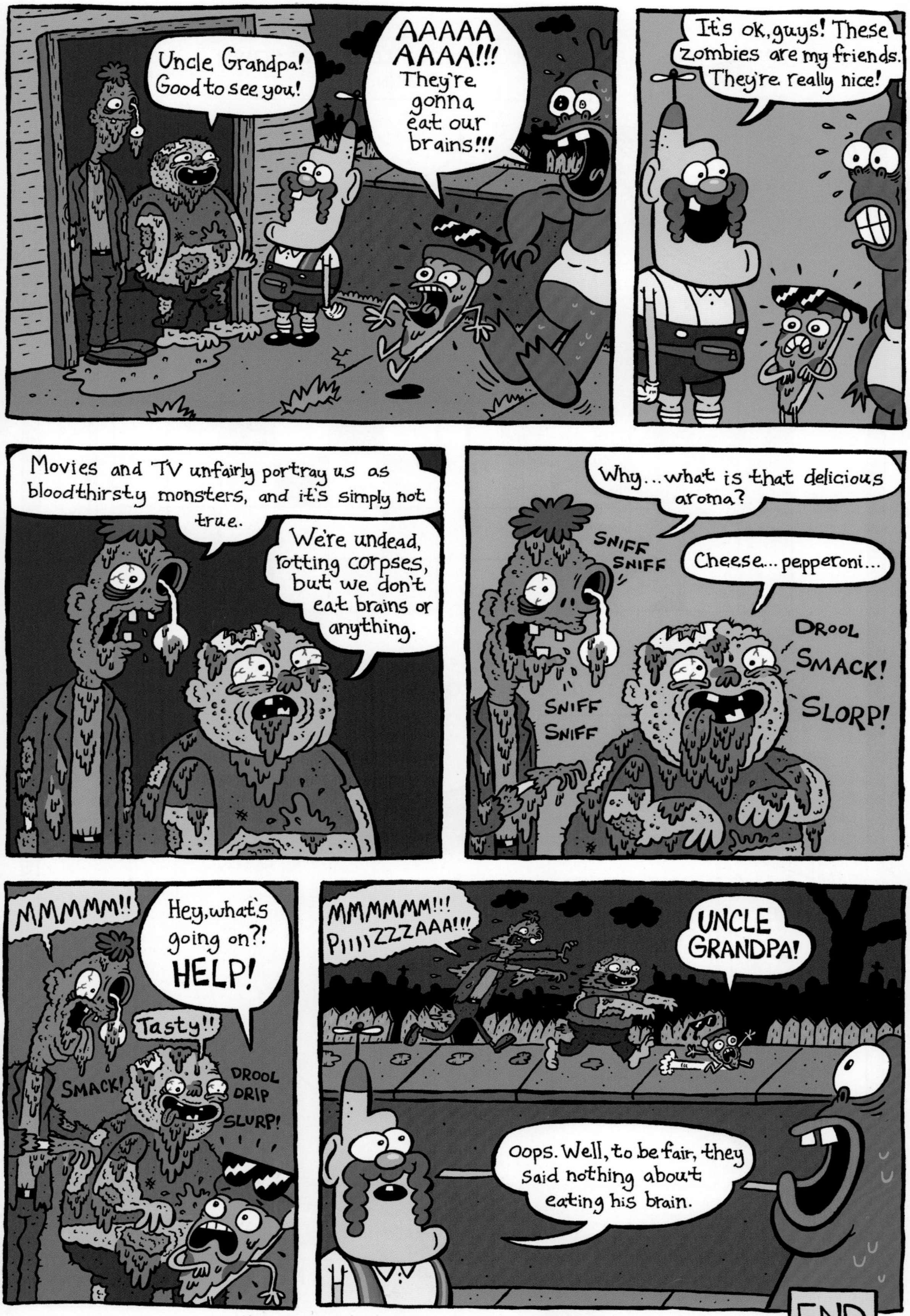
Uncle Grandpa! Good to see you!
AAAAA AAAA!!! They're gonna eat our brains!!!
It's ok, guys! These zombies are my friends. They're really nice!
Movies and TV unfairly portray us as bloodthirsty monsters, and it's simply not true.
We're undead, rotting corpses, but we don't eat brains or anything.
Why...what is that delicious aroma?
SNIFF SNIFF
Cheese... pepperoni...
DROOL
SMACK!
SLORP!
SNIFF SNIFF
MMMMM!!
Hey, what's going on?! HELP!
Tasty!!
DROOL
DRIP
SMACK!
SLURP!
MMMMMM!!! PIIIIZZZAAA!!!
UNCLE GRANDPA!
Oops. Well, to be fair, they said nothing about eating his brain.
END

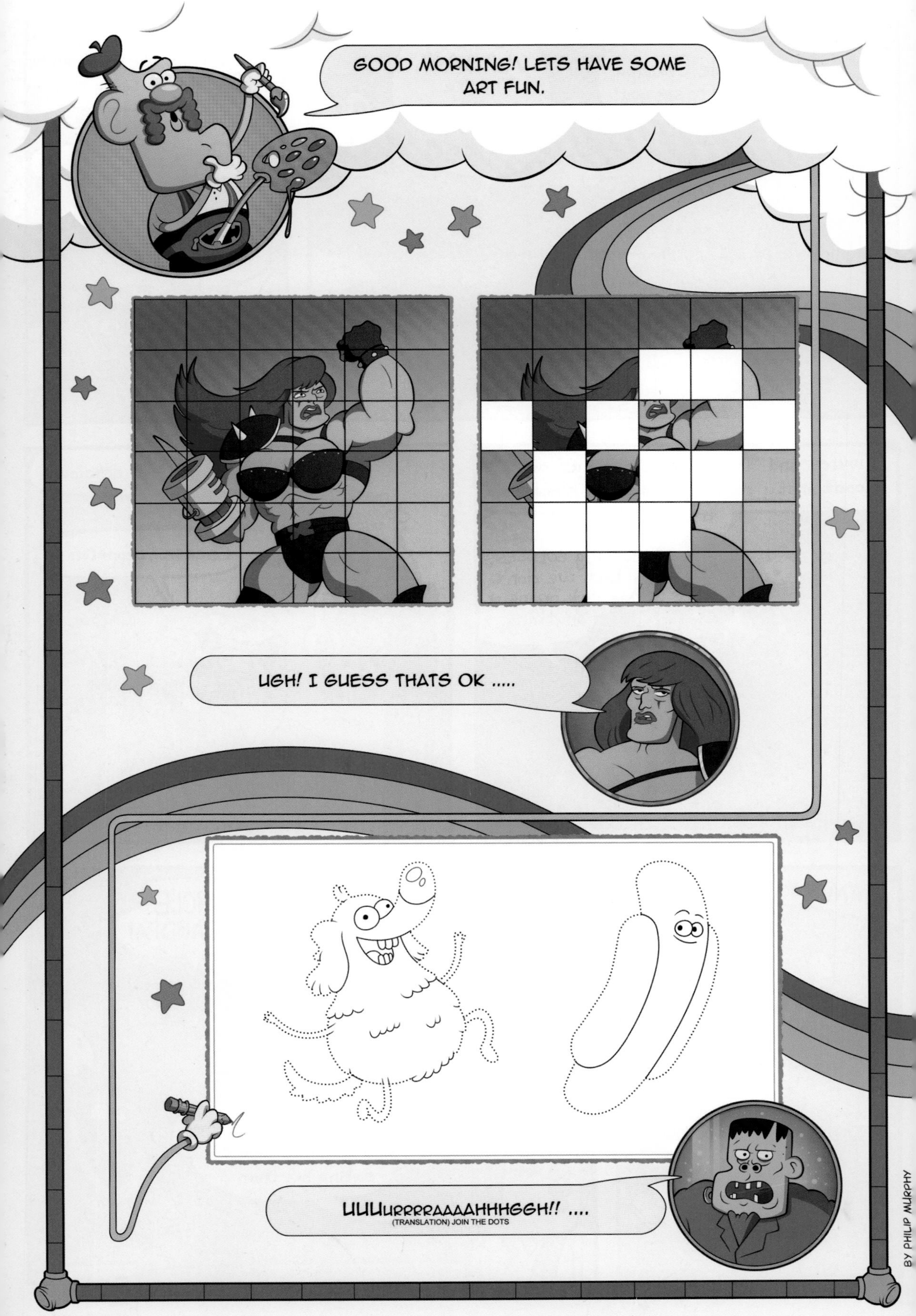
GOOD MORNING! LETS HAVE SOME ART FUN.
UGH! I GUESS THATS OK .....
UUUurrrraaaAHHHGGH!! ....
(TRANSLATION) JOIN THE DOTS
BY PHILIP MURPHY

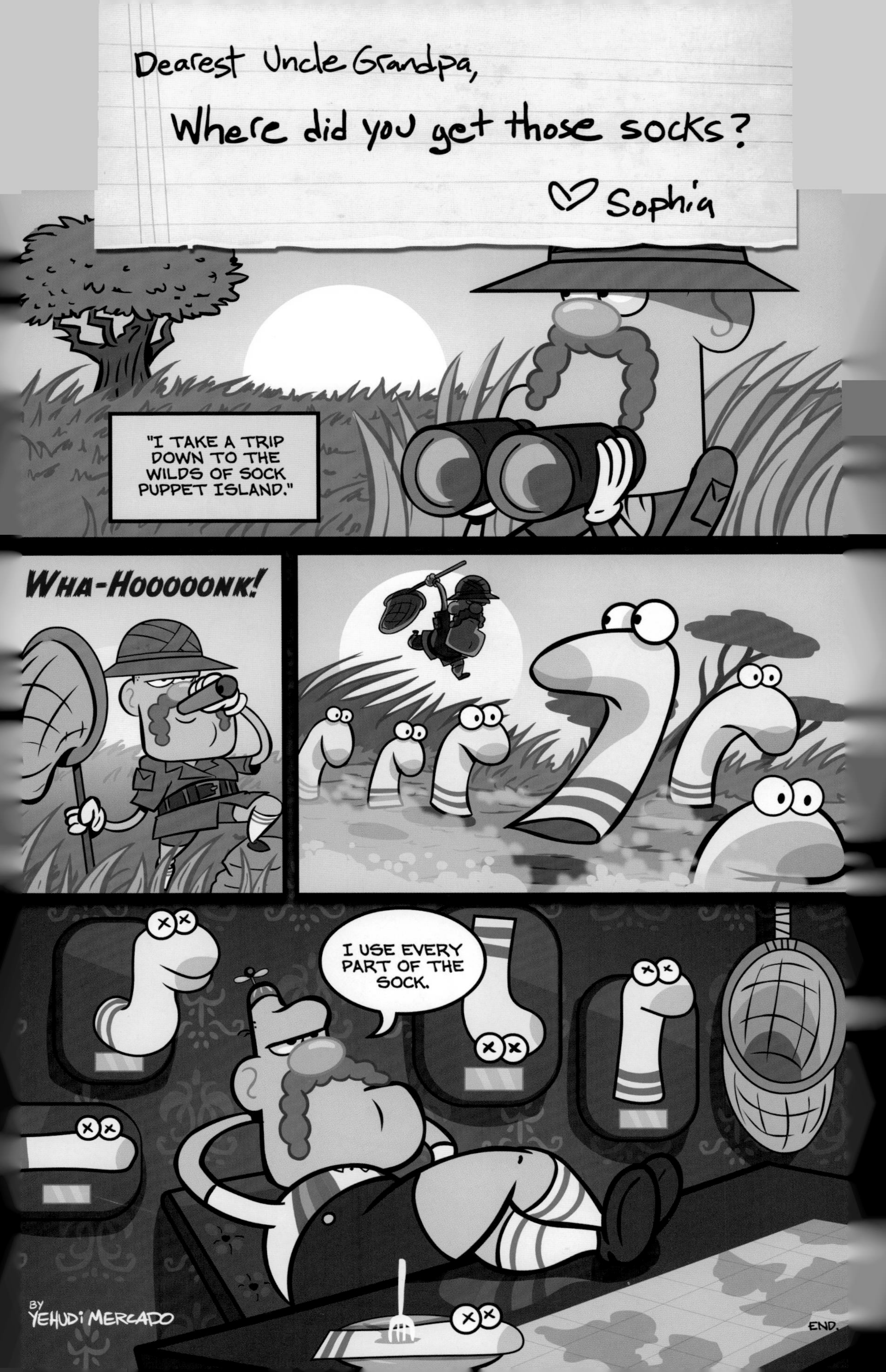
Dearest Uncle Grandpa,
Where did you get those socks?
Sophia
"I TAKE A TRIP DOWN TO THE WILDS OF SOCK PUPPET ISLAND."
WHA-HOOOOOONK!
I USE EVERY PART OF THE SOCK.
BY YEHUDI MERCADO
END.

ISSUE #4 VARIANT COVER
CHRISTINE LARSEN

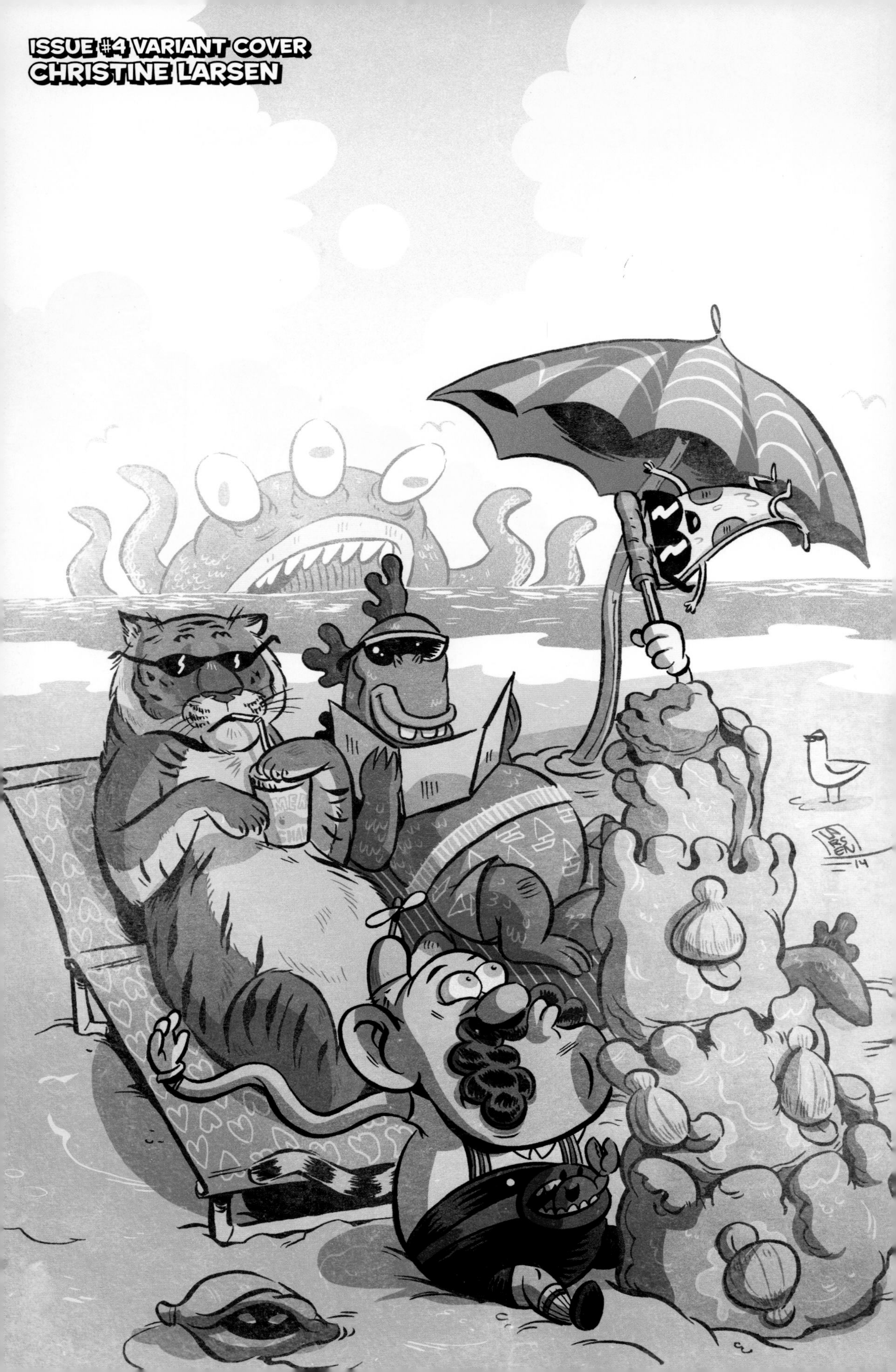
LARSEN '14

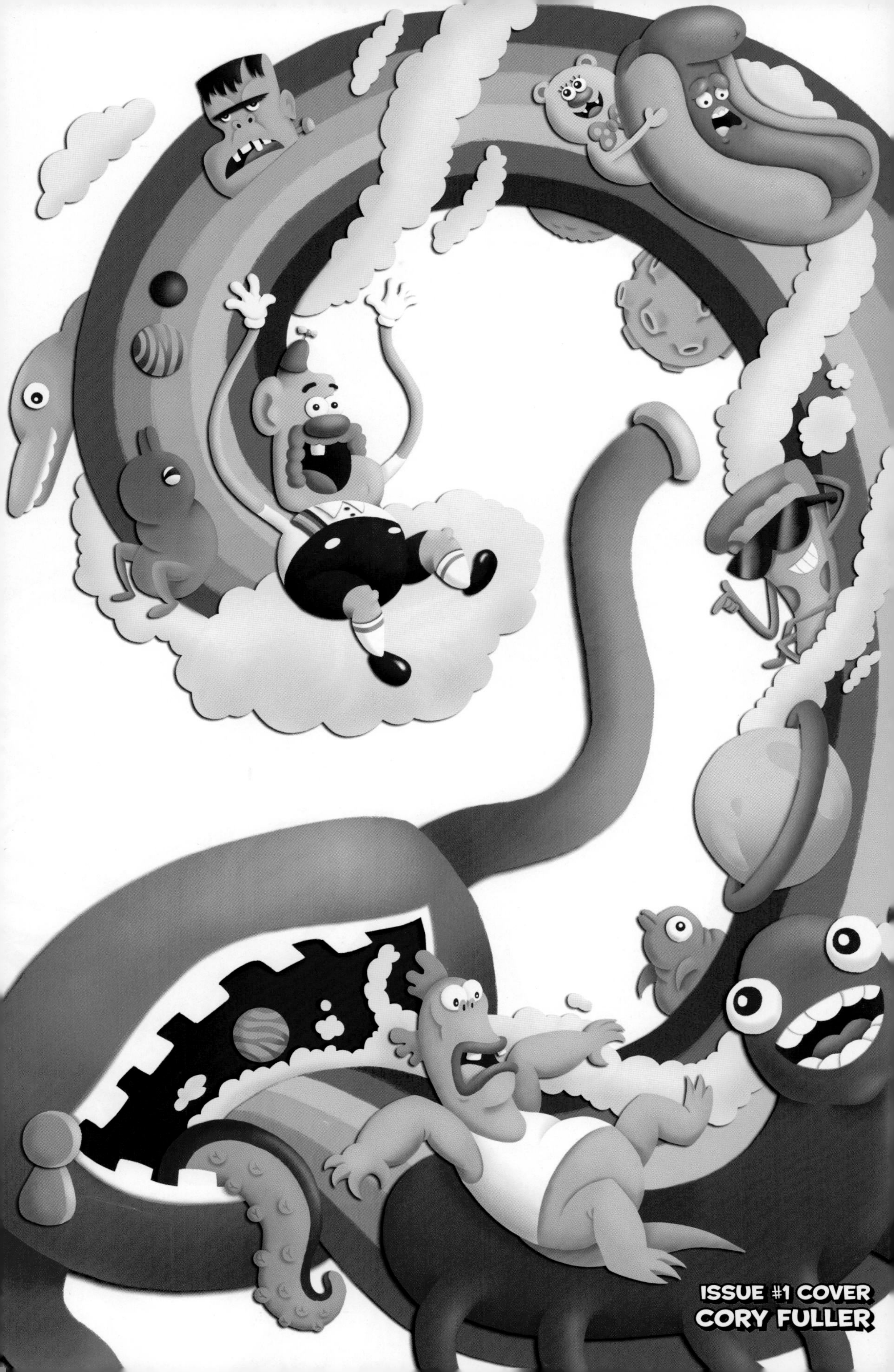

ISSUE #1 COVER
CORY FULLER

ISSUE #1 VARIANT COVER
TROY LITTLE

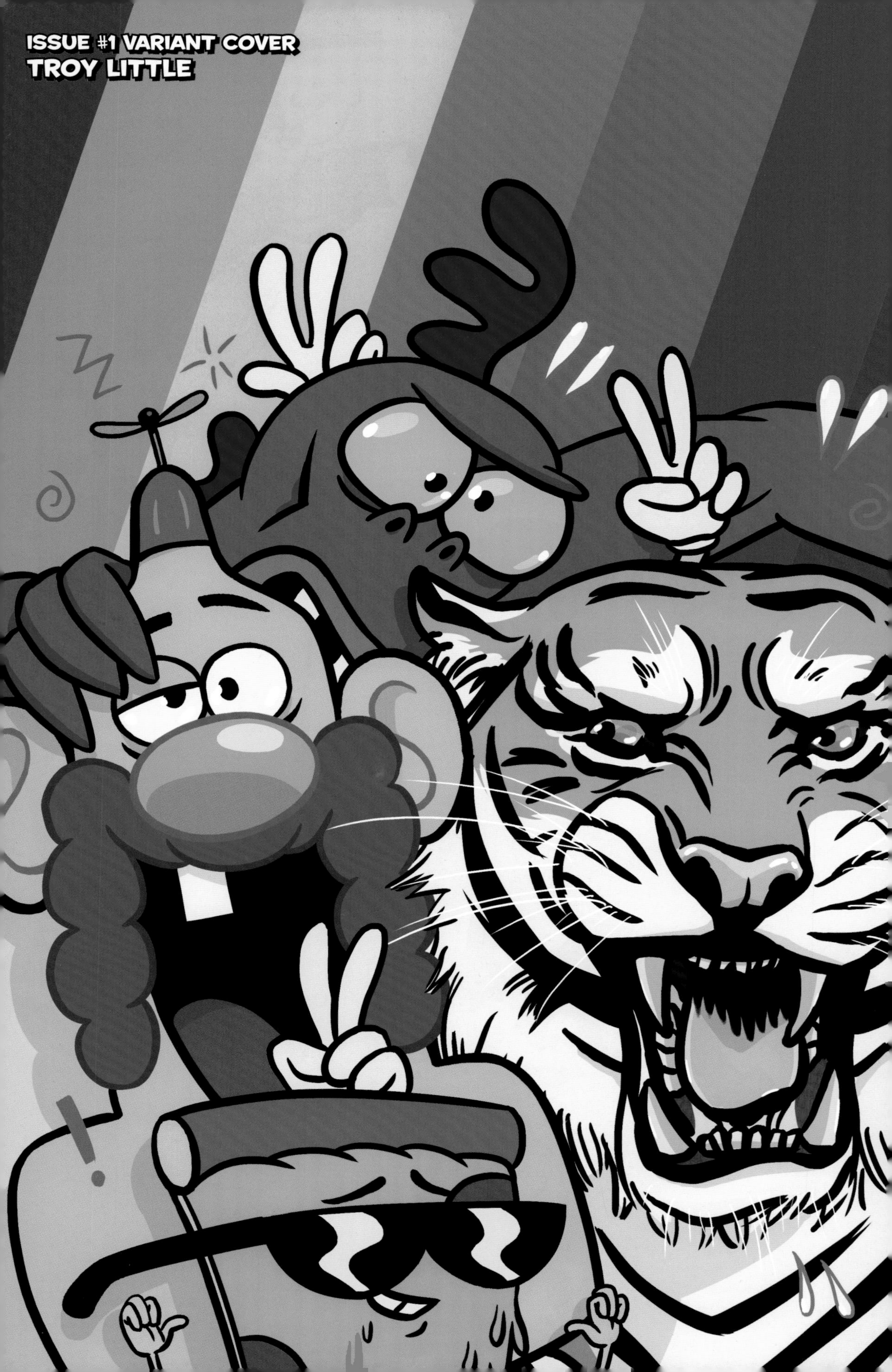

ISSUE #1 BOOM! STUDIOS EXCLUSIVE COVER
TRAVIS HILL
WITH COLORS BY WHITNEY COGAR

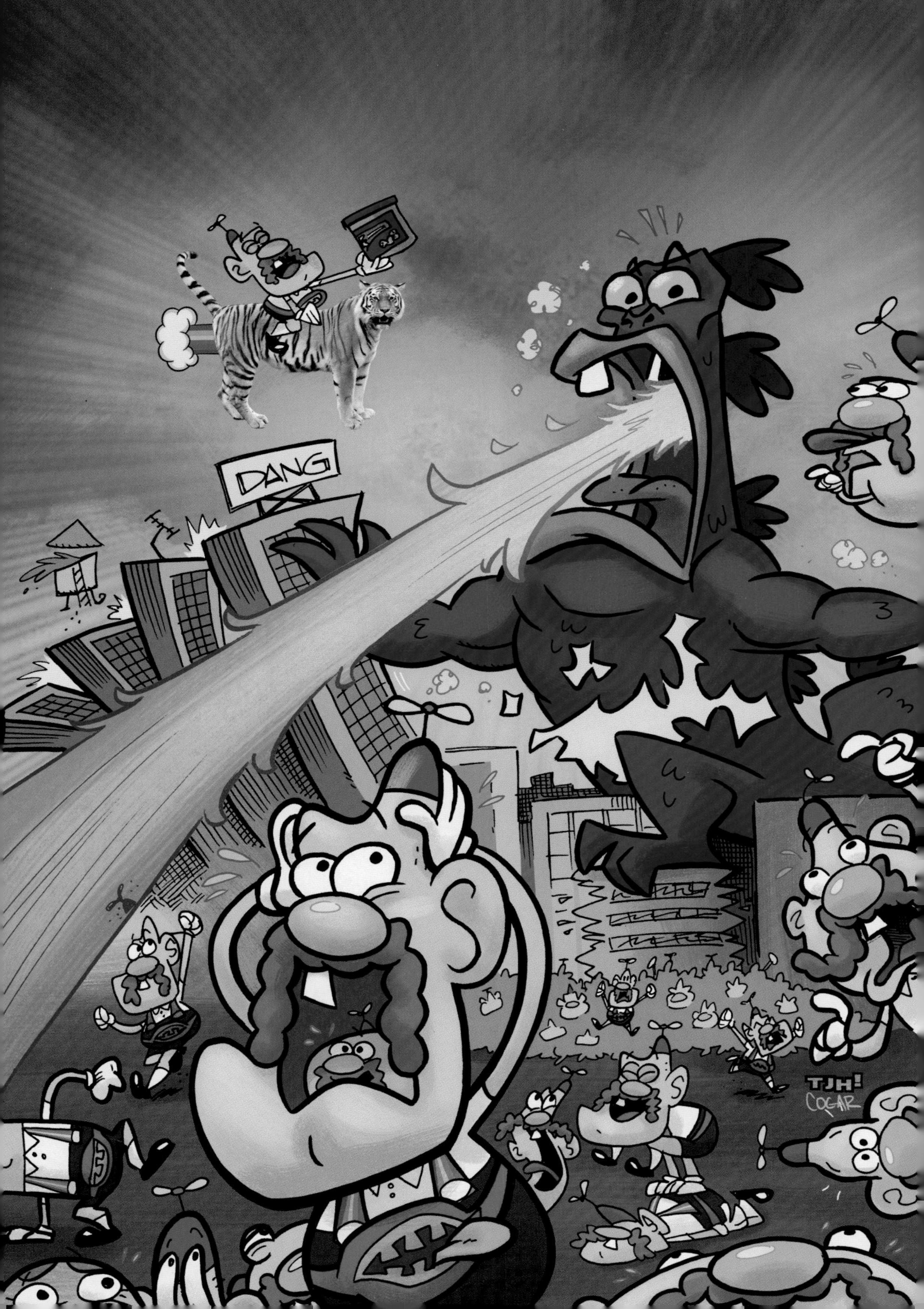
DANG
TJH!
COGAR

ISSUE #1 NEW YORK COMIC CON EXCLUSIVE COVER
ALLISON STREJLAU

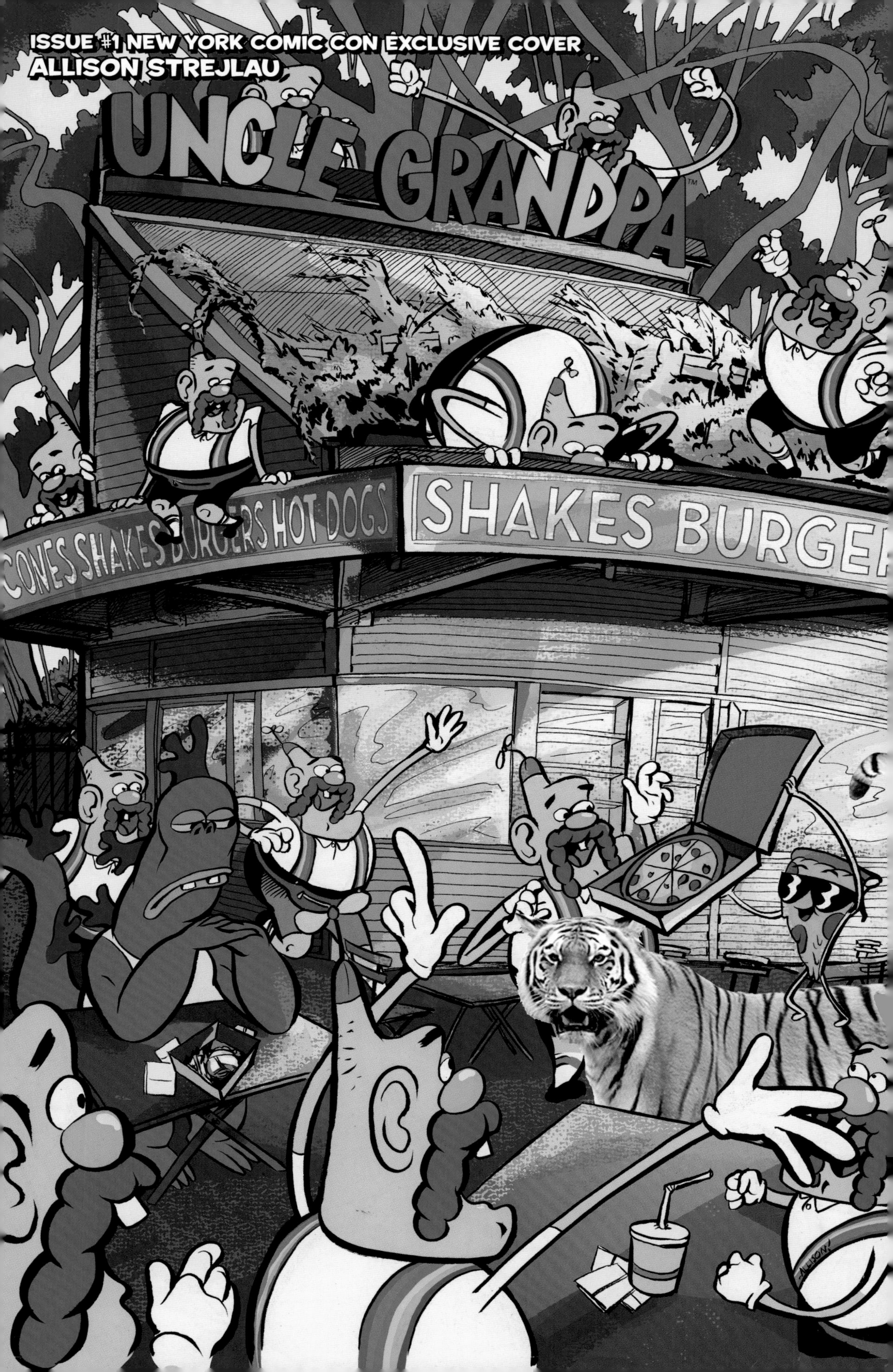
UNCLE GRANDPA™
CONES SHAKES BURGERS HOT DOGS
SHAKES BURGEF

ISSUE #1 COMICAZE EXPO EXCLUSIVE COVER
YEHUDI MERCADO

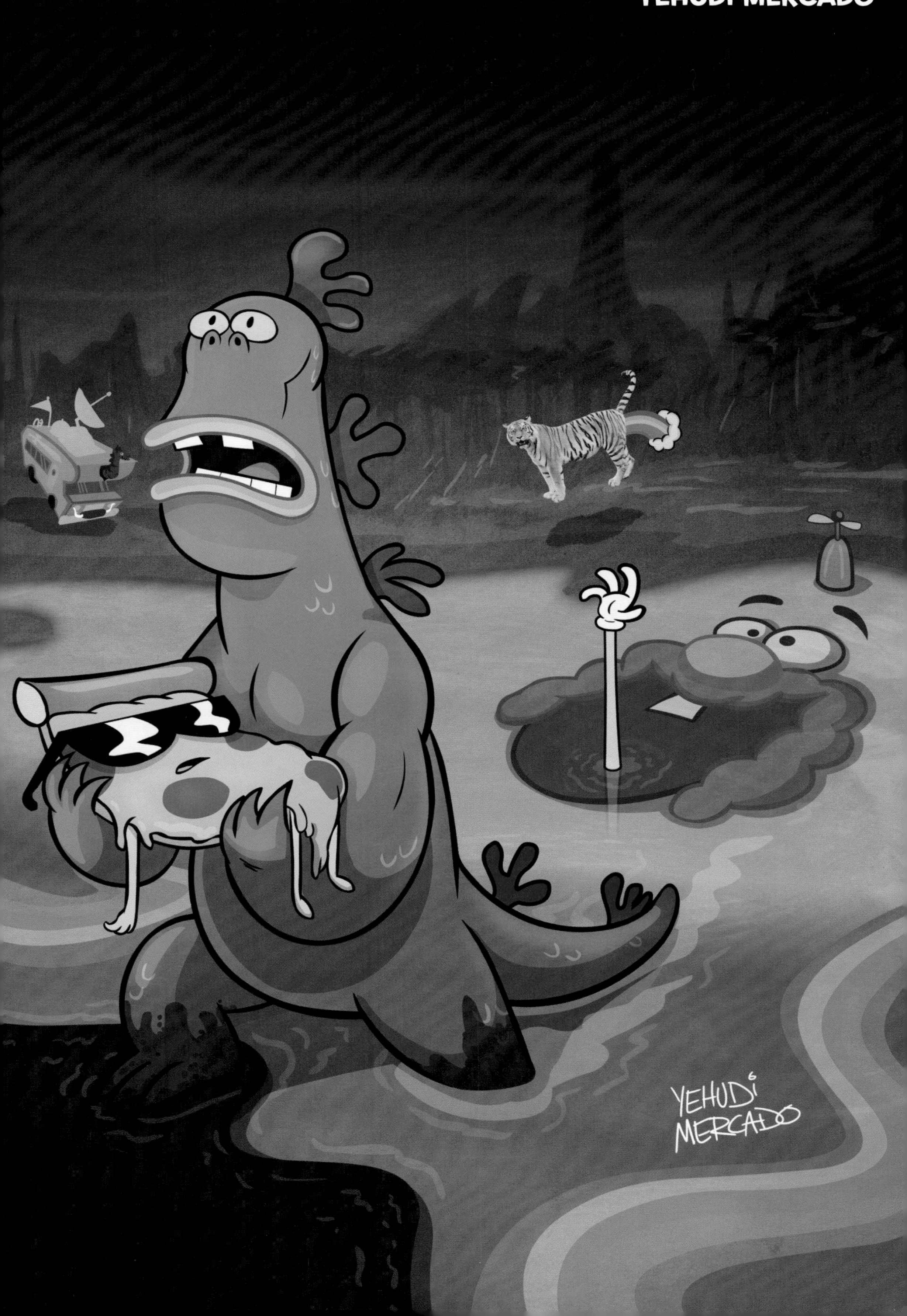
YEHUDI MERCADO

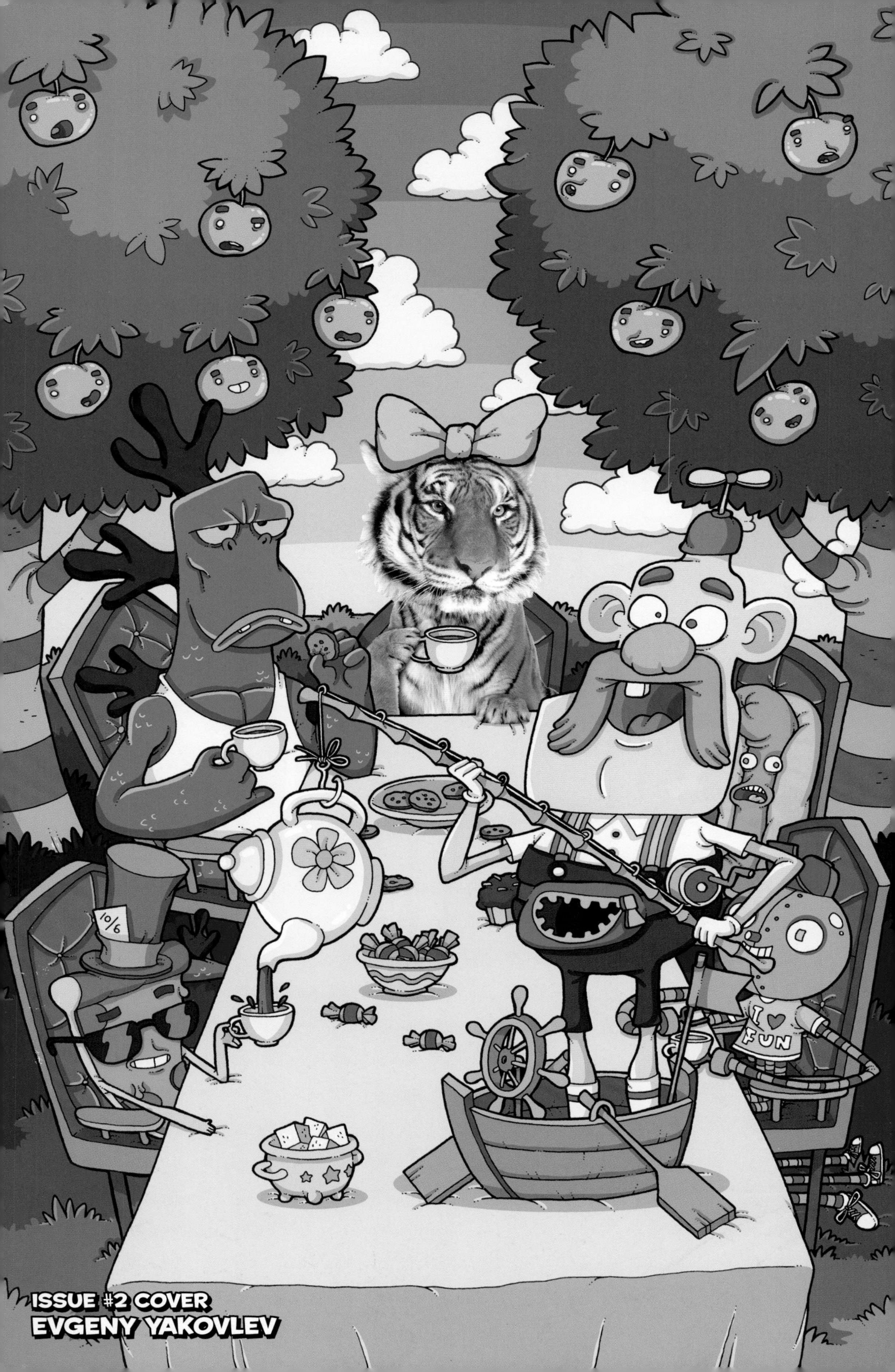
10/6
I ♥ FUN

ISSUE #2 COVER
EVGENY YAKOVLEV